Still Learning to Love

12 Days til Summer

Still Learning to Love

12 Days til Summer

Ann Hoff

This is a work of fiction. Names, institutions, events, and incidents are completely fictional.

ISBN 979-8-218-95488-8

Cover Design: Diren Yardimli
Bookcoverzone.com

Printed in the United States of America

Dedication

Daryoush, without whose support my dreams would not come true. To our lifetime of dreams to share.

Rowell, the poet and writer, my inspiration. Caroline, the most avid reader I ever met.

To Adelle, Felix, Primrose, and Remington.

True happiness has no meaning
without experiencing true sadness.

JOHN R. "JACK" SCHAFER, PH.D.,
RETIRED FBI SPECIAL AGENT,
PSYCHOLOGY TODAY

Chapter 1

Friday, June 9, 2017
New Smyrna Beach, FL

Beach waves crash onto the shore. A silver glow from tonight's full moon is an omen for death and a curse.

Jan Crawford's head is full of noise. She stumbles out of bed. Again, the pounding. Her unconsciousness unravels awake, and she tries to make her feet go in the right direction. A bolt of pain travels through her right hand. She trips and steadies herself leaning onto something but instead hits the sharp corner of the bedroom dresser. The floor tiles feel so cold. The room is dark. *Where is the light switch?!* Again the pounding, louder. She is still groggy from sleep. *Stop! Stop!* 'What the hell is going on?! George, is that you?' The noise is coming from down the hallway. She feels her way along the walls as her eyes adjust to the slither of moonlight piercing through the gaussian glass panel at the front door. Her hands touch the doorknob but slip. Half-dazed she tries to make her brain react and tell her how to hold and twist the handle. The door vibrates some more. The pounding. She puts her hands on her ears. 'Stop! Please! Stop!'

'Ma'am, please open the door. It's the police. We need to speak to you.'

Her neurons suddenly synapse enlivening her senses. She opens the door and leans on it, 'How can I help you, officers? What time is it?'

New Smyrna Beach Police Officer Chris Gwynn says apologetically, 'Sorry to disturb you, ma'am. It's after one in the morning. Can we come in? My partner, Officer Foster, and I would like to speak with you. It's important.'

Jan turns her head and squints. She wonders, *Where is George?* 'George! The police are here!' Chris and Foster look at each other and raise their eyebrows. Jan turns her head back, she releases the door and opens it, 'Sure, come in. I don't think my husband is here, though.'

Chris says, 'We know.' They follow her in. 'That's okay. We need to speak to you.'

Chapter 2

Tuesday, June 8, 2021
New Smyrna Beach, FL

Purplish blue puffs of clouds hang over the ocean. The ocean waves sound like wind creeping up the shoreline. For four years Jan has tried to fill up the hole George left in her soul when he died. Every year she comes back in an attempt to relive the years she was happy. She still thinks that by repeating her yearly escapades with George to the "Beach House" they rented every summer since their honeymoon, she can hold on to some semblance of the life she had.

Returning to where George died is about contrition, a sort of pilgrimage, but also her best work happens at the beach. Jan doesn't fool herself, the novels she writes don't resemble her love life, they never did. How could they? The key to writing romance is living happily ever after, and for her, that's been elusive. Jan still thought she and George were happy, comfortably in love, taken with each other. That is, until that dreaded night when everything changed.

Jan believes her marital bliss was because of their yearly escapades. The beach also helped her work as a writer. Her imagination and creativity are ripened by the gossip, characters, and stories she's found here over the years. She's met many locals, snowbirds, and foreigners. Here it's summer year-round plus it's intriguing and captivating.

When George was alive her work challenged their relationship because she spent so much time alone writing. Every summer she came to the beach to write and he followed her a few weeks later so they'd take a holiday. As the years went by though, she had been spending more time writing than vacationing with him, and then he died.

As she escapes again this year from the isolation she feels in the mountains of North Carolina, she ventures back to Florida where days of summer tan her skin. The unbuttoned blue muslin sleeveless shirt drapes her shoulders and covers her red tank top, matching her blue shorts. Her brunette layered, somewhat unruly, shoulder-length haircut emphasizes the square frame of her face and medium-length neck. The only makeup she wears is soft pink lip gloss to protect her from the sun and wind. Her tan is all she needs to bring out the hazel color in her eyes.

As she does every day, Jan walks along the New Smyrna Beach coastline. Barefoot, her feet feel chalky and dry, an effect of the humid gray sand. The air is muggy, a combination of the sea mist and normal Florida humidity. This year she is thankful for being able to spend time at the beach because it frees her from the constraints of wearing a mask everywhere she goes.

Every morning the sun creeps up on the horizon kissing the water, wrapping its orange rays around the porches of all the houses lining the shoreline. Sea Grape trees and Southern Wax Myrtle bushes cover the backyard inside the rustic ranch-style fence of Jan's cottage. The grayish-green vegetation also spreads onto the property next door, which is not fenced in. Jan's one-story concrete block white cottage with a red tiled roof has an unassuming rear porch. The two-story home next door totally contrasts her cottage. Its more modern design combines a naturally burnished gray cladded exterior resembling sea-washed wood, with customized long windows and French doors opening to the rear deck. The living room seems to merge onto the deck, an effect caused by its wall-to-ceiling glass windows.

Jan dabs her bare feet in the ocean and turns toward her cottage. The gate's latch gives off a soft clang as she enters the yard of her "Summer Beach House" as she likes to call it. She approaches the steps to her porch and notices to her right someone clearing the soft varnished wooden deck next door. He's shirtless and wearing shorts. *Someone is also trying to get a tan.* She tries to avoid being noticed staring at his muscular build. She quickly reaches the sliding doors and enters her cottage.

On the deck next door, staring out at the hues of blue which blend the sky into the ocean, Tim Evans is nursing a drink in a hydro-cup. His brown hair matches his brown eyes but not his untanned torso. The cell phone on the table rings and vibrates lighting up the name Mandy on the screen. Tim looks at it and ignores the call. *What does she want now?* They just argued over the phone a couple of hours ago, he's not in the mood for Mandy right now. She will get here eventually; all he wants is solitude. That's why he came ahead of them, to sort himself out. He closes his eyes and raises his face to the sun to take in the sun and salty air. He wants to cleanse or lighten some part of his soul. Today Tim is in search of meaning to the years of the making of himself. Building a family and a business, he's lost his zeal, that passion to create, and his ambition and motivation have disappeared. He thought Mandy was the love of his life, and that's why he married her. That's why Elsa came along to fulfill them both. So, why does he feel half his soul is hanging over a cliff?

After a few minutes, Jan returns outside with a book and a coffee mug and walks to the opposite side of her porch, away from the neighbor, and settles into the lounging chair.

Tim's phone rings again. This time Tim doesn't even look at it. Turning a page in her book, she realizes she can't remember a thing she's read. Again distracted, Jan stealthily peeks over the rim of her book and above her eyeglasses. Maybe he won't notice her. He turns and looks in her direction so she quickly lowers her stare pretending to be reading. He turns around and disappears into the house.

Fifteen pages later, which is a slow pace for her, the man next door has come out and gone back into his house several times. She feels he has been staring at her every time he comes outside. Now she's nervous about possibly having started *something.* The new neighbor has caught her eye for some reason. It's not only that he's handsome, Jan feels lonely. She has submitted herself to solitude these past four years. Work has been her only companion. Is this why her spirit is yearning for interaction?

She looks at her reddened skin and touches her bare shoulders. She decides it's enough sun for now. Plus, the new neighbor has not re-appeared during the past fifteen minutes she heads inside. Her laptop is on the dining room table beckoning for attention. The screen is dark, so she softly touches the power key to wake it up. As the desktop lights up she closes her eyes, *I'm definitely not in the mood right now.* It's been a few weeks of finding no inspiration to write. During the pandemic lockdowns last year all she could do was write, so where has her momentum gone? She walks away from the table, grabs her purse from the sofa, and takes out her car keys. Her mini-cooper is parked outside on the pebbled drive in front of the house. She gets in and backs out onto the street.

Walking out onto the deck and down the steps, Tim heads to the sand but the hot quartz burns the bottom of his feet. He hops in a zig-zag toward the shore. When he reaches the water he jumps head-first into the water. The shock of the cold water almost paralyzes him but he swiftly strokes deeper. He swims a bit further into the ocean then stops and stands. The waves hit his face, and he laughs. He sees a new one approaching, so he jumps right into it. 'Woooohoooo!' He yells and hits the water with his hands making it splash all around him. He looks up at the warm ball of light in the sky.

~

"See you tomorrow." Mandy Evans drops her phone on the kitchen counter after texting Tim. *I can't anymore!* She rolls her eyes as she walks down the hallway, 'Elsa, dear, have you finished packing your suitcase?'

Scrunching her nose, Elsa looks up from her book. She's propped up in bed by a pink bed lounger, her legs crossed, the book on her lap.

Mandy opens the bedroom door, 'Elsa, please take off your shoes when you're on the bed. Did you pack?'

Elsa points with her foot at the four-wheeled carry-on bag leaning against the closet door, 'Yes, Mom. I packed everything you told me to take.'

'Good. Are you excited?' Mandy smiles, 'I'm excited to go to the beach. Daddy's waiting for us.'

'When's dinner gonna be ready? I'm hungry.' Elsa says now sitting on the edge of the bed taking off her tennis shoes.

'In a while Elsa. Why don't you get some yogurt or something for now? I still have to finish packing. I'll let you know.'

~

The sun retreats smoothly behind the houses and wraps a cool shadow around them. Jan approaches from the north walking on the wet sandy bank of the beach. Once more she sees the neighbor staring at the ocean from his deck, still shirtless. She puts her hand over her eyes about to raise her hand to greet him but quickly pulls it back so he doesn't notice. Her movement makes him look over.

He waves, 'Hello neighbor.' His smile matches his eyes.

'Hello. Lovely afternoon.'

'Yes, it is. Quite soothing. Much needed change.'

Jan nods, reaching her porch. She shakes her feet on the stairs and walks toward the sliding door, rubbing her feet off on the area rug. She slides her toes and feet into some slippers. 'Well, have a good evening. Enjoy the view!' She waves, opens the door and walks inside.

Jan approaches the kitchen sink grabs a paring knife and some strawberries and peeks out her kitchen window which overlooks the neighbor's side of the house with a clear view of the deck. He's now staring at the emptiness ahead. Her eyes travel from his bare feet up to his waist, his chest, and then his brownish curls. A few deep lines and a 1-day beard accentuate his face. His arms are not delineated by bulging muscles but reveal some workouts. *I like it.*

She nips a tiny cut on her index finger, red liquid oozes slowly. She hurriedly runs her finger under water, brings her finger to her mouth, and sucks on it for a few seconds. Her brain is alert to the sting as she lifts her head up again. Across the walkway, there's light blue fabric unfurling through the open French doors dancing in the evening wind like a lost Sarong. Disappointment hits.

Chapter 3

Wednesday, June 9, 2021

The ocean water sparkles under the bright blue cloudless sky. Eyeing a now familiar shape in the distance walking toward her as she returns back from the North Environmental Park, Jan smiles. He is wearing something resembling a Hawaiian shirt, 'tourists.' Jan chuckles., she can barely distinguish the palm trees on it, but the pineapples scattered over the fabric are pretty bright. Their paths cross.

Stopping Tim puts his hands in his pockets, 'Hello neighbor, beautiful morning.'

'Yes, it is a beautiful morning.' Jan smiles and extends her hand, 'Welcome to our piece of paradise, my name is Jan.'

Until yesterday they were strangers. Jan fighting her way back to normalcy, embracing life again. As for him, Tim is feeling out of his depth on a journey of self-discovery. Meeting today on this beach like waves that meet the shore, Jan and Tim are about to drop their needs, wants, desires, and regrets at each other's doorsteps; just like the soft stream of water that touches the sand bringing in shells, foam, grains of sand, salt, and silt.

Fascinated by this stranger, Jan shakes Tim's hand, hoping she doesn't seem overly attracted to him. Tim doesn't want to let go of her hand, a soft warmth rising through him. Jan's smile opens some sort of door for him. Still holding onto her hand, 'Hello Jan, I'm Tim. Paradise indeed.' Tim points to his chest, 'First timer here.' There's a brief silence before he lets go and stares into her eyes.

Jan interrupts her and his thoughts with, 'Good to meet you.' She slides a strip of hair behind her ear as she tilts her head, 'I'm right next door, let me know if you need anything.'

Now running through his head are many excuses he can use. Tim doesn't want to break it off just yet, so he gives one of them a shot. He asks her if she knows a good place where he can get stocked up on food and snacks. Indeed, she does, so they arrange to meet up in an hour to go to some food stores in town. They say goodbye. Tim continues up the shore opposite the path Jan takes to return home.

Alerted by the ringing of her phone in her pocket, she pulls it out and answers, 'Hello?'

'Jan! How are you doing, dear?' A pleasant and cheerful female voice seeps through the speaker. That's who Dianne Taylor is, always positive and always cheerful. Dianne, Jan's agent, lives in New York but they are both from North Carolina. An interesting coincidence how they met. Jan is from a smaller town nestled among the pine trees in the mountains and never ventured to the big metropolis to find an agent. She had given up on finding one, much less a publisher, but a few years ago Jan ran into Diane when she was visiting her family. Jan was reading from one of her self-published books at a bookstore in Raleigh. Dianne was visiting the bookstore owned by her friend and was impressed by Jan's style, so she approached her. After a meeting, Diane offered to represent her. Since that day Jan's writing career took off. These days Jan and Dianne see each other now and then, and she's practically the only person Jan interacts with on a personal level, other than her sibling, since that awful night when her life changed. Considering Jan has to be chained to her laptop writing non-stop most of the time, they don't meet that often but through the years they've also become close friends. Jan can't say she really has many of those. Dianne's natural cheerfulness helps her stay grounded even through her worst days. Jan's work, her ventures down to Florida each year, and Dianne's friendship have given her strength and resilience.

'Dianne. Hello. I am well. Who couldn't be in these surroundings, eh?'

'Yes, yes, I envy you. I wish I could be there too.' Dianne looks out of her home office window onto the street, no sunny beach or a garden of red roses outside her brownstone, only asphalt, bricks, and concrete.

'Well, you can come, and visit, any time, I'll show you around.'

Dianne cuts the air with one hand, 'Are you kidding? I need you to finish that book, girl. If I go there then you'll blame me for not meeting your deadline. You are going to meet your deadline, right?'

She rolls her eyes, 'Yes, Dianne, I promise. The book is way underway, and right now I have a feeling the beach life is coming through for me. Plus, you know, I have the benefit of "real-life" research. In any case, yes. I promise you should have the final draft in two or three months, way ahead of schedule.'

'So, research, huh?' Dianne asks, 'Tell me more. Of the romantic kind? Or just that murder stuff?'

'Ha! Ha! Dianne, you want me to have the romantic experience, don't you? I'm not sure about that just yet. In any case, there are unanswered questions about the murder, so we'll see how it goes. Plus, you know this place inspired the story.' Jan walks past Tim's house and turns to her cottage.

'Mmmm, just be careful Jan.' Dianne is now staring at her computer screen, her eyes sifting through a long list of emails, and their subject lines, 'I'll let you go now. Stay on task, and don't let that beach swallow you up, you hear?'

'It's okay Dianne, I will; talk to you soon.'

'All right. Bye.'

Jan puts the cell phone on the dining table and walks toward the kitchen window, her mind wanders off to the new neighbor. Flirtatious, like a fifteen-year-old, she wants to give herself the opportunity to be ready for someone again, nothing serious. *Could Tim be that for me?* Needing to let go of the past and finally of George, she is also concerned for where she'll take her characters, Rose and Otto.

Not feeling an attraction to anyone since George died four years ago, Jan isn't quite sure how to handle this burgeoning allure for her new neighbor. After George died she spent two weeks crying herself to sleep. George's sudden death was a blow she was not prepared for. Neither was she ready for the revelations that came with his death, learning about George's secret.

To pull herself out of depression she delved into her work and avoided relationships altogether. She wrote and published an average of a book and a half a year since he's been gone. Everything's been about work, her thoughts, actions, and results. She's unsure of where this could lead, should she accept the rush and excitement enticing her today? What if he's married or has a girlfriend? What if he's not into it? *I could see how he looked at me this morning, how he's spent so much time out on his deck staring back at my house.* What if he's wrong for me? What then?

Otto and Rose are venturing into an affair, is that why she feels inclined to do this? If Tim's off-limits… Isn't that exactly what she wants? Someone she doesn't have to commit to, someone who can help her swoop deeper into inspiration for her new book, a relationship in which all she has to invest is a little time and effort? She doesn't know it yet, but she's about to take a winding road. Danger and heartbreak are just around the corner.

An hour after meeting Tim on the beach Jan hears a car horn blasting outside. The lots of Jan and Tim's rental houses are separate, but they share the driveway. Jan's front door opens to face the street. Tim's home opens to the side of his house and to two parking spaces. After hearing the horn Jan lifts the front window's curtain, and waves at him. She grabs her handbag, and sunglasses, and rushes out the door.

As she gets in the passenger side of the black Mercedes SUV, she reaches back for the seatbelt, 'Ahh, we could've walked there you know?'

'Really? Oh well, let's just go in the car, in case we buy too many things,' he winks at her.

Jan shrugs, and points to her right, 'Okay, go ahead there, and turn right. After a couple of blocks, there's a pink house on the corner, and you'll turn left.'

They ride along and arrive at a quaint one-story white building with a terracotta tiled roof. Tim nods approvingly as he maneuvers the car into a parking spot on the property. Jan gets out and waves for him to follow her into the building, 'Come on, you're gonna like it here.'

As they walk in, their senses are hit by a mixture of sweet fruit and flower fragrances, weaved into a soft fresh breeze winding through the shop. Stalls of sunflowers, chrysanthemums, roses, and lavender at the entrance draw Jan into the store where she catches the view of yellow, orange, green, and red colors where the fruit and vegetables are laid out on table-high stalls. She turns and watches Tim standing at the entrance taking it all in. She has mixed feelings but she still smiles at him.

Tim heads to the rear of the establishment, curious about something behind the cashier counter. He picks a rag doll from a stand. It has red hair and tiny shell earrings and is wearing a blue and green bikini top with a matching skirt. He places it in his basket and roams around picking some goat cheese, honey, and natural orange juice from the fridge. As he walks to the cashier he looks toward the vegetable stalls. He watches Jan scratch a lime, bring it up to her face and smell it. She places some in her basket. She doesn't notice Tim looking at her, but he chuckles and stares as she reaches over for some tangerines and a couple of oranges. Tim walks out. She picks a few green vegetables, tomatoes, and avocados.

As she pays for her groceries at the cashier, Jan leans her head left and right looking for Tim. She walks out to the parking lot and finds him leaning on the car with his arms crossed. A glint of sunlight shines on his hair and Jan feels a soft warm rush go through her. She waves at him. He waves back.

Outside the market, Jan carries her large paper bag filled with groceries, and Tim opens the rear door for her to place it in the car, 'Now, where to?'

Smiling Jan says, 'Well, depends on what else you need. But, we could walk around the corner for a mid-morning smoothie?'

'That sounds great.' Tim locks the car and strides next to Jan. He leads her by softly touching her back. Jan feels a tingling sensation run up her spine, making her skin perk up, she tries to hide a shudder. She smiles and puts on her sunglasses.

Gathering their smoothies from the truck vendor, Tim says, 'Let's walk toward the water, might as well take in some of the great salty sprays.'

'I guess. It should be healthy, huh?'

'Perhaps, ha!' Tim laughs and slurps some liquid through the straw.

Walking along the shore they stride on the sand avoiding the low waves trying to reach their feet. At the same time, small sandpipers run away from them and from the water foam. Jan and Tim laugh at the tiny birds returning now toward the receding water as they dive their tiny beaks into the wet sand to pick into minuscule air bubbles looking for snails.

'So, what do you do Jan? What brings you to this paradise, as you call it?'

She shrugs, 'Well, I come here for the solitude.'

'Solitude. Hmmm. As in getting away from someone? From work?'

'I guess you could say both.' She looks out into the distance and takes a sip out of her straw, 'I may be trying to get away from myself, and I'm not running away from work but come here to work. I'm a writer.'

Tim raises an eyebrow. He is a couple of inches taller than Jan, but his reaction is not lost on her. He looks at Jan expecting her to say something. She doesn't. She runs her fingers through her hair and he notices the emerald and diamond ring on her wedding finger. 'Let's see then. So, you're a writer. Is that why you are here alone? Is this a work trip where you leave your husband to tend to the kids and the dog?'

Jan smiles and looks at him, 'I like where you're going with that.' Now she feels more relaxed, 'That would be kind of ideal.' She stares out at the smooth froth from the waves rolling up to the shore. She thinks that after all, why can't she have the *happily ever after* she writes about in her books? All her life she's been the good girl and look what it got her, deception. Maybe she needs to change the outlook of her novels and her life. Should she venture for a one-night stand?

Tim gives up on finding out anything else, so he follows the path in the sand, that of other people's footsteps that are disappearing as the water recedes back into the ocean. Jan speaks up again, 'All right, so here goes. I don't have a dog. My husband died a few years ago. No kids. This is kind of a work trip and a vacation. I live in North Carolina and come here during the summers. It's just me.' She tilts her head toward him, her lips forming a line, not quite a shy smile.

Tim pulls back, surprised, 'Whoa! That's intense.'

Now she smiles and looks ahead, they're about three hundred feet from their homes, 'Too bad, we could've walked home from here.' She swerves her head covering the expanse of ocean and looks down the shoreline toward where their houses are.

'Go ahead and walk from here, sounds like a good idea. I can get the car and meet you there.'

'No, that's okay.' She swerves her head to her left, 'let's get back to the car.'

The summer sun feels incandescent on Jan's shoulders as she gets out of the car. She reaches over to softly touch her bare shoulder and test the temperature of her skin. Her hand feels cool on her hot skin. Tim pulls Jan's bags out of the back seat, 'Looks like you'll need some protection there, your back is looking quite red right now.'

Jan tries to look behind her shoulders, and winks, 'It does feel a bit steamy.'

'I can help you with that if you like.' He carries the bags and follows her up the driveway toward the front door.

'With what? The bags or my back?'

Tim looks confused. Jan laughs and touches her shoulder. Tim winks, 'Ah, yes, okay.' He shrugs, 'Both, I guess.'

Jan walks toward the front door. She unlocks it. There's something stuck on the doorframe with a nail. Tim is standing right behind her when he notices a Tarot card pinned to the doorframe. He tilts his head to the side, his hands are full so he can't reach for it, which was his first instinct, 'What is that?'

'What?' Jan says and turns to look at him, he tilts his head toward the door, 'That.' He raises his chin to point at the door. Jan turns and sees the card showing a heart at the center with three swords slashing through it. She shrugs. 'Oh, that. Well, that's probably Buford. He leaves me these little mementos now and then.' The door is open now and she tears off the card from the doorframe, 'Come on in.'

'That seems pretty ominous, Jan.'

She tries to seem unconcerned but deep inside she's troubled, 'Nah, don't worry about it. Buford's harmless. He's probably gone through half the deck already.'

'He's done this before? Why is he doing this? Who is this Buford?'

'He's a local. He's still lamenting the death of his Cassandra. She was the beach psychic and Tarot card reader. She passed away a few years ago.'

'Oh, that's sad. Why does he do this to you, though?'

'Forget about Buford. Look, I have.' She's lying, of course. Buford and she are more parallel than she wants to admit. But she's not going to share that with Tim, at least not now. As they reach the rear of the house she points toward the kitchen counter, 'You can put that there. Give me a second, I'll get some aloe if you don't mind helping me with it.' She walks toward the hallway.

'Sure, no problem.'

As Jan walks back toward the living area she has a bottle of clear green liquid in her hands. Tim is staring at the Tarot card which Jan left on the counter. She hands him the Aloe lotion and is holding a towel over her front so her back can be bare, 'Here, please lather some on my back if you don't mind.'

Jan flinches a bit as Tim's fingers and the cold liquid touch her skin. Tim smiles, 'Does it hurt?'

She shivers slightly, 'No, it's just so cold. Thanks.' When he's done she turns around, and Tim hands her the bottle. He stares into her hazel eyes for a few seconds. Her cheeks warm up, her throat feels dry, and her knees feel weak. Jan holds his stare, challenging herself to take another step. *What will happen if I do this? Am I setting up a trap for myself? Or just for him? Is this worth it?*

He breaks the spell whispering, 'You're welcome.'

Her heart beats a little faster but she decides to break away, 'Do you need some as well?'

'No, I don't burn that easily, I'm okay. Thanks. I better get going, Mandy's waiting. Thanks for showing me around, Jan.'

'Sure, my pleasure. Say hello to the family.' She watches him walk down the hallway and out the door.

~

Elsa is sitting in the waiting area of the airport at John F. Kennedy Airport in New York. She kicks her pink glittered suitcase in front of her. A boy across the aisle of seats looks up from his portable video game. Elsa sticks her tongue out at him. Mandy Evans softly grabs her arm to get her to stop kicking the luggage as she balances the cell phone by her ear with her other hand. The phone is ringing. Elsa doesn't stop kicking the bag so Mandy looks at her sideways with that "Mommy" look. Elsa stops. The call goes to voicemail and Mandy mutters under her voice in frustration. After hearing the voicemail tone she says, 'Tim, I just wanted to tell you our flight got delayed by an hour so you don't have to wait for us at the airport. Call me back, please.' She ends the transmission and puts her phone in her handbag.

Now playing with one of her braids, Elsa asks, 'Is everything okay, Mom?'

'Yes, pumpkin, everything's okay.' Mandy pats Elsa's arm wishing this next hour to go by quickly.

~

The afternoon is now winding down. Jan takes a break from her laptop. To her amazement, the story flows non-stop for a couple of hours which surprises her since her mojo has been barren during the past few weeks. She looks up from her computer toward the sliding door, which is open.

'Daddy!' A child's voice rings in her ears slashing through the scene, the words, Rose, and Otto's lovemaking, the walls. She hears it again, 'Daddy! Can you help me put the vest on?' It's coming from outside her cottage, not in her head. She closes her eyes. It's coming from next door.

Walking over to the kitchen window, Jan looks over to Tim's deck. She sees a young girl with red hair run over to Tim with a life vest jacket in her hand. He puts his beer can down on the table and complies. A slender, beautiful woman walks through the French doors. Her red hair bounces off her shoulders onto the white tank top and shawl enfolding her. She sits down next to Tim.

Looking at the redhead Tim says, 'You're not going for a swim?'

'No, why don't you do it? I'd rather sit here and watch the ocean.'

Looking through the window Jan is trying to define what she feels right now. Is it dismay, frustration, or a letdown? It's definitely a lump of something hanging in her chest. Is it just disappointment? A range of emotions sweeps the spectrum. Selfishly, she's been allowing herself to open up to someone but this changes everything. Jan shuts her eyes as she leans over the kitchen sink turning on the faucet. She's looking for sound, something to stop herself from hearing the thoughts ringing in her head, *How could you be so stupid, Jan?*

Chapter 4

Thursday, June 10, 2021

The swoosh sound of an email as it lands in Jan's inbox distracts her from the page on her screen. The weather is cool so she's sitting on the porch under the umbrella. She closes her eyes, touches the mouse, then withdraws. *Don't go there!* She knows, once she clicks into her email software, there will be no turning back. Intrusions are hard to fend away. Links is the right word for connecting pages online. Like an addiction, once Jan goes to one page the links seem unbreakable. As far as distractions go, she watches as Tim opens the French doors and walks outside onto his deck. He is dressed only in his trunks. Again. Is he trying to torture her? Jan feels a tinge of electricity. He stands looking out at the ocean from the deck and takes a sip from a coffee mug in his hand. *Might as well engage him.* Jan waves and greets him, 'Good morning!'

Tim looks over, 'Good morning.'

Mandy walks outside wearing a pink silk mini kimono that barely covers her thighs, also with a coffee mug in her hand. Today her long curly red hair bounces off her shoulders onto her back. She isn't wearing makeup but her complexion is radiant, hydrated and supple. A few freckles accentuate her nose and cheeks matching her copper-red eyebrows. She smiles and looks over toward Jan.

Tim points toward Jan's house and says to her, 'Honey, this is Jan whom I was talking to you about.' Jan can't hear them. He looks at Jan and yells, 'Jan this is my wife, Mandy.'

Jan nods and yells back, 'Hello Mandy, nice to meet you.'

Jan waves raising her coffee mug as if in a toast. Both Mandy and Tim do the same. Jan lowers her head to continue reading her laptop screen. Tim places his arm touching Mandy's back who stares ahead looking at the glitter-like jewels dancing on the water.

~

After a few hours, a gust of warm salty wind blows through the open sliding door swaying the shades in the dining area of the cottage caressing Jan's skin and hair as she reads her computer screen.

The sound of the keys on her laptop as her fingers transfer her thoughts onto the digital page is music to her ears. The words stare at her from the screen. Watching Tim for the past couple of days has allowed her to romanticize what it would feel like to be with him. Now that she knows he's married, she's tried to focus on what it would have been if there was something more between them. Those emotions she's invented for her and imagined for Tim are helping her lay down Rose and Otto's emotional and physical outbursts in her book. It doesn't feel very convincing to her, however. This is going to need a lot of work.

She hears the young girl out on the deck again. Walking over to the kitchen window Jan peeks over toward the deck next door. She sees the young girl with red hair wearing a blue bathing suit and jumping up and down on the deck in front of Tim. He's reaching out to her as if trying to make her stop the hyperactive girl. He gets out of his chair as she rushes down the steps and he follows her to the beach.

Oh no. Jan turns around, a chill runs down her spine. She walks toward the sliding door and slams it shut. *What is happening? My imagination is getting the best of me.* She reaches for her headset and hooks it up to music from her phone app. Sitting at the dining room table again she takes a seat in front of her laptop searching for an escape. The pages, *read, read, read. Write. Don't think about it! Write!*

Chapter 5

Friday, June 11, 2021

Brainstorming is an exercise for the persistent. At least that is what Jan believes. It is easy to come up with scenarios, plots, ideas, dialogue, and characters by using this technique in the simplest form. However, Jan believes persistence is what pays off for her. She is not one to just throw words on a wall or a whiteboard and hope to come up with quick storylines. Sometimes it takes days for her to wind up with a convincing and compelling scene for a story. It's like weaving a piece of cloth or carpet. The warps and wefts on a loom thread the stories together and tighten up making a strong fabric. When Jan searches for more sources and references, the more prompts she is able to generate, the stronger her stories become.

Searching for inspiration and information, today she finds herself at the library. She's read a few reference books on police procedure and down the line, she'll *interview* her friends at the police department. For now, walking up and down the aisles of books at the library is her happy place, to be surrounded by books.

Reading down the list of Dewey Decimal Classification numbers she has written down on a piece of paper, she glances along the spines of the books on the shelves in search of books on bronze welding, her character Otto's vocation. Turning around to the other side of the bookshelf, she continues scrolling up and down the shelves looking for the right number and bumps into a gentleman who is walking over from the other end. She barely looks up but says, 'Sorry!'

Tim turns around, 'Jan! Well, hello there!'

Jan suddenly pulls out of her distracted concentration, 'Oh, Tim. Hi!' She looks behind him and behind herself, 'Where's Mandy?'

'She's in the Children's room with our daughter, Elsa. They have story time. So, I decided to see if there was something more interesting for me around here.' He smiles.

Jan raises her eyebrows, 'Ah. I see. Have you found anything interesting?'

'I'm glad I found you here.' He stops as if trying to find something to say, awkward silence. Jan turns her head to look over some more Dewey Decimal numbers on her list. Turning around Tim imitates her and searches for some numbers and titles on the shelves. Again he turns to Jan and says, 'So, I was wondering.' Jan turns her head in attention. Tim continues, 'I watch how you go out walking on the beach every day. Would you mind some company? Maybe Mandy and I could go with you sometime?'

Jan pauses and tilts her head, 'Eh, sure, sure. I usually go out in the mornings when it's cool. That should be nice.'

'Great. I'll tell Mandy and maybe we can try tomorrow.'

'Sure.' Jan turns around and looks through the shelf for the book she had pinpointed before Tim startled her. She pulls it from the shelf and starts backtracking her steps, 'So, I guess I'll see you around, then.'

'Yes, yes, of course.' Tim waves, 'It was great seeing you.'

Jan walks to the guest counter to check out her book as Mandy and Elsa are walking out of the "Children's Room" behind a group of young ones and parents, 'Hello Mandy, how are you?'

Smiling Mandy says, 'Oh, Hello, how are you? Is it Jan?'

Jan nods. Mandy continues, 'Elsa, this is Jan, our neighbor at the beach house.' Elsa looks up but is silent. Mandy touches Elsa's shoulder and she shyly says, 'Hello.'

Jan nods and smiles, 'Hello. Yes, I'm doing great. I see you've found the library. Did you enjoy Story Time, Elsa?'

Elsa shrugs, 'It's all right.'

Picking up the book from the counter which the librarian checked out for her, Jan feels a bit jittery, 'So, how are you finding New Smyrna up to now?'

'Great, great, though we haven't been out that much.' Mandy raises her shoulders, 'Elsa's been enjoying the beach so much we haven't ventured out. This is the first place I've visited.'

'There's a lot to see here.' Jan says adding a wink, 'I know you'll like it. How about you come over for coffee tomorrow morning? I make the best Espresso in town.'

'Well, that sounds great. I'd love to.'

'Great, see you tomorrow, then. Any time before nine is okay.' Jan extends her hand, 'I usually get up at the crack of dawn, so whenever you're ready.' Mandy shakes Jan's hand.

'Looking forward to it.' Mandy catches Tim's eye and softly pushes Elsa toward him, 'See you tomorrow.'

Putting Mandy between herself and Tim is what Jan is doing, as it should be. The draw he has on her is threatening to overpower her control. After four years of staying away from any type of relationship or commitment, her attraction now is a tad off the charts to someone who's off-limits. Is her Rose and Otto story getting the best of her? *What is wrong with you?!*

~

Happy with the results of making a new recipe of baked enchiladas which she just put in the oven, Mandy walks out to the deck. Elsa is up in her room reading, so Mandy is going to take advantage of that. Tim's sitting at the round umbrella table watching beachgoers and swimmers. She sits down next to him, 'I thought you'd be in the water.'

He shakes his head and purses his lips, conversation is not something he's welcoming right now. Mandy runs her hands over her lap and persists, 'Tim, I've been here for almost two days now, we have to talk. We came here so we'd get out of our normal and find a way out of the sluggishness we're in.'

Tim turns his head to Mandy, 'Is that why you came?' He shakes his head, 'I'm not feeling it, Mandy.'

Mandy squints in order not to show the tears she senses pooling in her eyes. Tim thinks she's reacting to the sunshine. He's making it so much harder for her to reconnect, 'Tim, what are we doing?' She turns placing both elbows on the arm of her chair trying to get closer to him, 'I don't want to fight anymore, I'd like it if we could share things like we used to.'

'Mandy, I'm trying. I don't get why you don't see that.' He turns around to face her, with his elbows on his knees, he takes her hands in his, looking down to the floor, 'Look, I don't like the pressure, and I feel a bit constrained here.' He looks up into her eyes.

'I don't want to pressure you Tim. I just want you to help me figure out what's happening to us.' She looks over to the house through the French Doors, Elsa is still upstairs. 'I want what's best for Elsa. Why are you so distant?'

'Elsa is my main concern which is why I agreed to come here this week. We both want what's best for her and I'm trying to figure that out.'

'Maybe you're not trying hard enough, Tim. Maybe we should try something new.'

'We're here, aren't we?' Tim now sounds slightly irritated. 'I came here because you suggested we get away. I have taken it as a way to also release a bit from work, since it's been so demanding lately.'

'I know, I know.' Mandy leans back in her chair and folds her arms, 'But you've been pulling away from me, Tim. You don't see it. I feel you're so far away.'

Tim gets up abruptly and a couple of bottles fall over on the table, 'I don't want to do this, Mandy.' Surprised, Mandy swerves up to catch the bottles, 'Tim! Tim!, please.'

Walking up the path of sand from the shore toward her cottage, Jan witnesses as Tim barges through the French doors. She watches Mandy pick up the bottles and wipe off the table with a napkin.

Jan turns her head so Mandy doesn't notice her. She focuses again on her phone.

'Can you hear me? all I hear is waves and wind.'

Jan hears Dianne's voice coming through the cell phone's speaker just fine, 'Yeah, I hear you.'

'Ah, all right.' Dianne continues, 'So, as I was saying, Missus Fairchild told me the edited copy of "Broken Time" will be at the printers soon. So, we can keep our calendars as planned for the mid-fall launch of your next book. Now, how's this one going?'

'Good, great. It's going great.' Jan lies, however, she's barely finished the first draft of the novel.

'Great, as in almost done? Do you have your second draft? Your third draft? I know how thorough you get, Jan. Missus Fairchild is aiming for a spring release for this book. Do you think we'll make it?'

Of course, Jan is not a great liar, but she has been stuck on where to take Rose and Otto's story. 'Mmmm, perhaps. I'm just finishing up a few strokes here, and there. You could say I'm in my second draft, heading toward a third.'

'That's pretty slow for you, Jan. A third draft doesn't mean much.'

'I know, I know.' She pulls the sliding door a bit too harshly and it slams, 'But I'll get there. Missus Fairchild will get her book in time. I just need a bit more time and inspiration.'

'Jan, are you all right? Don't tell me you're falling into a dark hole. Do you need me to come down there? Cuz you know I will.'

Jan closes her eyes, 'No, no, of course not! Look, I'll call you in a few days and tell you where I'm at. Let me organize my files. This is temporary. You know I do my best work here at the beach. It'll come out all right.'

'Okay, if you promise we can keep Fairchild happy. She is testy most of the time, and I would hate to test her testiness.'

Jan waves off the comment and chuckles, 'Don't worry, Dianne. It'll be fine. Now, I've got to get back to work.' Now in the kitchen, Jan turns on the electric teapot and leans on the counter, 'I'll give you your romance and your beach town murder, don't worry.'

'Well, goodbye dear, please feel better. I hear some of that sadness in your voice.'

'I'll be okay, just going through some stuff.' Walking every day on the beach by herself doesn't do much for her spirits. Her current mood does resemble the cool winds of dusk.

'Okay, I'll see you when you come to New York with a final draft, a final product.'

'Wrapped in a bow, Dianne dear, wrapped in a bow.' Jan hangs up and puts her phone in her pocket. She stares into the emptiness, looking for words and angles for her plot and characters. How much of her real experiences should she venture to use? Jan's life is about to take a turn much like the novel she is trying to write. In the end, how much truth she manages to thread into the fiction may be her weakness. How much will she be able to resist?

~

Looking at her reflection in the mirror as she scans the top of the dresser looking for her favorite perfumed hand lotion, she sees the image of George and herself smiling back at her; she frowns. She picks up the photo and stares at it. The smell of the pine needles fogs her mind as she remembers the day they took this picture in the forest walking along the trail behind their home in North Carolina. Home? Is where she and George spent their life before he died still home? The beach house feels more like home to her now. Sadness hits, the pang of hurt surfaces again, and it showers through her, she feels weak. She thinks of Tim. She closes her eyes, sets the picture back on the dresser, and walks away. She needs a break.

~

The fun in the sun got the best of Elsa, and she's fallen asleep on the living room couch in front of the TV. Mandy asks Tim to carry her upstairs.

As he walks out of Elsa's room and shuts the door, Mandy is standing in the doorway to their bedroom her head tilted to the side and her copper curls falling onto her shoulders. The white lace of her silk nightie frames her breasts. A pink silk bathrobe drops seductively off her shoulder. Tim approaches her putting his arms around her waist and kisses her softly. He then says, 'Not tonight, Mandy.' He walks down the stairs.

Mandy catches her breath and stands in the doorway. Her eyes water. She hears the front door close.

The streets aren't deserted but the coming and going of the day have quieted down considerably. Tim walks into the Honky-Tonk bar on Main Street. It's Karaoke night. For some reason, Karaoke brings in the most patrons to the joint. People love inflicting pain on their eardrums by listening to off-key singers belting out love songs, but maybe it's just the booze. Buford Hall is here. His blond hair matches his big blue eyes which roam around the room as he leans against the wall in the rear corner end of the bar watching the patrons. A heavy mustache covers his lips and his disgust as his face reddens when he sees Jan walking on the stage.

Shuffling her feet, Jan takes centerstage and grabs the microphone. She's wearing a short denim mini skirt and a sleeveless blue-rimmed loose white t-shirt which highlights her bronze-toned arms. Holding the mic near her face almost like a professional, she begins billowing out the lyrics of The Bee Gee's "Staying Alive." Buford stares at her, narrowing in on Jan's hand holding the mic and the emerald and diamond ring shining under the stage lights. He sets down his beer bottle on the bar and stammers off out the side exit door.

Tim is sitting at the bar watching Jan's performance and he laughs. He drinks his beer without taking his eyes off her. There are many high round tables around, and many patrons are nursing all sorts of concoctions, some served in glasses, others in cans. Most of them are watching Jan, others are trying to avoid the noise altogether, and maybe carry on a conversation.

Tim is intent on Jan's performance. It's between good and bad, though she isn't tone-deaf. He smiles at her. She smiles back. As she finishes, he raises from his seat. Jan walks off the stage toward a couple sitting at one of the round high tables. He sits back down.

'Fancy seeing you here, Jan.' the woman says, 'I don't think I'd seen you here since George was around.'

'Now, Linda, drop that, what do you expect?' the man says.

Jan waves them off and brings her "Sunny Cape Codder" cocktail to her lips, 'Don't worry Chris, it's okay. Linda's right. Ever since George, I hadn't come to Honky-Tonk. I wasn't ready.'

'There, there.' Chris Gwynn pats her hand, 'But go easy on the drinks, that's your third one tonight. They'll creep up on you, you know.'

Linda Hall watches her and smiles. Jan gets up, 'Yeah. I know. That's it. I'm wrapping it up. Great to see you guys. See you at the beach sometime.'

Linda hollers back, 'Sure. Great seeing you too.' Both of them wave as Jan walks out the door. Now out of earshot, Linda throws a friendly punch at him, 'Chris, you're always the cop, aren't you? Controlling people's drinks! It's not like she's gonna drive anywhere, let a girl have some fun.'

Tim's still sitting on his stool, eavesdropping on Chris and Linda.

Chris picks up his drink and swirls the glass to hear the clinking of the ice cubes, 'Yeah, I guess you're right. Ever since Cassandra was murdered and George died right there.' He points with his glass next to where Linda's sitting, 'I hadn't seen Jan have any fun. Guess I blew it.'

'Yeah partner, you did.'

Tim scoots off the stool, puts a ten-dollar bill on the counter, and hurries toward the door. He sees Jan's silhouette about a block and a half away going east toward the beach. She's already reached the corner of the ten-bedroom motel. He rushes his pace a bit more, 'Wait! Jan!'

Buford Hall pulls in from the corner of the motel hoping Tim hasn't seen him almost taking steps to follow Jan. He leans against the brick wall until Tim crosses the street. Buford takes off in the opposite direction.

Hearing Tim calling her, Jan stops and turns around. Tim catches up to her. 'Jan, hold up. Can we talk?'

'Hello Tim, how are you? I'm heading home on the beach.'

'Can I join you?'

'Sure. How are Mandy and Elsa?'

'They're great. I just came out to get some air and enjoy the beach at night.' He shrugs, 'By the way, you were pretty good back there.'

'Ha, ha.' She laughs, 'No, I wasn't. I'm not going to say I was a total disaster, but singing is not my forte.'

'But you're an artist, you could maybe pursue it.'

'I'm a totally different kind of artist. I'm doing okay with what I have now.' She stops and turns toward the ocean to watch what seems like a sheet of black marble unfolding before them. 'It's so dark tonight.' She's looking at the slim smile shape of the moon hanging in the distance. Tim touches her arm and raises his hand toward her face. He turns her head and leans in brushing his lips against hers. She drops the sandals she's carrying to the ground and puts her hands around his waist. Heat rises from her chest as her body reacts to his touch. Her knees feel weak as prickles of sensations travel from her loins throughout her body. Suddenly she pulls away, 'No!' She puts a hand on her chest and stretches her other arm putting distance between them, 'We can't do this. Oh, Tim.' She picks up her sandals and runs away leaving Tim standing in the middle of the empty beach.

Chapter 6

Saturday, June 12, 2021

Laying awake all night, Jan has tried to take apart the emotions that torment her right now. She imagines each of these as bright stars descending into her bedroom window their glare blinding her to the point she can't discern right and wrong. Conflicted she's falling prey to Tim's demands, she's realizing this now. Does she want to succumb to weakness or rise above this? *I must think of seeing the truth through my own eyes.* It's not about writing fictional stories anymore, but about living her own life. *What does that mean?*

It's early morning and she gets out of bed, grabs her laptop from the dining table, and heads out to the porch. She stares at the sky and the slightly brighter waxing moon ahead and sets herself to pour out onto the keyboard every description and scene that comes to mind. She wants to dissect the desire she feels for Tim. She compares the feelings she felt for George with her attraction to Tim. She never felt drawn like this to George. She shakes her head, *This is so confusing.* Is it because she knows better than to pursue him?

The sun slithers onto the landscape and a spectacular blip of orange spreads on the horizon. She stares at the wooden gate ahead and beyond toward the ocean. The waves softly crash onto themselves and the sound comforts her. She decides to spill these feelings of despair onto her novel. She would rather have her fictitious friends push through the mire of emotions than live them herself. Little does she know.

~

The sun's been up for an hour or so now as Mandy walks up the wooden steps to Jan's patio and notices there's a laptop on the table next to a tall coffee mug. She approaches the sliding door. The wide sleeve of her green drop shoulder top fans out as she lifts her arm to knock. She notices Jan standing in front of the stove in the small kitchen. Jan turns around at the sound of the tapping and smiles.

Opening the sliding door she says, 'Hello Mandy! Come in, come in, you're here just in time. I'm getting some more coffee ready.'

Mandy smiles, 'Good morning, I see. Are you sure? I see you're set up outside with your laptop. I'm not interrupting?' She looks around the living area of the house. She admires the open layout. The kitchen and dining room are right across from the sliding door, and to her left there's a larger area with a sofa, loveseat, and television.

'Oh, no. No trouble at all. I've been working for the past three to four hours, I need this break.' Jan chuckles.

Mandy opens her mouth in surprise, 'Oh, wow. You get up early.'

Jan waves her to come over to the kitchen, 'Only some days, when inspiration strikes.' She shrugs and winks at Mandy, 'I have to put the muse to good use when she hits.'

Handing Mandy a mug with some espresso coffee she points to the sugar bowl on the counter, 'There, get some sugar if you'd like. I recommend at least a little bit of sugar. Would you like some creamer or milk?'

Mandy waves her off, 'No, just some sugar will be all right.'

Outside they take a seat on the patio. Jan sets down her mug on the table, 'So, are you enjoying your vacation?'

'Yes, we are. It is wonderful to get away from the big city.' Mandy looks around at the beachgoers who are slowly pouring onto the beach setting up their beach chairs and laying out towels on the sand. She smiles. 'We both needed to get away from the big city. Life here feels so carefree.'

'Yes, I know what you mean, don't we wish we could just live here forever?'

'That would be wonderful! Maybe, retire here? Though that seems to be so far away right now for me. But maybe you could.'

'Mmm. It may feel different if I lived here year-round. I do come here often enough, though.' She sips her coffee, 'I love it here, but I do need to be in different places throughout the year on account of my work, plus I have a home in North Carolina.'

'Ah, yes. Tim told me you're a famous writer. Is that exciting?'

So, Tim told her about me... 'It can be. It can also be exhausting sometimes. Plus, writing is a very lonely activity.'

'Are you alone?'

Jan lowers her eyes. Mandy notices a bit of sadness on her face, 'I'm so sorry. I didn't mean to pry.' She puts her hand over her mouth.

Jan shakes her head, 'No, don't worry. It's okay. It's just that I lost my husband four years ago.'

Mandy reaches out and takes Jan's hand, 'Oh Jan.'

After a brief moment in silence, Jan shrugs and takes a breath, 'Well, that's in the past and life goes on. So, tell me about you, about Elsa. She is such a lovely girl.'

'Yes, she is our joy. She's a very delightful young lady and we're very proud of her.'

'I see why.' Jan smiles. At that moment Mandy's phone rings and she touches her pocket. Jan says, 'Go ahead answer it, no worries.' She gets up and picks the empty mugs from the table. She walks inside.

Mandy takes the phone from her pocket, 'Hello, Stacy. What's up?'

Stacy Delgado, her business partner up in New York, sounds a little harried. She's just received a rush order and it's for specific pieces only Mandy knows where to find. That means work follows you everywhere you go in these modern times. Vacations or holidays are meaningless, but Mandy is happy to help. It is her company, after all. When Jan walks outside again she hears Mandy finish off, 'It's okay Stacy. I'll let you know what I find. After all, I left you all alone holding down the fort. So, it's only fair that I chip in. Don't worry about it.' They hang up.

Mandy turns to Jan, 'Well, that was work calling.' She chuckles, 'I guess I'm not going to get away from it no matter how hard I try.'

'What is it you do?'

Mandy points to her cell phone, 'My partner Stacy and I own a Design Studio or boutique like we like to call it between ourselves.' She winks. 'We cater to different types of tastes in design. We design spaces, so furniture, decor, and accents, the whole feel of a room. Depending on the client, some like antiques, which is what I specialize in, and other times they like more of a modern style. That's what Stacy likes.'

Jan rises her eyebrows, 'That's fascinating.'

'Thanks. Well, Stacy has sent me some work.' She pulls out her phone and looks for the text that just dinged. She reads it, then gets up, 'So, I have to go. Thanks so much, Jan. It was lovely. Thanks for the coffee.'

'My pleasure, Mandy. I spend a lot of time here on the porch, so come by anytime.' She smiles and they wave goodbye.

~

It's still early, the temperature is comfortable but it will be demanding in a few hours. Jan decides to go on her morning run, it's better to get out now. She's changed into her stretch black running shorts, sleeveless light blue sports shirt, and this time running shoes. She walks out of her gate and heads north.

After a while she looks at her fitness watch, which has already tracked one mile, so she turns around. On her return, the waves are stronger, there are children and adults wading in the water and some laying on beach towels on the sand. In the distance she notices Tim walking toward her. He's becoming a familiar image now as she can distinguish his gait in the distance.

She paces in place as he advances toward her, 'Hello, Tim. Good morning.'

Smiling he responds, 'Nice morning for a walk, or a run.'

She lowers her pace still in place, 'Yes, very invigorating. You're picking up jogging?'

'Well, if I'm honest, I'm looking for you.'

She stops, leans down, and places her hands on her knees. Recalling the other night on the beach with him she tries to avoid looking at him. She takes a breath. 'Tim, I don't think this is a good idea.' Fearing that she will more than like Tim, she doesn't want to open up her vulnerabilities to him, either. Pursuing Tim to get "professional enlightenment" is the idea she's toyed with since she met him but she's told herself accountability and responsibility calls for not letting herself go.

'Yes, I know, I know.' Tim sounds a bit impatient, 'Indulge me. Right now, nobody's around. Just walk with me. We can talk, just talk.' He spreads out his arms.

'Okay, just talk.' She stops panting, and starts to walk, 'What do you want to talk about?'

Tim takes hold of Jan's hand. She doesn't pull back. They walk hand in hand for a while. She feels her body warm up and briefly shuts her eyes. A few years after she married George they stopped holding hands. Their marriage had become comfortable. What she gave, he took. She gave love and support. She received love, security, and warmth. They had folded into each other, not quite taking shape as anything exciting or provocative, but neither was it disastrous. Their relationship was just comfortable and dependable. They each gave enough to make it work.

Holding Tim's hand Jan wants to to stamp the impression in her memory of how she feels at this moment.

To their left, the line of houses disappears into patches of green Florida Sea Grape and Saw Palmetto trees. 'Come.' Jan pulls Tim's arm, 'Let me show you the North Environmental Park.' They turn from the shore toward the shrubbery. 'It's okay, the sun is up now, but nobody will be there yet.'

They follow a wooden boardwalk into the park and walk around that trail. Jan points him to a picnic table at the end of the path and walks toward it.

'This is a nice area.' Tim tails after her, 'It's pretty secluded.'

'Yes. It is. Many people use the park's parking area and walk to the beach. There isn't much parking for the crowds to come, and now that the city commissioners doubled the parking fees, it takes a while to fill up. Hold on, I want to take a break.' She laughs as she sits on top of a picnic table with her feet on the bench. Now looking serious, 'Tim, why are you doing this? You know I can't do this. You have too many ties.'

He places his hand on her shoulders and looks into her eyes, 'There's a lot you don't know about Mandy and me, Jan. It's been a while now that our marriage is in trouble.'

'I'm sorry to hear that. The fact is you still have a beautiful wife and an amazing daughter.'

'We came on vacation to see if we should stay together.' He shrugs, 'At least that's what she thinks. She wants this trip to be our way to bond again, to see if we both had it in us to continue, for Elsa's sake. But I can't anymore.' He looks up to the clouds above them and laughs, 'Wow, that does sound so cliché.'

Jan turns her mouth downward, 'It sure does.' What a dilemma. On the one hand, she feels very attracted to him, but on the other, he's just looking for a rebound and he doesn't even know it. That is definitely not what she wants. She puts an arm on his shoulder, 'Let me be honest with you Tim. When all is said and done, maybe we can check in on it. What do you think?'

'Perhaps that would be wise. It's the grown-up thing to do.'

Jan then pulls Tim in and kisses him. Tim's eyes widen. During the next few minutes, they transfer heat, and energy with their lips and delve into their wants. Tim breathes in what he can to satisfy his craving for her, the thirst for an adventure, for something to wake him up. She finally comes up for air and says, 'This is goodbye.' Jan gives in to the idea it will be quite some time before she finds someone who would be able to fulfill her desires. Future goals.

She breaks it off, 'Now, let's walk back to the shore, like normal people, and head on with our lives. Okay?'

Tim is still standing in front of her holding onto her arms, 'Jan, I didn't know what I was missing in my life, but I want you to know you would fill up a void I didn't know I had.'

Jan lowers her face. Tim softly puts his hand under her chin and raises her head. He stares into her eyes. He sees a tear threatening to fall, and he softly wipes it off Jan's cheek, 'I know we have to stop, and I will do my best.' He kisses her again, 'Let's go.' They don't speak another word until about half a mile later when they arrive at the edge of their houses.

Mandy waves from the deck, 'Hey there!' She has a tall glass in her hand of what looks like orange juice from afar, 'Good morning!' Both Jan and Tim look up, and Jan waves. Tim heads over to the patio deck and walks up the steps, 'Hey there, Mandy, good morning.' He walks past her into the house. Mandy's disappointed. She watches as Jan walks up her patio steps into her house. She then stays on the edge of the deck admiring the sun, clouds, and birds hovering over the horizon.

~

As the words keep flowing through her fingers Jan tries to translate her new feelings into coherent sentences. This evening the dialogues are pouring out onto the page as she digests lust, rage, grief, dread, and frustration, and explores the perspective of her main characters. Her new feelings nourish her writing. This is a good thing. Nothing like raw emotion on the page. *Will my readers react to these feelings? Will they get it?*

In her restlessness, Jan waves her arms and knocks over her mug from the table. The mug crumbles to pieces on the tile floor and tepid coffee splashes all over. 'Shit!' Jan looks over at the ceramic pieces commingled with brownish liquid on the floor for a few seconds and turns her head back to the screen, ignoring it.

Chapter 7

Sunday, June 13, 2021

Wading through the water chasing after a bright squishy ball floating near her, Elsa grabs it and tosses it to Tim. He catches it and throws it back. She misses the catch and wades back a bit to get it. Tim splashes some water to make it harder for her to find it. 'Daaaddy!' Elsa complains. Tim laughs and splashes some more. He looks toward Jan's house, the light in the rear patio is on, and there is no sight of her. He finds it strange to have the patio on during the daytime. He frowns.

They can't see the face of the slender woman wearing a navy blue bathing suit, and a large white sunhat walking toward the shore. Tim whistles gallantly. Mandy waves him off. She stands on the wet sand, letting the ripples of water touch her feet as they creep onshore.

'Mommy, Mommy, come, and play with us.' Elsa shrieks raising her hand and holding the squishy ball.

'No, darling, this is as far as I'll go, I'll watch you having fun.'

'C'mon Mandy, join us.' Tim gestures waving her in.

Mandy holds onto her sunhat and shakes her head. Elsa splashes showing off her swimming skills, Tim rushes the water in, and out with his arms. Elsa giggles. Fun in the sun.

~

The day goes as Sundays go. For Tim it's been a quiet day. Reading the menu his thoughts wander to Jan. He thinks of how he's been able to watch her every day sitting on her porch, walking on the beach, or taking in the sun. But today she's been absent. Where did she go? Why did she go away? After he arrived he felt a new door opening in his life. He has found what he's been looking for. He now knows Jan is fighting some of the same feelings for him. These days he has been trying to rationalize a relationship with Jan while keeping also trying to figure out his future with Mandy and Elsa. He's not even sure that is what he wants or if he can achieve it. He's distracted.

'Yuck.' Elsa shakes her head, 'no.' The waitress smiles.

Mandy points to the menu, 'Honey, are you sure you don't want any veggies, maybe some carrots or broccoli?' Elsa sticks her tongue out and Mandy looks over at Tim.

Mandy clenches her jaw, 'All right, all right, chicken and fries it'll be. So, that'll be all for us.' She hands the menu to the waitress. Tim pulls his head back and lowers his eyes to avoid getting into this silent conversation about Elsa's food habits.

'I'll bring your drinks right away.' the waitress shuffles the menus in her hands and walks away.

'So, I like this table right next to the ocean.' Mandy says as she looks around checking the rest of the patrons on the restaurant deck nursing beers, cosmos, martinis, and downing shrimp and calamari appetizers. Of course, the kids with their colorful sugary drinks. The sun is setting on the west and the beach is like a canvas of purple, dark blue, and orange-pink brush strokes on the horizon.

'Yes, I think it's very nice.' Tim says.

'This was a great idea, honey.' Mandy reaches for Tim's hand, 'I'm glad we did this. We needed the break, Elsa needed to get away as well, and venture out. As it is, we never have time to leave the city. Do you like it, honey?' She looks at Elsa. Elsa nods, slurping the drink the waitress just placed in front of her.

'Good, good. I'm glad everyone's happy. Are you happy?' Mandy says.

Tim shuts one eye and curiously looks at Mandy, then at Elsa. He smiles. 'Of course I'm happy!' he chuckles embarrassingly. Mandy shrugs, and continues, 'Yes, I guess we're happy.' She smiles at Elsa, 'right pumpkin?' she winks at Elsa. Elsa giggles.

After dinner, they walk on the beach to get home. Elsa runs ahead of them, stomping her feet in the water, splashing, and jumping along the way. Mandy carries hers and Elsa's sandals in one hand and takes Tim's hand with the other. He smiles, she rests her head on his shoulder and wraps her arm around his waist. He reaches around her shoulders. They've reached the edge of Jan's house. He looks up, the porch light is on, and that slither of brightness also shines through the sliding door, but no movement inside. They walk onto their property and up the path. Elsa is still splashing around the shore. 'Elsa, time to come inside.' Tim hollers. Elsa rushes up the stairs, Mandy goes inside, and Elsa follows. Tim says, 'You both go ahead, I'll stay out here for a little bit.'

'Would you like me to join you?' Mandy asks.

Tim shakes his head, 'No, that's okay. You and Elsa do your thing. I'll be okay.' He focuses on the purplish hues quickly disappearing in the distance.

After a long walk, Tim returns and finds Elsa and Mandy watching a movie on TV. Leaning behind Mandy, Tim lightly nuzzles her nape, and whispers in her ear, 'I have something to show you, come on!' He signals with his eyes to Elsa who is entranced watching the TV screen.

A flurry of soft electricity runs through her and her skin prickles up. She follows him up the stairs, coquettishly winking. Tim smiles, beckoning. Once at the top of the stairs, she unleashes her sundress as it slides off her shoulders showing her bare shoulders and back.

With the repressed energy Tim has from yesterday morning he feels his arousal increasing, he grabs Mandy and kisses her, guiding her into their bedroom and shutting the door behind them.

Chapter 8

Monday, June 14, 2021

Walking down aisles of shelves, Mandy and Elsa admire glass and porcelain dishes, platters, and glasses at "Anna's Antiques." She hears the soft murmur of two ladies speaking at the back. She picks up one of the platters which she thinks may be a French Limoges porcelain antique. She asks Elsa to hold the dish upside down so the can take a quick picture with her phone. She quietly sends the photo by text to Stacy. She types, "Check out the marks on these platters and let me know if authentic." She quickly puts her phone back in her purse and takes the platter from Elsa and they walk over to the counter. Anna, the store owner, looks up from speaking to Linda Hall to greet them. Mandy hands over a couple of platters to Anna, 'Could I ask you to reserve these at the counter for me? I can come later today to pay for them and pick them up.'

'Sure, sure. I'll keep them here for a day if you like.'

'That should be fine, thanks so much.' Mandy smiles at Anna and turns to Linda.

Linda smiles back, 'Are you visiting?'

'Yes, yes, we got here a few days ago.'

'Well, that's great, we love visitors!'

Mandy pulls out her car keys from her handbag and she places that over her arm, 'We love it here. I'd never been. Do you live here?'

'Yes.' Linda points at Anna, 'Anna and I are long-time residents here at the beach. I grew up here, and Anna, well Anna has probably been here longer than I have.' She laughs.'Where are you staying? At the hotel? Or do you have friends here?'

'Oh, no. We've rented a house just on the beach. It's a few doors down from the restaurant and the condos, not far from the beach gate.'

'Oh, that's prime real estate, very nice homes there.'

'Yeah. We like it very much, especially since we're right on the beach. I am inclined to maybe buy property here, I like it so much!'

'That is great! You came to the right place, I'm Linda Hall, a real estate agent. I could surely help you with that.' She pulls a card out of her purse, 'Here, take this and maybe we can meet up for coffee sometime. I can give you a tour of the real estate that's up for sale, and show you around.'

'That would be great! Wonderful.' Mandy puts Linda's card in her purse.

~

Finding himself alone in the house sitting on the sofa with nothing to do, Tim rushes up from the sofa and walks out the front door to go for a walk. As he locks up the door he hears someone scuffling their feet behind him on Jan's property.

A blonde blue-eyed man wearing a khaki shirt and pants is at Jan's door. He looks startled, his eyes squint and he promptly sprints. Tim follows him, 'Hey! What do you want? Who are you?' Tim chases after him but gives up when he reaches the corner of Main Street.

He returns to the house catching his breath. As he reaches the driveway he notices Jan's front lamp light is still on. He shakes his head, she must still be away. As he gets closer he notices something stuck on the door frame. Again. *That must've been Buford!* He knocks on Jan's door. After a few seconds, he knows she's not coming to the door. He picks the card, it has a drawing of two dogs who seem to be howling at the sun, but the bottom portion says, "The Moon." He frowns and puts the card in his pocket. He turns around and walks back onto the street.

~

The evening breeze is soft and smooth on their skins. Elsa shrieks as a couple of fake money pieces of paper are blown away by the wind. She gets up and rushes to catch them. Mandy and Tim laugh, 'C'mon honey, it's your turn to roll.'

Tim looks up and stares at Jan's porch. The light is still on. Everything there is quiet and still. A slither of light shines through the kitchen window. He thinks back to the first time he desired to touch Jan and how he held back thinking about Mandy. He shakes his head as Elsa yells, 'Got 'em!' She turns, and sits back down, placing the fake $10, and $20 bills under the Monopoly board next to the rest. Monopoly has become a favorite game of Elsa's, 'I'm getting $200 right after I roll, Mr. Banker, so pay up!'

'First, roll your dice, honey cup, you could get a pair of ones. Let's see how it goes first.' Tim answers. Elsa rolls her dice, picks her 'Car' token, hops around the board, passes GO, and stretches her hand out waiting for her fake money. She wiggles her fingers, 'Pay up!' Tim laughs, picks out 2 $100 bills, and hands them to her.

Mandy stares at the ocean, breathes in the salty air, and smiles. She watches as a lace of white moves along the shore edging along the blackness of the night. The horizon looks like a blank movie screen, and all she can hear is the waves rushing in, and her husband and daughter's laughter. She is content and happy. Her life is full tonight.

Chapter 9

Tuesday, June 15, 2021

Watching the beach from her patio porch, Jan stares at the shoreline as Tim and Mandy are strolling along the sand while Elsa runs after the sandpipers who try to avoid her and the water. Mandy wears white well as it contrasts her shiny copper hair flowing under her large summer hat. Tim is wearing the same trunks he had the first time she saw him. Again, no shirt. *Nice little family.*

As they now approach both properties Mandy takes off her sunglasses and waves at Jan, 'Hello there, Jan!' She puts her hand on her head to prevent her hat from blowing off.

'Hi, good morning.' Jan waves back. 'Nice day for a morning walk.'

Tim smiles, relieved to see Jan has returned. All he does is nod and look at her, his hands in his shorts pockets. Mandy turns around, 'Come on Elsa, let's go inside, you can come out later to play in the water.' Elsa runs past them toward the house.

Mandy waves at Jan again and follows Elsa into the kitchen. Tim stays outside on the deck. He steals a few looks toward Jan's house. Jan goes inside her cottage.

As Mandy walks upstairs, Tim strolls over to the kitchen counter, 'Elsa, do you want a snack?' He pulls out a couple of slices of bread from a bag and begins to smother them up with peanut butter. He's about to dive the knife into the strawberry jam. 'Daddy, no!'

'What?!' He says turning to Elsa.

'Don't make the jam yucky! The knife is dirty.'

'But it's all going to the same place.'

'No, Daddy.' She rushes over to the drawer and pulls out a clean knife. 'Here, use this one.' She passes it over to him.

Mandy watches from the top of the stairs and pauses reading something on her cell phone and says, 'You can learn a thing or two from your daughter, Tim.'

'All right, here you go Elsa.' He hands her the PB&J sandwich, 'Now, go over and watch those cartoons you wanted to watch.'

Mandy walks down the stairs signaling for Tim to follow her outside to the deck.

Mandy takes a breath, 'Well, guess what?'

Tim sits down next to Mandy. She continues, 'We have to go back this weekend. Elsa is going to need some remedial classes which start on Monday.'

'What happened?'

'She didn't do very well in Language Arts. She needs to test again, and since she is going to switch to the better school in the Fall, it's best she go in with better grades.'

'Oh, no. How bad is it?'

'Very.' Her lips turn down, 'I had no idea it was this bad. I knew she was struggling, but I thought she had overcome it, at least to an average grade. Plus, she needs to be ready for Middle School in a couple of years.'

Tim closes his eyes. 'What should we do?'

'Well, for starters, get her into the remedial class, and have her make the effort this summer. That means taking classes most of the summer, which I'm sure she's going to hate.'

'But she is having such a wonderful time here.'

'Yes, she is.' Mandy shrugs, 'And so am I but she has to understand what responsibility is, and this is a consequence she has to learn how to handle.'

'Do you have a plan, then?'

Mandy gets up, 'I say we take advantage of the days we have left, and we should head back up on Saturday. That gives us Sunday to unwind from the traveling and all that and be ready for a Monday start. I'll have to change our flights.'

Tim stays silent. Mandy goes back inside leaving him on the deck.

Later, Tim is packing the dishwasher with the dirty plates from their light lunch. Mandy stealthily slides over to him and hugs him from behind. 'What do you say we go snuggle upstairs while Elsa is distracted?' She kisses his back and reaches with her hands down his front to entice him to some intimacy. Tim pulls back and turns. He kisses her but pulls away. He opens the French door and leaves it open, the sound of the ocean seeps through into the house. Mandy feels hot, her chest wet, and she touches her warm cheeks. She breathes in, disappointed, and closes her eyes.

~

In the shower, Tim hears a knock on the door.

'Tim!' Mandy hollers.

'Yeah!' He answers.

'Will you be long?' Mandy asks. 'We're going hiking up a trail I found south of here. Do you want to come? We can wait for you.'

Tim thinks for a few seconds, shakes his head, and slides it under the shower. 'No, Mandy, I'm okay. Just go ahead. I'll figure something out here.'

'C'mon Tim. We only have a couple of more days. Don't you want to share them with Elsa?'

'Mandy, I don't feel like going. Look, I'll fix dinner for us, that way when you get back you won't have to wait. So go ahead. Have fun!' He dabs some shampoo onto his head and lathers it into his scalp with his fingertips.

'Okay. Tim. I thought we were supposed to try our best here. We'll go. See you later.' Mandy stammers out pursing her lips, frustrated about the turn her now very short vacation at the beach has taken. She wonders if she misread the signs of what she thought was Tim's re-commitment to their relationship.

~

Dinner has come and gone. Mandy is snuggled on the sofa with Elsa under a cotton fleece blanket, reading her a story. She loves reading the story books to Elsa, especially the ones that rhyme. This one is about two naughty squirrels and an acorn. She looks up as Tim walks by the rear toward the door, 'I'm heading out.' He says, 'I'm gonna grab a beer, and see if I meet some locals. Don't wait up for me.'

Mandy knows what this means, she'll be going to bed alone. Just like when she's home. She thought this vacation would be a change for them, for their lives. It sure looked like it. *I guess habits die hard.* Her eyes are wet, she blinks, looks down at Elsa, and hugs her for comfort, 'So, where were we?' She winks and hopes Elsa doesn't grow out of this ritual any time soon.

~

On his way back from the bar Tim sees Jan's car in the driveway. He turns, and goes to her door, knocking, and ringing her bell, continuously.

Jan forcefully opens the door as his hand is rising up to knock again. She yells, 'What the hell are you doing?!'

He brings his finger to his lips in a gesture of silence. 'Can I come in?' he asks as he hands her a tarot card he found stuck on the doorframe just now.

'What for, Tim?' she looks at the card. A knight in black armor riding a horse and the word "death" written at the bottom. She turns around leaving the door open; he walks into the hallway.

'I have another card at home also, the "Moon" card, whatever that means.'

Jan shrugs as she walks ahead of him down the hall.

'Jan, where were you? I was going crazy.'

Jan is in the living area, she drops the Tarot card on the table and leans a hand on one of the dining chairs, 'What is this all about Tim?'

'I can't believe you left without telling me! I thought something happened to you! I missed you!'

Jan's eyes open wide and then she frowns, 'There is nothing between us, Tim. Do I have to remind you that you have a wife and kid next door? They probably heard you making all that racket at my doorstep, you know. That's the only reason I let you in, so you wouldn't throw away what you still have.'

Tim tries to approach her and she raises her hand midway to stop him, 'Jan, the truth is Mandy and I are not doing well. Our relationship has run dry, and I don't think there will be any turning back. Since I met you all I want to do is be with you. I'd like to try. Why can't we be together? Look, I know I will have to leave Mandy eventually and you don't have any ties. This is doable.' He moves toward where she's standing. Jan moves away, and stands behind the table, putting more distance between them. Tim walks around the table and reaches for her. She lets him embrace her, but her arms are against his chest in semi-resistance.

'Tim, I'm married to my work. I have ties, and I don't want to break them.' She lies as she tries to pull away from him. He softly grabs her arm, pulls her in, and searches for her lips. A brief but deep kiss strengthens Tim's resolve. They both hold their breath. He rushes his hands down her arms, toward her front, looking to release her clothes. She takes one step back and pushes him away. 'No, no, no, Tim. I can't.'

'Please, Jan. These past few days you were away I've realized that I need you.'

'Do you always get want you want Tim?'

He doesn't reply.

She is still trying to put up a barrier between them, 'I have to go to bed, I have an early start tomorrow.'

Tim tries to reach for her again, and Jan puts him at arm's length, 'Please, you have to go. This is not going to work.' She waves a hand between him and herself, 'We are not going to work out!'

Tim looks confused, 'How would you know if we haven't even tried?'

'Where's Mandy? Go to Mandy, please. I refuse to break up a family, I can't do this to Elsa. Please understand.'

Tim takes her hand, and puts it on his chest, 'Do you feel that?' Jan lowers her head. He says, 'I know you do. As I know you feel something for me. Why reject it? All these years I have never strayed from Mandy, not once. But now… all I want is to be with you and make you happy in some way.' He lifts her chin with his finger, 'I know you want it. I know you want it as much as I do. Your body doesn't lie to me.'

Tim brings her closer and Jan's resistance is failing. She closes her eyes as he finds her lips again. The heat of his passion softly caresses her, and he wraps his arms around her, pulling her in. Jan pulls away again.

Tim's closeness is breaking down all the barriers she promised she would put up to fight her newfound urge to be with him. She must be strong. Jan doesn't want to live in regret, hiding in the shadows of deceit. She refuses to be a mistress, loving on borrowed moments, living a lie. Jan takes a deep breath feeling a heavy weight on her chest. She exclaims, 'Please stop Tim, please! I don't think we'd make it Tim.' She pulls away and walks down the hallway to the front door, 'I need you to go.' She opens the door.

'I want you tonight, Jan. I want to be with you.'

Jan doesn't say anything as she leans against the open door.

Pain forms on Tim's face. A flash of white scrolls across it as the torment travels from head to toe through his body. It's not that he believes she won't take him. It's that he recognizes life sometimes shows you glimpses of happiness and that maybe it's only that, glimpses. 'I wish our paths had crossed before, Jan Crawford.' He says with a thickness in his throat, 'There will always be a spot in my soul for you.' He turns around. A chill runs through his arms. His arms feel so heavy as they drop to his sides. He doesn't realize his shoulders and body show how defeated he feels.

Jan bites her lip as she sees his reaction, a stab of agony also in her chest. She knows what he does to her. She knows she is not able to account for her actions if he gets close; if he touches or kisses her. Again, she's gotten something out of this flirting but now she has to stop before it gets out of hand. She doesn't want to play this game, this experiment she thought could be research. Now she knows she's been a complete fool. She vividly remembers what she felt when George died and all his truth came out. She knows lies and deceit take you down hidden, forbidden, and painful paths; how it feels to be lied to and betrayed. She doesn't want to go there again, nor be the cause of lunacy for anyone else.

Remnants of torment run through her quickly, like water struggling through river rapids on a chilly afternoon, as reality resurfaces reminding her of when she felt smothered by George's lies. She had been oblivious to his escapades and trysts with the local Tarot card reader and psychic, the medium's daughter as some locals called her. Cassandra and George had been having an affair for a few years. On and off, of course, since he only ventured here during the summer. But perhaps it was enough for them to cement their feelings for each other. The night he died that truth glared at her head on. The night he died, she also died, murdered. So, for the last few years, she has carried the weight of his deception and of his guilt. In the end, the police accused him of her murder. Case closed.

It took her a long time to come to terms with that chapter in her life, so this is where she stops this nonsense. At least it hasn't even really begun. Of course, Tim is going to feel bad, but he doesn't know the pain he was about to inflict on his family or himself by pursuing it. She stands still watching Tim walk toward her down the hall.

She furiously wipes off the tears rolling down her face. 'Tim, I'm so sorry.' She wraps her arms around herself. 'I know I could have feelings for you, but you have to go to them.'

He walks through the door and turns around, 'That card is going to be an omen for you.' He keeps walking without looking back.

Jan closes the door and starts shaking uncontrollably. She leans against the wall and slowly slides down to the floor, sobbing.

～

Both windows in the bedroom are wide open, and a cool breeze sifts in as Mandy turns in her bed. The sheets slide off of her revealing a sliver of lace from her soft-pink silk nightie sliding along her slender tanned thigh. She moans in her sleep. Some lace also barely covers her breasts, and her red curls cascade onto her chest rising and falling in tempo as she breathes. Tim watches her. He stands next to her side of the bed and starts taking off his clothes. All of them. The shuffling wakes Mandy up. She leans up holding herself up on one elbow. Tim, now completely naked, leans in and kisses her furiously. He moves on top of her, fully aroused. She takes it. He is meticulous, touching all the right spots with his lips and his tongue. From her face, down her neck, her breasts, and her groin. He lays on her, covering her body completely with his. He hungrily drinks in every inch of her, and she takes in all the sensations she's feeling. So many sensations she had not felt in so long. She enjoys every second of pleasure.

Chapter 10

Thursday, June 17, 2021

Reaching over Tim's plate, Elsa tries to get to the syrup. All three of them are sitting at the table on the deck eating breakfast. Tim doesn't notice Elsa, he's looking ahead across the yard toward Jan's house. Jan is on the patio sitting under the wide beach umbrella with her laptop open, and a mug of coffee next to it. Mandy looks at Elsa, 'Elsa, please ask your dad to pass you the syrup. It's not polite to reach over people's plates.'

'Oh. Sorry, Mommy.' She says embarrassingly.

Tim snaps out of his thoughts, 'Oh, sure.' He gets the syrup and passes it to Elsa, 'Here you go honey.' Elsa takes it and pours the liquid over her waffles.

Mandy turns her head, covering her eyes with her hand, 'Oh, there's Jan!' She waves, a big smile on her face, 'Hello Jan! Good morning!'

Waving back, she smiles and rises her coffee mug as in giving a toast, 'Good morning.'

Tim also waves and says 'Good morning.' Elsa mimics all of them as well. They smile and get back to talking. Jan leans back into looking at the laptop screen, slithering her eyes upwards now and then taking a peek at the happy family. She smiles to herself. *Good. Good. Concentrate on your book. Dianne needs this last edit, and I'm bound to finish it by the end of the week. Almost there.*

~

As the sun is setting behind their house the Evans family is enjoying the shore. The water is warm as Tim and Elsa excitedly splash around.

They count and ride the waves, and take it all in. However, Mandy is sitting in a beach chair near the shore. She wouldn't dream of going in the water. Mandy gets up, waves at them, and gestures she's going back to the house. She folds the chair and picks it up along with her book, a novel she's reading, *The Blooming Sun* by Jan Crawford. She leans the chair against Jan's wooden fence and looks up toward Jan's porch, and waves at her. She ventures to open the gate and walks through.

'Hello there, neighbor!'

Jan looks up, 'Hello Mandy. How are you? Enjoying your time at the beach?'

'Yes, very much. Can I sit for a minute, so sorry to intrude, I know you must be working.' Mandy tucks the book close to her bosom which doesn't go unnoticed by Jan. Mandy continues, 'Yeah, I'm reading your book. I like it.'

'I'm glad you like it. But yes, sure, come in, please have a seat. I needed a break anyway. Can I get you anything? Iced tea, coffee, wine?'

Mandy waves her off, 'Oh no, no, please, I'm interrupting, and I don't want to take any more of your time than necessary. I just want to say hello. It's exciting to meet a celebrity.' She makes quotes with her fingers.

Jan smiles, laughs in fact, 'Ha! Mmm, not quite, but somewhat well known.'

'Well, I'm glad I've met you. You're delightful, and I want to invite you to come with us tomorrow. We're heading to St. Augustine. I've never been. Have you?'

'Yes, once or twice, an interesting place. I love the old buildings and the history.'

'Great! That's what I hear. Would you join us? It'll be fun.'

Jan looks at her laptop and shrugs. Mandy senses she's going to say no. She says, 'Come with us, really. You need to get away from work now and again. Believe me.' She puts her hand to her chest, 'I know! I have work back home, even if it's not that much. I work part-time, but I needed to get away.' She looks down at Tim and Elsa in the water. She points to them,

'Look at them! They're so happy, relaxing, and playing. It's been so long since Tim had any time for Elsa. You see, you need to take some time off.' She's still smiling.

'Well, okay. If you insist. I do like St. Augustine. I would very much like to join you. It should be fun.' Shutting the screen of her laptop, Jan takes a sip from her mug. 'And, maybe a day off will get me away from so much caffeine.' They both laugh.

'Okay, I'm aiming for leaving around eight thirty, is that a good time for you?'

'Sure.'

'Great.' Mandy gets up, her book still close to her, 'See you tomorrow morning. Glad you'll be able to make it.'

'Me too.' Jan smiles and watches Mandy head down the stairs onto the path toward the wooden gate.

Chapter 11

Friday, June 18, 2021
St. Augustine, FL

Running up to the Gazebo in the middle of the Spanish plaza in the middle of town, Mandy tries to keep up with Elsa. Tim and Jan are still about half a block away walking down Saint George Street in the Spanish Quarter. They had been at the Oldest Wooden Schoolhouse museum. As Tim brushes his hand against Jan's she doesn't resist and lowers her gaze. He holds her hand to cross the street. Over on the other side of the park, Mandy raises her arm so they see where they are.

Leaning over a railing in the Gazebo, Elsa swings her feet off the ground, 'Mommy, Miss Jan told me there's a house here made of seashells. Can we go see it?'

'Seashells? Wow. That should be interesting.' Mandy is distracted watching Tim and Jan walk toward them.

As Jan approaches she hears them and adds, 'Yes, it's called coquina, and back in the day when the Spanish lived here they extracted the tiny seashell rock to build the Fort of San Marcos to protect the city from invaders. They also built some homes. There's a museum just around the corner with coquina walls we can go visit.'

'Fascinating.' Tim eyes Jan, and she nods.

'I want to go!' Elsa squeals.

'All right, then.' Mandy interjects, 'Jan, lead the way.'

They continue walking down tight sidewalks and narrow alleys. Turning a few corners, Mandy is now next to Jan. She says, 'Do you write any historical novels? This town seems like an interesting setting for one.'

'Actually, I don't. I like history, and St. Augustine is a fascinating place. But I have not written anything like that.'

'Well, you seem to know quite a lot. Maybe you should think about it.'

Jan smiles. 'Maybe I should.' She raises her hand, and points at a two-story bone-white colored building sitting at the corner of two streets with Spanish names, 'Here she is. Let's go inside, and you will be fascinated by all this.' Her eyes beam with delight.

Elsa pulls on her mom's hand, who leans in to hear her whisper something in her ear. Mandy says after listening to Elsa, 'Okay, let's go inside.' She winks at Tim once inside, and she pulls Elsa with her, 'We'll be right back, you guys just go on. We'll catch up with you.'

Tim looks at Mandy, then at Jan, back at Mandy who is now walking down the hallway, 'Okay.' He shrugs. Jan swerves her head indicating for him to follow along to the left. They go up a flight of stairs to the upper part of the museum. They find a hallway with doors on the left and on the right. They walk into a scantily furnished bedroom with a baluster bed and a medium-height dark wooden armoire. Jan reaches over to the side of the bed and examines one of the wooden balusters, 'This craftsmanship is exquisite.'

'I am just wondering if these folks enjoyed making love here.' He smiles looking at her from across the bed, 'It seems like their mattresses weren't very soft, though it's roomy enough.'

Jan blushes and shakes her head, 'Come on, let's continue.' She walks out of the bedroom and Tim follows.

As they go inside a library Jan approaches to look at the books on the bookcase. She smiles and touches the spines of some of the old leathered books. Tim walks to the other side and watches her. He turns around to check out the door. They're alone, so he moves toward the door and swings the door almost shut. Now closer to her he reaches in holds her arms and kisses her. Her face heats up, her breasts feel hard. She gives in.

She closes her eye and he says, 'I couldn't help myself.'

Jan seems to wake up from her daze and pulls away, 'I'm sorry.' She turns toward the door, opens it, and runs outside.

Tim hears Mandy and Elsa walking up the stairs, his cheeks are still a bit warm but he manages to say, 'There you are.'

'Where's Jan?' Mandy asks.

Tim points down the hall, 'I think she's in one of the bedrooms, we got split up. Come, and see this incredible library.' He guides them toward the library. As both Elsa and Mandy enter the library, he feels his face start to cool off. He walks over and stands between Mandy and Elsa, wrapping his arms around them.

~

All afternoon Mandy has been in her element visiting rose gardens and admiring so much old architecture. Jan has barely spoken since Tim's kiss. They've been in and out of shops, had lunch, and visited houses converted into museums. Mid-afternoon, the smell of bread and sugar draws them to the tall storefront windows of a sand-colored two-storied corner building with a wraparound Mediterranean porch iron railing on the second floor. It's a bakery displaying the most delicious-looking cream cannoli. Of course, they have to try some.

The sun is down as the car rides onto the driveway shared by their rental homes. Elsa is sleeping leaning her head against Jan's shoulder. Jan stares out the passenger window. Tim stops the car and Jan waits for someone to come fetch Elsa, she doesn't want to wake her. Tim takes Elsa out of the car and carries her into the house.

Jan gets out of the car and says, 'Thanks so much for inviting me, Mandy. It was a wonderful day.'

'Yes, it was. Poor Elsa, we really wore her out.' She laughs. Jan reaches over to Mandy and gives her a hug, 'Thanks. See you in the morning.'

'Oh, I'm not sure about that, we're leaving early.'

Jan feels a muscle in her jaw tighten. She catches her breath, 'I didn't know you were leaving so soon.'

'I'm packing tonight and leaving very early. But it was great to share today with you.' Mandy extends her hand to touch Jan's arm. 'I hope we can meet again sometime. Look me up if you ever come to New York.'

Jan smiles, 'Sure, sure. Have a great trip back.' She walks away toward her front door.

~

After tucking Elsa in bed, Mandy comes downstairs, and heads to the kitchen to get a glass of wine. 'Tim?' She calls out. No answer. She sees the French doors are open and walks out to the deck, glass in hand. At the edge of their property, someone is heading toward Jan's gate, he pushes it and heads up the path. Mandy watches, then yells out, 'Tim?'

Tim looks up and quickly swerves his face toward the right. The color leaves his face, and he stammers, 'I…I was going to check, and see if Jan had seen my Ray-bans. I can't find them.' He turns back, down the path, out the gate, and walks toward Mandy.

'I was looking for you, we need to put the luggage in the car. I'd rather pack it tonight, and leave for the airport early without the hassle.'

'About that.' Tim sits on one of the chairs, 'I've given it some thought, and I would like to stay a few more days.'

Mandy takes a sip of wine, and gestures her glass toward him, 'Do you want some?' Tim shakes his head. Still standing facing the ocean she takes another swig of the red liquid and puckers her lips. 'Any reason?'

'What?' Tim looks up at her, as he leans back in the chair extending his legs, and putting his arms behind his head, 'No. No reason other than relaxing for a few more days. Look, I don't want to go back to the city. It'll be there when I get back. I need to unwind. So much to do when I get back, and here is what I need right now, absorbing the sun and the good vibes. I'll still be cutting my vacation short. I can drive you to the airport but I want to stay a few more days.'

Mandy, who is still standing next to Tim's chair watching the ocean, balances her hand under her elbow, holding the almost empty wine glass in her hand, 'I know, we are having such a wonderful time. I wish we could continue but I want you with me, Tim. Why do we always have to split up like this?'

'Split up? What are you talking about?'

'You came alone, I came down a few days after you. Why can't we all go back together? Be together? We hardly have any time to be together once you start to work again. How are we going to make this work?'

'Can we make it work, Mandy?'

'I'm trying, Tim. I've put every effort into making us work. Why is it not ever enough for you?' She looks at him, the pain strained upon her face, 'I thought we were working. I would just want you to give us more of your presence, your time. Now Elsa's going to take summer school. It's going to be so hectic we won't even have a real summer!'

'Mandy, I get it. I do, but my job is very demanding, and I just need a few more days here. Okay?' He looks to the beach, not at Mandy. Mandy turns around and walks inside.

A few minutes later Tim hears commotion inside as Mandy starts hauling suitcases out the front door toward her car. She opens up the trunk and puts two large suitcases in. She walks past him toward the door and heads upstairs.

Chapter 12

Saturday, June 19, 2021
Daytona Beach Airport, FL

Crouching down to Elsa's level, Tim gives her a hug in the airport lobby, 'Come here pumpkin.'

Elsa says, 'Bye Daddy! Come home soon.'

Tim kisses her on the forehead, 'Now be a good girl, and keep reading your stories. Okay?'

Elsa wrinkles her nose and nods, 'Sure Daddy. I will.'

Mandy is quiet, pretending she doesn't care that Tim is staying behind, but the truth is she feels like there's lava flowing inside her stomach. She shakes her head and pouts her mouth.

Tim rises and tries to hold Mandy, but she pulls away. He tells her, 'Honey, have a safe trip, I'll be back in a couple of days. I promise I won't go back to work right away, we'll do something together when I get back.'

'I hope so, Tim.' She pulls the handle of her carry-on bag, 'Come on Elsa, let's go, the line is getting long.' She strides toward the security area.

Tim follows them until they reach the Security agent. 'Bye, sweets. You two think of me.' He winks and waves at them. Elsa smiles but Mandy doesn't look up as she takes her driver's license back, and walks toward the baggage check.

~

Jan hangs the pink canvas shopping bag across her shoulder as she walks out of the produce shop heading east toward the beach. Her pace is steady. As she reaches the beach car park where day beachgoers park, a gust of wind blows her airy cotton skirt. She slides her hands down her front, but the heavy bag and a crack in the sidewalk make her trip a step. She doesn't fall but she drops her shopping bag.

A few cars down Buford is leaning against his truck watching her. His arms are crossed and he doesn't move an inch as he observes the chaos. Jan picks up her bag and a few oranges that fell out of her bag. She gets back up. As she walks past Buford he says, 'Have you been receiving my messages?'

Jan continues walking, ignoring him. She feels a string of electricity travel down her spine and her breath quickens.

'You should go to the police and turn yourself in, Miss Crawford.'

Jan turns quickly around, 'What are you talking about?'

Buford's brow is furrowed and he sneers, 'You know what I'm talking about. You killed Cassandra and you should go tell the cops.'

'I may just go ahead and talk to the cops and tell them how you keep harassing me, Buford. Just leave me alone!'

'I'm going to prove it, Miss Crawford, I'm working on it.'

Jan rolls her eyes, holds onto her shopping bag, and turns around toward the ocean. She walks onto the beach, her steps brushing up sand on her way home.

~

Back at the house, Tim puts on some light shorts, a T-shirt, and a cap. He feels he has enough of a tan now, so he smothers some sunscreen on his face, arms, and legs. He walks out of the house and stares to the right to see if Jan is on the back porch. She's not. The house is quiet. He heads north, taking the usual path Jan takes when she goes for a walk. Maybe he will find her along the shoreline, maybe.

He doesn't see her. He looks at his watch. This is the usual time she goes out for her walk. He turns around and heads back.

In her cottage, Jan is nervously washing her vegetables in the sink, brushing the tomatoes, and placing the lettuce and kale in a bowl with water and vinegar to let them stand for a bit. She hasn't been able to calm her nerves. She thinks maybe if she sits down to edit the novel, it will help her forget her encounter with Buford, so she goes to the dining table and wakes up her laptop. Maybe this will quiet her down.

From his deck, Tim looks over to Jan's porch but doesn't see her. He decides to go knock on her front door. No answer. Her car's in the driveway, he knocks again. He turns around to leave and Jan's door opens. 'Oh! it's you!'

Tim turns around, 'Well, happy to see you too! Were you expecting someone else?' He frowns.

Jan lowers her head, 'Sorry, sorry, that came out wrong, so wrong. What are you doing here? I thought you'd be on your way to New York.'

'I'm not, I stayed. I took Mandy and Elsa to the airport this morning but I decided to stay a couple of days.' He approaches the doorway. She opens the door to let him in, 'Come on in. Would you like some coffee? A beer?'

'Sure, coffee works. Are you all right?'

'Actually, I'm glad you're here.' She shrugs. Now in the kitchen, she spoons coffee out of the canister and prepares the coffee maker.

'So, what's up?'

She frowns her lips, 'I just had an encounter with Buford up by the beach gate, and it kind of creeped me out.' She shivers thinking about it again.

Tim's eyes widen, 'What did he do? Did you talk to the police? You need to do something about him, Jan.'

Jan waves her hands to try to calm him down, or maybe calm herself, 'He didn't do anything. He just talked. But he's a bit unnerving. He accused me of killing Cassandra, which is a total lie. I had nothing to do with that.'

Tim stays silent and sits on the kitchen stool at the counter. He's holding his arms in front of him. After a while he says, 'Jan, maybe you should tell me the whole story. What do you say?'

Jan quietly pours coffee into two mugs. She looks up, 'Sugar?'

Tim nods. She stirs a teaspoon of sugar into each cup, picks them up, and guides Tim outside to the porch.

Jan raises her head and looks into Tim's eyes. She sighs, 'Okay. I guess you're right.'

Jan begins recounting the worst day of her life, and how the beginning of that ordeal was the easiest part. How the police woke her up in the middle of the night and she was so confused about the pounding on her door and not finding George in bed with her. She tells him how she felt when they told her that her husband was gone, that he dropped dead in the middle of the Honky-Tonk bar.

She tells Tim about grieving George's passing. How he succumbed to a sudden heart attack though he was healthy, strong, and young. She cries reliving the scene of watching the love of her life lying on a stale and cold slab in the morgue of the hospital where he was taken. She says she doesn't remember how she managed to arrange for the funeral home to take him back to North Carolina so she could bury him near his parents. After a few days of his passing the police called on her again to let her know that before George died he had been having an affair with the town psychic, the Tarot card reader; a young and very beautiful fortune teller who sold gemstones, potpourri sachets, and scented oils. He had not only had an affair with her, but she died the same night he did…Murdered.

That wasn't the worst part, not even close. She continues on how she had to delay the funeral for weeks because the police asked her not to leave town after he died. The police questioned her for hours on end about Cassandra, she was a suspect in her murder. Eventually, they cleared her. Case dismissed.

After speaking non-stop for about fifteen minutes and shedding tears along the way, Jan stops. They both sit in silence looking out at the ocean. There are birds flying over the water and one dives in head first, its wings splashing the water around him. The bird quickly pulls out flying away with a fish thrashing in its beak trying to break free. As seconds go by, the fish is squirming less forcefully flying high above, up in the air.

Chapter 13

Saturday Late Afternoon
New Smyrna Beach

Walking barefoot near the water, Tim puts his arm around Jan's shoulders and pulls her in. Her mood hasn't improved much since she opened up to him about her whole ordeal. She leans into him and puts her arm around his waist. They walk in silence.

'I don't know quite what to say, Jan.'

She shakes her head, 'There's nothing to say but thank you for being here. Buford has brought up so many sad and stressful memories. I'm glad you're here.'

'Me too.'

The sand is wet and the waves spill over their feet. Tim is concerned about Jan's encounter with Buford earlier in the morning. 'Jan, I think you should talk to the cops about Buford. It's not about leaving Tarot cards at your door anymore.'

'Yes, I know. I've talked to Chris, Officer Gwynn, before though. I brushed it off to depression and his sadness. He received a heavy blow when she died. I know his sister, Linda, since way back. Cassandra's death hit him very hard.'

'That's all right, but him having accused you of murder and leaving those cards as a message can escalate into something dangerous. Maybe you should file a complaint or a restraining order or something.'

She frowns, 'Isn't that too drastic? Plus what proof would I have?'

'How about the cards? Those are proof enough, I would think.' He shrugs.

'I threw them out. I don't keep them.'

'Well, you're in luck. I have a couple of them at home. The other day you were away I found one and put it in my pocket. Did you throw out the other one?'

'Maybe it's still lying around.' She turns around, 'Let's head back, it's getting late. What do you think about staying for dinner? The company would be good.'

'Sure. If I can bring something.'

'Don't worry about that. It's just something simple and I have everything we need.'

They walk watching the mile-long beach ahead of them. The blue water skirts the golden sand with foam laced along the edge, like a choker around a woman's neck.

~

Jan kicks off her sandals and props her feet onto the wooden legs underneath the patio table. She smiles at Tim, 'So, now that you know pretty much everything about me, I think it's time for me to know more about you. Don't you think?'

Tim pours more beer into their pilsner glasses and sits back down in his chair, 'I have to say my life's been pretty boring.'

'What about your family? Your parents? Where are you from?'

Tim briefly touches on growing up in upstate New York where his parents still live. He has a younger brother who lives on the west coast. He talks about going to college and his early days working for a financial firm in New York and how he eventually ventured on his own with his college roommate creating their own company. He leaves out about his parents' loveless marriage and that he and his brother left home as soon as they could.

Jan prods about his love life. He chuckles, 'There isn't much to tell. I had a relationship in college. I thought she was the one, but it was not to be.' He shrugs. 'A few years later, when Josh and I were launching our company, I met Mandy. After the company was taking off I felt it was time for me to settle down and that's when Mandy and I got married. So, that's it. Nothing exciting. All I am is just a big-time money man.'

'Oh, you're out of my league, then. I know nothing about money, other than spending it, ha!' She takes a sip of her beer, 'So, you work with stocks? I guess we won't have much to talk about.'

'I can think of a few things we can talk about. By the way.' He looks into the house, 'What smells so good?'

Jan winks, 'Just wait, you'll see in due time. They're not ready yet.'

Tim appreciates she's smiling again. Her eyes pull him in, magnetizing him, and a rush of heat swims through his veins. She leans her face on her right hand, and he notices again the emerald and diamond ring on her wedding finger. George seems to still be present in her life. He tries not to frown, 'Let's see then. I know you're working on a novel now, how is that going? Are you almost done with it? When will it come out?'

Jan takes a sip of her beer, and smiles, 'My publisher wants it to come out next spring.' Now more relaxed she brings her feet up on her chair balancing herself by holding her glass with both hands and leaning her elbows on her knees. 'But there are a few kinks I have to iron out which I'm having a hard time with.'

'Is there anything I can help with?'

Jan places her beer glass on the table and wraps her arms around her legs and rests her chin on her knees, 'No, I don't see how you could.' She lies and stares at Tim. At this very moment, her body is feeling again. How she missed the flow of desire wave through her, the want of a man's touch, and how she can feel that again by just looking at him.

A strand of her hair falls over her face making Tim want to touch her and move it away from her eyes. He moves his hand close to her face and caresses her with the back of his hand looking into her hazel eyes. She holds his stare, her lips form a slow smile as she tilts her head to acknowledge his tenderness. A slow heat tickles his chest and cheeks but is immediately distracted by a beeping sound coming from the kitchen.

'All right, let me get those, I'll be right back.' Jan heads inside. In the kitchen she takes chicken wings out of the broiler, sets them on the tray next to the cut celery, broccoli, ranch sauce, and hot buffalo sauce, and heads back to the porch.

'Oh my, that smells so good.'

'Just wait til you taste my special seasoning or you can also choose to dip them in these sauces. Plus there you've got your veggies.' She says as she places the tray on the table.

Tim picks a few pieces of chicken, some celery and broccoli, and puts them on his plate.

'Don't be bashful, take some more.' She leans in, picks more chicken wings, and places them on his plate. She grabs one, dips it in the hot buffalo sauce, and feeds it to him, laughing. 'There, try that delicious homemade hot sauce. My recipe.'

He grabs her hand, and takes a dab at the chicken wing, then licks her fingers. She smiles and then backs down in her chair.

As the minutes go by, slithers of orange turn to purple and blue on the horizon. There isn't much sunlight left from the west to shine on the east. And on the platter, all that is left are droplets of orange and white sauces. They both laugh and take a swig from their almost-empty beer glasses. Jan slowly steadies hers with her lips and keenly stares at Tim. She sighs. He stares. Their eyes lock firmly. No words. The only motion is the lifting and sinking of their chests. He raises an eyebrow, his pupils imperceptibly moving, trying to read her thoughts but finding it hard to hook up with them. Her hazel eyes shine and seem to smile but he feels her thoughts still hang behind a curtain. She's present and an alluring temptation concealing a mystery he wants to explore.

She breaks the spell, the silence. 'The ocean looks lovely.' She says turning her face toward the east, shutting her eyes as the ocean breeze kisses her face, 'I think I'm going to get my swimsuit on and go in. Want to go for a swim?'

Tim frowns slightly, 'Mmm, sounds like a treat. I've never been in the ocean at night.'

'We can go for a swim and then have what I am sure is a delicious cheesecake you brought for dessert.' She gets up from her chair picking up some of the trays and glasses.

Tim's phone rings. He nods at Jan, 'Yes, go ahead, I'll meet up with you when you get dressed. I"ll go get my trunks.' He answers the phone as he's walking down the steps toward the gate.

Jan giggles and walks inside.

Tim reaches the gate and notices he forgot to leave a light on in his house, it's dark. He finishes talking with Mandy, who is fixing dinner at home and hangs up. He stares at the ocean for a few seconds and turns around back into the house.

Jan has her aqua blue bikini shorts on and is staring at the long mirror located in the corner of her bedroom trying to latch on her bikini bra, her hands behind her. She stops as she looks up and sees Tim's reflection in the mirror standing at the threshold of the bedroom. He stands still and his gaze weakens her. She doesn't turn around but locks onto his eyes. He walks in. She still doesn't turn looking at him through the reflection. Now close to her, standing behind her, his hands lay on her bare shoulders. Tim unties the strings of her bikini top around her neck. She doesn't stop him. The piece falls to the floor. His hands begin to tour from her shoulders down her arms. She closes her eyes and takes in the sensations as he draws nearer to her and wraps his arms around her waist. She leans her head into his shoulder, her eyes still closed.

Tim slowly kisses the nape of her neck. His lips feel hot but soft. For a moment she opens her eyes and watches their reflection in the mirror, her breasts now bare, his hands caress them and elicit sensations and feelings she had buried long ago. He leans his head onto her neck, and briefly, she thinks she sees George's image. She stretches her arm behind her to touch Tim's head. It's been years since she's been with someone. In this house she has only been with George. But no, this isn't George, it's an unfamiliar face. Someone she met just a few days ago, someone who has lured her into opening up to experience what she has refused to feel for years. She knows she has provoked him and she reminds herself it will only be this once.

Tim lifts one of her arms, folds it softly, and lays kisses along it straight down to her fingers. She turns around, and he brings her fingers up to his lips. She smiles remembering the chicken wings and hot sauce. He frowns, 'What's so funny?' She shakes her head. Her hair bounces and a soft grin slides across her mouth as he kisses her. He lifts both of his hands to hold her face, he holds it still and searches for depth, awareness, and knowledge. *Who is she? Why am I here?* He can't fathom to answer any of those questions as his want increases and his lips descend on hers yearning to unravel her secrets.

The heat and wetness of his lips runs a ripple of current through Jan's body. Her reaction weakens him. She quickly lifts off his shirt and brings her hands down to touch his chest. She leans in closer so her breasts also touch his skin, her lips hungrily searching for his and her hands continue exploring him. Tim moves in closer. Her hands snuggle under his pants releasing him. At the same time, he removes her bikini shorts. Their thighs touch, and overlap. Now she moves in closer. She places each palm of her hands on his, lifts her arms, and guides their arms upward wiggling her fingertips. They linger with their arms above, reaching for the ceiling, all this time kissing, making every inch of their skin touch, slowly moving in sync, in a sensual dance where the energy emerging from each of them wants to outsmart the other, and entwine, looking for a way to collide and combust. This way, naked, thigh onto thigh, chest against chest, skin onto skin, their pulsating bodies plunge onto Jan's bed and swim to its center.

Tim lays on top of Jan and she lifts her hips up to shrink the gap between them, 'Now!' she whispers. Tim slowly, and softly entices Jan as his body's throbbing reaction on entering her threatens her responses to climb, and she moans with every push. Tim groans in unison as they both climb together to a point where their rhythms become parallel to each other. Jan's moans and Tim's groans increase in speed as their bodies spasm uncontrollably in pleasure, as wetness, energy, and orgasmic sweetness become a potion of fulfillment for them both.

~

Jan's thoughts jolt awake with the piercing sound emanating from the tea kettle as Tim walks into the kitchen wearing only his navy-colored undershorts. She shivers and shakes her wet hair trying to hide her real reaction to Tim's masculinity. She pours hot water into two mugs. She hands him his mug and grins as she takes a sip from hers. 'So, how about that dip in the ocean now?' She says.

'You look well in your bikini. I'd say you look awesome in your bikini, and without it, if I might add, but I don't feel like going next door to get my trunks.'

'You don't need trunks! Who's gonna know the difference, your underwear can pass as a swimsuit, it's dark out there.' She points out the sliding door, 'Plus, we can go for a swim close to the shore, and it will make this evening complete.' She lifts her shoulders as she holds the mug in both hands, standing right next to him. She gives him a quick kiss.

He winks, 'Okay, I guess you're right. Let's finish this, and we can go.'

'Great!'

A few minutes later the ocean crashes onto the shore, but Tim and Jan are a few feet deeper in the water, swerving up and down riding the waves as they come in, avoiding going under them. They hold onto each other, their hands tied, in order to avoid the pull from the water. The wind is mellow and they get closer to talk. Jan's leg touches Tim's, provoking him. She feels his leg like silk under the salty water. She says, 'What are your thoughts about one-night stands?'

Thoughts! His pupils expand, his eyes widen, and in a neutral voice, he says, 'A one-night stand… I can't say I've ever …'

'Oh, come on! Surely you have.' She splashes the water a bit, 'A young, powerful, rich guy like yourself? No way you haven't had a one-night stand.'

He shakes his head, and rolls his lips down, 'Is that what this is?' He pulls her in wrapping his arms around her. The ocean pulls but he tries to hold steady. He wipes away hair from her face and kisses her. Water splashes on their faces making them release their lips.

She's still holding tight, 'I think that's what this has to be.' Tonight she let go for only one reason, or maybe two. She needs to feel wanted and she needs to delve into real emotions so she can gather momentum again.

'I once had a short relationship.' He shrugs, 'But that was when I was in college. I guess it wasn't an affair or a one night stand since we were steady. My relationships tend to last more than one night.'

'Tell me about it.'

'There was this beautiful young woman who worked for me. When I was in college I opened a house cleaning business.'

'A house cleaning business? When you were in college?'

Tim nods, 'Yes, can you believe it? It was easy. I set it up one summer, and once it was set up, it pretty much ran itself! So, one of the ladies who I hired to clean homes, was young and beautiful, very shy. Anyway, she and I had a thing for a few months.'

'Ahh, so you've always been an entrepreneur. And, what was her name?'

'Her name was Tania.' His eyes brighten up as he smiles.

'Was she your first love?'

'No, I wouldn't say my first, but she was significant.'

'Where is she now? Have you kept in touch?'

Tim looks down a saddened expression clearly on his face, 'No, she died in a car accident.'

Jan quickly reaches to touch him, 'Oh Tim, I'm so sorry!' He looks into her eyes, she reaches for him and kisses him, then leans her forehead against his, 'I'm so, so sorry.'

They stay like this for a few minutes. Tim takes her hand and lifts it to his lips, 'It was quite a long time ago but it still can hurt. I'm okay, though.

'Yes, I know how that goes.'

Tim smiles trying to make the environment more cheerful, 'Okay, how about you? Have you had many relationships?'

'Truthfully, no. I have not. I had a couple of boyfriends in high school and college. Then I married George. He was from my home town. Since George, I haven't been with anyone. You're my first.' She tightens her arms around his shoulders as she feels another pull from the water. 'So, then this is your first one-night stand? I guess it's my first…'

'I have never been unfaithful to Mandy. Until now, that is. I'm not sure if it counts as being unfaithful, though.' He shrugs, his lips form a line and his eyes look saddened.

Jan runs her fingers through his hair staring into his eyes and places her index finger on his lips, 'Your secret is safe with me.'

Tim looks into Jan's eyes wondering what will happen now that he's walked through this door. It's been so long since he asked himself to feel or think about where he wants to be in life, and what has meaning for him. He's forgotten that fire that drove his actions, what fulfills him. He's forgotten the enthusiasm and adrenaline which create his euphoria for life. Today he realizes he's probably found some of that with Jan and isn't sure he wants to give it up. He kisses her again and a current thrums through both livening up their bodies.

They walk out of the water and sit on the sand. Water rolls softly onto their feet. He moves wet hair away from her face.

Jan looks at him. She reaches over and softly brushes her lips against his. She then draws his name in the sand. He laughs. Jan shrugs and looks over at him, 'Tim, you're amazing. I don't want to wish you any harm. I don't have the attachments you do…'

Tim puts his index finger on her lips. He lifts her up and they kneel in the sand facing each other. He takes her face into his hands and silences her with a kiss. He whispers, 'Shhh, tonight is gonna last forever.' and Jan understands the want Tim shares in this kiss. His need and deep desire pour inside coating her longing and tearing down the loneliness she has become used to. Tonight they are perhaps naive about the intensity of the difficulties to come as they stare at the horizon tracing the path of light shining onto the ocean and reaching the moon ahead.

Chapter 14

Sunday, June 20, 2021
The first day of summer

Snuggling under the covers, Jan stretches in her sleep as Tim reaches over and kisses her nape. He eases out of bed and walks over to the long mirror in Jan's room. He looks at himself in the mirror as the memory of the previous night overcomes him. Twelve days ago he set out alone in search of his inner self, his past, his future…he isn't sure what. He felt drawn to the south certain he would find it. He knew he had to leave New York alone and that fulfillment was out there for him to find. He would know when he saw it. Today he thinks he's found at least the answer to one of the questions he didn't know he had. Is Jan his answer?

He touches his face and wonders. *Have I lost weight? Has my hair grown? Do I look younger? Older?* He stares at the reflection of his naked body in the mirror. It seems as if he's looking at someone else. *Who is this?* He touches his arms and his chest. His eyes trace the image in the mirror. Tim turns and looks at Jan lying in the bed. Her back is bare. He fights an urge to slide in next to her and touch her all over again. He looks over at the dresser to get his watch and check the time. He sees a picture frame lying face down and reaches for it, slowly lifting it up; Jan and another man are smiling at him. *George.*

Tim feels the rustling of sheets and turns around, 'Good morning gorgeous.' He smiles. Jan smiles back and stretches. The covers slip revealing her naked upper body, her skin is shining, her supple breasts inviting.

'Coffee?' Tim steps over to the bed as she extends her arms out to him. He reaches in and kisses her.

'Mmm, that sounds great, but I'd prefer something else and I think you are ready for it.' She pulls him onto her and they roll in the bed. Their skin awakens to the smooth discovery of fresh sensations as every inch of their bodies touch.

They manage to face each other. Jan caresses his face and looks deeply into his eyes. She holds her stare and admires his brown eyes, sifting her fingers through his hair. He watches her eyes move rapidly trying to read him. Her silent quest into his soul, traps him in her own mystery. He feels as if he might drown in the pool of her eyes, 'What have you done to me, hazel eyes?' he whispers.

Jan's lips softly stroke his provoking a tingling on her own lips as she travels from his mouth to his face, and she kisses his eyes one by one. Tim grabs her face with both hands and brings his lips down on hers with fire and passion. She responds deepening her kiss as the rest of her body reacts and she stretches alongside him, aligning and alloying into sensuous ravishment. They live in this deep fury today. Today is all they have.

~

A few hours later sitting on the porch with her laptop in front of her, Jan smiles calling to mind each detail of being with Tim yesterday. She revives in her mind every sensation, not wanting to lose this newness, wrapping it up in the present to keep for as long as she can. She is experiencing the story she is to write, but she knows her reality is avoidance. She tries to focus on the laptop's screen but the words seem to be running away from each other, she can't make any sense of them. *Maybe if I relax a bit and search for a while online.* The mind does play tricks on you, doesn't it. *Get away from that mouse!*

She hears the sliding door open a soft wave of recognition brings her back to the porch. Tim looks over, 'So, I missed the sunrise?'

Jan nods, 'Yup, you missed another beautiful sunrise. But I guess you were just too worn out from last night, or should I say, the whole day yesterday.' She winks, 'Don't worry, there are more sunrises ahead.'

Tim smiles, 'Well, that could be.' He takes a sip of coffee, 'What are you up to?'

She chuckles, 'Work. Can't get enough of it.'

Turning his face serious, Tim takes her hand. Jan isn't quite sure if he's going to play a joke on her or if he is actually serious since she doesn't know his personality that well yet. He runs his finger over hers one by one, 'Jan, we have to do something about Buford.'

She looks into his eyes, 'Yes, I know. Yesterday was a bit scary.'

Tim puts the mug on the table, 'What if we go to that policeman you've mentioned is your friend and talk to him about it?'

'Today? Today is Sunday. I'm not sure he'll be at the station. Why don't we wait until tomorrow?' She pats his hand with her free hand. 'I promise. I will look into it tomorrow.'

Tim agrees, for now. He proposes they spend the day together. He wants to make her his special breakfast, and later take a walk down the beach. They have to compromise, though, because she needs to work on her novel. She wants to be able to infuse it with some of her new inspiration before Dianne calls her because she knows she wouldn't be able to lie to her again.

Tim leans in close to her face and nudges her nose with his, 'You won't be able to say no when you smell what's coming. So, stay put, get to work, and leave the rest to me.'

Jan opens her computer back up.

Tim points toward the kitchen, 'I'll head over there, and get busy. Do you want more coffee?'

'Sure.' Jan nods and passes him her empty mug.

Close to noon Jan and Tim are walking along the shoreline, 'So, how did you manage that scrumptious breakfast? Waffles, whipped cream, berries, that was quite the spread.' She skips through some water and watches Tim's footprints sink through the wet sand.

He takes her hand, 'I had the ingredients at the house. Waffles are Elsa's treat, there were some leftovers when they left.' He winks as he avoids some of the sun rays getting into his eyes. A slight chill runs through Jan, she rubs her arms to hide the goosebumps. *Elsa's treat.*

Tim covers his forehead with his hand and looks upwards toward some seagulls flying over them. 'Watch out!' Jan points toward the sand, 'There!' Tim pulls back startled by her cry, and looks down at what she's pointing at, a transparent blob of what? 'What is that?'

Still pointing she says, 'That thing can sting hotter than those chicken wings I gave you last night. You don't want to touch it, much less step on it.' He leans in and crouches to get a closer look.

'That is a man-o-war, or what's left of it, probably. It looks like it's dead. I don't know much, but I keep away from them dead or alive. They're poisonous, and sting like hell, they say.'

'So, you've never been stung by one?'

'No, and I don't plan to.'

'Well, thanks for saving me.' He pulls her in toward him, embracing her. He looks for her lips and kisses her. His warmth turns to heat. Her body responds and their kiss deepens. She catches her breath, and puts her hands on his chest, 'Tim.' She looks up into his eyes, 'I do really want this, believe me, but we're playing with fire.' She is so afraid of not being able to pull away from him for good. If they keep this up, the vine of lies she's tying around her neck may strangle her.

He lowers his head, 'I know, I know, but I can't get enough of you, Jan.' He looks up and down the beach, 'I don't want this to end. I think we have something we shouldn't lose.'

'But it must, Tim. It has to end.'

'It will after tomorrow.' He stares at her hair blowing in the wind and takes her hand in his, 'But today we have each other. We will make the best of today and right now believe it will last for a long long time. How about we go back to the house and relax, then later on we go out for tacos.' He winks at her.

Jan smiles, 'All right. I like that. The sun's getting a bit hot. Let's get back and maybe we can go hit the town at sunset.'

Sunday night at the bar is noisy. Tim rushes Jan into the the Honky-Tonk thinking about how he saw her here just a few days ago and started falling in love. She's laughing. 'Tim I don't want to re-live the embarrassment of the other night. What are you doing?'

'Come on, go in, let's get a drink. You were so sweet singing "Staying Alive." You did great.'

'Oh, all right. Just one drink then.'

They move inside, he walks slowly behind her, puts his arms around her hips, and pulls her closer to him. They head to one of the round high tables toward the back of the bar. They're approaching a table where Linda and Chris are sitting. Jan waves, and gets closer, 'Hey there guys!'

They nod and smile, 'Hello Jan. How are you doing tonight?' Linda asks.

Jan introduces Tim to Chris and Linda. She knows Linda since the first few years she has been coming to town every year. Jan explains Linda's a Real Estate agent, her office is just down the street from here. Linda smiles, 'Hello Tim.' Jan tells Tim she met Chris, however, under somewhat dire circumstances when her husband passed away. He's a detective at the New Smyrna Police Department. Chris raises his eyebrows and nods. Tim smiles and says, 'Nice to meet you both.'

Chris intervenes, 'But who wants to talk about dark times, that's not why we're here. Right, Jan? We're here on a Sunday night to have a good time.'

Linda adds, 'Would you care to join us?'

Jan looks at Tim. He shrugs, so Jan says, 'Sure, why not.' Tim leaves them and goes to the bar to order some drinks.

Linda leans in toward Jan and asks about Tim. Jan looks over toward the bar and smiles, 'Tim? Right, right, Tim is renting the house next door to my cottage. He's in town for a few days.' Linda nods and raises her eyebrows, 'Ah. I see.' She takes a sip of her Cosmo.

Tim returns with their drinks. He leans in and whispers in Jan's ear, 'How about you tell Chris about Buford?' Jan shakes her head and slightly puckers her lips. She leans her head toward Tim trying not to let Linda hear her, 'No, not now. It's okay.'

Tim shakes his head. They socialize for a few minutes. Linda asks Jan and Tim if they will be staying long in New Smyrna, 'The summer is just beginning.' Jan shrugs, she may cut her visit short this year. Tim mentions how he's heading back to New York this week. After Jan and Tim finish their drinks they say their goodbyes. As soon as they are out on the sidewalk, Tim blurts out, 'Why wouldn't you tell Chris about Buford?! You have to do something about that. What if he attacks you when I'm gone?'

Jan touches his arm, 'Don't worry about it. He won't. I have a good reason not to have said anything.'

Tim shakes his head. Jan explains that Buford is Linda's brother and she did not want to get Linda involved in all of this. She will contact Chris privately at the police station sometime. Until then she should be all right.

The night is waning into the midnight hours as they walk back strolling along the shore. When they hold hands Tim feels as if he can't let go. Jan feels the summer is just beginning and that it just has to end. She plans to keep these past few days, along with what is about to happen, and pack them in nicely where she stores the precious moments in her life. She will carry tonight with her as a token of what could have been. Looking at the almost full moon she feels comfort in the resolution she makes. Tonight's the night. Sorrow and regret for later.

The window shades at Tim's place are drawn and the room is dark and quiet. Jan stands in the middle of the living room watching as Tim comes down the stairs. She holds her stare as her white cotton dress slowly slides down her shoulders, she lets it fall to the floor. Tim approaches Jan and takes her right hand bringing her fingers up to his lips. He kisses them one by one. She smiles and he stares entranced. She pulls up his shirt making sure she touches every inch of skin. Up to now, it's been slow loving but the passion turns on, accelerating into fear, and starving for completeness. They fall onto the sofa looking for support. Their fingers travel searching for depth and satiety. They touch making their nerve endings come alive, their lips connect, their bodies meld, once again reaching where most likely only forbidden love can dwell.

Will Jan and Tim's souls connect as their bodies have? Only time will tell.

Chapter 15

Monday, June 21, 2021
New Smyrna Beach, FL

The night died late for Jan and Tim. He opens his eyes and watches slithers of morning sunlight draw lines across the blue walls of the bedroom. He rolls around in bed, a smaller bed than he's used to, searching for Jan. She's not here.

They shared the bed in the guest room of Tim's house because she refused to sleep in the main bedroom. He sits up, scratches his day old beard and gets out of bed, 'Jan?' No answer. He walks downstairs now in his underwear, maybe she's made coffee already. 'Jan? Do you want some coffee?' He walks into the kitchen and the coffee maker is on, coffee in the carafe, it smells fresh. 'Where are you?'

She's nowhere to be found. Tim goes upstairs and quickly dives into a pair of jeans and a loose t-shirt, walks down to the kitchen for a cup of coffee to go and heads out of his house to knock on Jan's door.

Her car is not in the driveway. There's another Tarot card nailed to the middle of the door with a pocketknife. Another card. This time he pulls the card off almost tearing it in half. He grabs the pocketknife and puts it in his pocket. The card has the image of a naked man and a woman standing below some sort of angel-like effigy and the words "The Lovers" written under them. He rings the bell. No answer. He pounds on the door several times. No answer. He puts the torn card in his pocket and heads back to his house.

As he enters the house and places the house keys in the tray on the credenza in the entryway he sees the note. He opens it:

Tim,

I am not very good at goodbyes so I'm leaving before we have to confront the fact we shouldn't see each other again. We live on, I wish you happiness.

Jan

Tim stares at the note wondering what went wrong. Until now he has been building up the courage to change his life. These last few days he has realized Jan completes him. He had been searching for so long for an anchor in his life. He once thought Mandy was able to moor him to the pillar where he felt secure but he's always felt he has been sailing through life, navigating the open seas in search of a port. Mandy has not been that port. Now that he's found it, he realizes he's lost it. He has also lost his resilience to continue without Jan. He doesn't want to go on without her. He is willing to live on stolen time, on brief encounters, if that means not going back to how he was living before. But she's gone. He takes out his cell phone from his pocket and calls her. It rings until the voicemail catches on. He hangs up and sends her a text: *Why?*

He climbs up the stairs two steps at a time and rushes into his bedroom. He searches through his shirts and finds the other Tarot card, the Moon card he found a few days ago. He places both in his hands, comparing their messages. He has the proof he needs. He takes the pocket knife in his hands. *This is all I need.*

As he walks out the door he says out loud to himself, 'Why did you leave like this Jan?'

~

Looking around from her table in the far corner of the coffee shop, Jan feels a familiar buzz in the environment. She got off Highway I-95 a couple of hours after she left the beach and stopped at a shop just off an exit ramp. She sips on her Mocha-flavored coffee and lights up her laptop. She needs to write, she is restless and can only reduce it by drowning her thoughts onto her book.

No matter what Tim says now about how his marriage is falling apart, she would have to forget him. He is still committed to his wife and daughter. She let her guard down and enjoyed a wonderful couple of days but having a relationship with Tim isn't going to work. She has to give herself the opportunity to forget Tim. Now she needs to forgive herself for falling for what she promised herself she would never do.

As the vividness of her recent experience jumps off the page, a heatwave brews inside her, recalling every detail of the pleasures she's lived. She hasn't erased yet the soft touch from her skin, the trembling lust and passion still running through her veins, the heat of his lips. She transfers her hunger, shame, and passion onto Rose and tries to bring out the same in Otto as the characters fight to live and experiment on stolen time. Hers was momentary and brief. Can she make it last for Rose and Otto? Should it last?

Of course, this is hitting her hard; harder than she thought.

~

Tim sits in the lobby sifting through the cards in his hands. A uniformed woman sits behind a tall counter at the New Smyrna Police Station. She has her hair pulled back neatly in a bun and is wearing soft makeup. Her deep green eyes stand out. She slants her head toward Tim as Chris walks through the door at the side of the room. Chris says, 'Thank you, Officer Sutter.' He walks to where Tim is sitting.

Tim is uneasy, a bit jumpy as he sees Chris, 'Hey! Good morning.'

'Good morning, Tim. How can I help you?'

Tim hands the two Tarot cards over to Chris, 'Here, I need to give you these. I believe Jan could be in danger and you need to investigate.'

'What are these? Where did you get these?'

'Over the past few days they've been showing up on Jan's door.'

Chris nods and folds his arms across his chest.

Tim takes the pocketknife out of his pocket and hands it to Tim. He explains today he found the 'Lovers' card nailed down by this knife. He continues to explain he believes Buford is a threat to Jan, that he harassed her the other day while she was walking home. He's willing to sign a statement, if needed.

'Do you know if Jan is pressing charges? Can you ask her to come in and make a complaint?'

Tim lowers his head, 'No, I can't ask her that. She left.'

Chris motions to Tim to sit down and sits down next to him, 'The only way I can pursue this is if Jan presses charges. I know you are concerned, but there isn't much I can do.'

'You can't be serious!'

'Look, let me give you a bit of background. This is a very unpleasant situation but harmless, really.' Chris looks down at the Tarot cards in his hands. 'I know Buford can be a bit intimidating. Have you met him?' Chris flips the card between his fingers and passes them back to Tim.

Tim shakes his head, 'No, I have not met him but I've seen him. I chased him away from Jan's house the other day. He also harassed her on the beach. Jan explained it to me and I think she is concerned. I think he is dangerous, wouldn't you think? These are threats.'

'I can tell you he is harmless. He is Linda's brother and I promise I have my eyes set on him, he's not too far out of my reach. He's been doing this on and off for a few years now when Jan comes down and stays here at the beach.'

'But why? Why do you think it's harmless? I for one find it alarming. This card today was nailed to the door by the pocketknife.'

'We've talked to him. We have also approached Jan to let us know if she feels threatened, and I can take further action only if she files a complaint. Buford has just had a bit of trouble with depression and alcoholism. Sometimes he doesn't know what he's doing. He won't harm Jan.'

Chris asks him, 'Has she explained why Buford does this? How well do you know Jan?'

Tim shrugs, 'Not that well. I mean, I met her when I got here about a week ago. She told me about her husband dying, about Buford and his girlfriend, and about the cards. That's it.'

Chris sits up, 'Well, let me fill you in on the town's past, maybe Jan left a few things out. So, here goes…'

Chris tells Tim the story of Buford and Cassandra's on-again-off-again romance since Cassandra moved here. Buford once had a promising future and today makes a living doing landscaping for the expensive properties around the beach and the town. Cassandra was into reading rocks, tea leaves, Cristal balls, cards, and palms. She was quite good, she came from a family of psychics so must've grown up around all that. 'Have you heard of Cassadaga?'

Tim shakes his head, 'What's that?'

'It's a town not far from here. It was formed in the eighteen hundreds as a spiritualist camp. That's where she was from. Cassandra was very beautiful and had a lot of flair and panache, she had a following. She looked like a gypsy and she dressed the part. Here the tourists ate that all up. Anyway, after one of their breakups, it seems Cassandra and George hooked up one of those summers he and Jan were in town. Linda told me it was quite a love affair. Jan never found out, at least not until they were both dead. I guess George wandered out when Jan was busy with her writing and he felt bored or something. The fact is they had an affair. We are not sure how long it lasted and now it doesn't matter.'

Tim sifts his fingers through his hair. Chris continues, 'Cassandra was murdered and George died that same night at the Honky-tonk bar where we met.'

Tim nods, 'Yes, Jan told me as much'

Chris shifts in his chair, 'Did she tell you we believe he murdered Cassandra?'

Tim looks at Chris alarmed, his cheeks redden, 'George killed Cassandra?'

Chris shrugs, 'After investigating Cassandra's murder we concluded George to be her murderer. We found a weapon with Cassandra's blood on it which belonged to George. Buford could never forgive George for taking away his Cassandra. He doesn't believe George murdered Cassandra. He's always insisted Jan did it, though. So that's why he puts the Tarot cards on her door, I guess.'

'You have to be kidding me.' Tim shakes his head, 'No way Jan could've done that.'

'Buford seems to think so.' He leans back in his chair.

'Do you believe that?' Tim asks in alarm, 'Do you really believe that?'

'No, I don't. I don't think Linda does either.' Chris says, 'Chief Walter Brooks and I…he's retired now, but he and I don't think Jan had anything to do with it unless other evidence comes up.'

Tim is silent staring ahead, his complexion a bit ashen. Chris continues, 'The Chief and I had many suspects, including Buford. Don't bring that up with Linda, she will have none of that. We investigated Buford and he didn't do it. There's no evidence to support that. All we had was the hammer, which had George's prints on it, so that's what led to George and not Buford but to this day Buford accuses Jan of doing it.'

'Does Jan know this?' Tim asks.

'Sort of. She is aware of his accusation, and as you've seen, he leaves her reminders now and then. But that's it.'

'Hell, that's some story.'

~

Linda walks into her home from the side of the carport and turns on the light switch. She hears the sound of glass hitting the ceramic tile in the living room and quickly turns around.

Buford swivels over getting his feet on the floor. He must have tossed the glass with his leg while taking them off the living room table, 'Doggonit!'

'Buford! What are you doing here?!' Linda drops her purse on her desk, 'Oh, Come on! You're drunk?'

Buford's gruff appearance and overall demeanor these past few years are such a contrast to the young and vibrant man he once was. Today it seems his future is behind him, and such a promising one. He had climbed a ladder of sorts reaching the title of Construction Project Manager at a renowned local home builder, but he threw it all away. After Cassandra's death he slowly let go, day by day, from week to week he became less reliable. After a few months his employers lost respect for him and fired him. He never seemed able to regain the stamina to get back on his feet and all he could manage to make ends meet was to clean people's yards and work the landscape around office buildings. Linda tried to be there for him, but after a few years, she had to make him move out to his own place.

Buford tries to balance himself as he gets up from the sofa, 'I was sleeping. Why did you wake me up?'

'Buford, you don't live here anymore. What are you doing here?'

'I couldn't get home. I didn't feel good.'

Linda reaches out for him and puts her arm around his back and makes him lean on her. 'Oh, come on, I'll take you to the guest room, you're lucky you have me or you'd be out on the street!'

Buford smiles. Though his smile is barely noticeable under his unkempt mustache, Linda sees it. *I wish you'd come back, brother. I wish you'd come back.* She hugs him and puts him to bed.

~

It's almost midnight and the beach is dark. Tim stands at the edge of the deck and looks to his right. Jan's house is completely dark. There's no light simmering through the kitchen window. The porch light isn't on. Forlorn and angry he stares at the ocean. He's all alone, Mandy and Elsa are gone. Jan is not with him either. *Where are you, Jan Crawford? Where have you gone? Why did you go? I need you.* He jumps off the deck and walks down the path of his yard in his trunks, bare-chested, barefoot, and heads into the water. It's a bit chillier than during the daytime, but he takes a plunge. He does a few strokes swimming ahead a short distance and turns back. Closer to the shoreline, he lies on his back, floating on the water, staring at the sky. The keenly bright moonlight shines on the ocean. The sky is crisp with sparkling tiny lights glittering in the dark sheet of black above him.

Chapter 16

Tuesday, June 22, 2021
New York City, NY

The first day of summer should've been a vacation for Elsa and Mandy and yet, they are home, back to their four-bedroom condo in Astoria with little time to adjust. Today, two days later, Elsa is in the full swing of summer classes. Tim is flying back tonight. He stayed longer than she expected. Now there would be no time to do anything fun since he's going back to work tomorrow.

As Mandy opens the door to her store, she is not looking forward to going back to work. Stacy shrieks with joy when she sees Mandy walk through the door. Stacy is tall and slender. She likes to wear slacks and high heels, which tend to visually make her seem taller. Her outfit is a two-piece navy jacket with contrast-lined sleeves which accent her ankle-length slim slacks. Promptly she makes a sad face to be sympathetic to Mandy since she had to cut her vacation short. But that frown doesn't last long.

'Am I glad to see you, girl!' Stacy says as Mandy walks in the door. Mandy tosses her large orange handbag into a drawer next to her Louis XIV-style desk. She pouts.

'What's going on, Mandy?' Stacy asks concerned.

'Oh, nothing. Just the same old Tim.' Mandy is stressed, and it shows. She brings her hand up to the side of her forehead where she feels a small bump coming out. She closes her eyes. 'We were having such a wonderful time. Then we had to head back home because Elsa needs to go to summer school!'

'Oh, wow. That's a bummer.'

'Yes, it is. That's not the worst of it. Tim stayed down there at the beach, while we were here back in reality. We won't be able to do much. He's going right back to work. I hate it!' She stammers and stomps her feet on the floor.

Stacy walks over to her, 'But, of course!' she says slowly, 'I can see why that's upsetting.' She reaches over and puts her arm around Mandy's shoulders, 'Do you want to take a little while to adjust?'

'No, let's get on with it.' Mandy sits down behind the desk.

Stacy stands across from the her and as usual, starts talking gesturing with her hands, 'Okay then, let's get down to business. So, you know how we got that large order for the newlyweds. Well, that's all taken care of, packed, and shipped. They're enjoying it in their new home.' She places her index finger to her chin, 'that is if they're back from their honeymoon.'

'Oh, Stacy!' Mandy broods, 'that's where I thought I was this past week! On my second honeymoon!'

'Now, now, dear.' Stacy walks around the desk and leans on it, 'let's concentrate, and let me tell you what we need right now. We need you to focus and look over the list of things we have here on this piece of paper.' She nods her head as she speaks, 'These are the pieces we don't have, but we could very well get, for this beautiful newlywed couple, this very rich, newlywed couple. Can you find these or some similar ones?' She places the strip of paper in front of Mandy.

'Yeah, yeah, you're right. Let's concentrate on work. Let me take a look at that.'

Stacy suggests Mandy add one of the platters she found at the beach and walks away so she can work. Mandy is a connoisseur of everything antiques, passed down heirlooms, auctions, and estate sales of the rich and wealthy. Stacy loves the work she does, and the business they've built, but Mandy's the one with a lot of the skills and knowledge behind it. She knows where to look, and what to look for. Stacy smiles to herself and silently claps unnoticed, *Mandy is back, it's all good.*

Chapter 17

September 2021
New York City, NY

Characters populate Tim's cell phone screen as he types a message, 'Jan, I hope you get this. I Miss you. Can you call me?' He puts his phone on the desk.

Popping up on the text phone of his app, a red notification bubble makes Tim's heart race faster. He touches the screen to open the app. Jan has sent a text, 'Hi.' He frowns. *That's all I get?* That's the only word. Staring at his phone, his shoulders fall as he holds it with both hands, disillusioned. He deletes the conversation and places the phone in his pants pocket.

Chapter 18

October 2021
New York City, NY

They live in Astoria so Elsa can be close to school. Though it seems she is struggling, the new school is a 10 on a scale of 1 to 10. Elsa has improved and will be all right in the end. Tim doesn't mind the one-hour commute both ways during rush hour to the financial district, though that does strain their family life. He also works long hours and Tim stays late at work most nights.

Summer receded and New York City is now submerged in orange, brown, and yellows. Tim is sitting at his desk swirling his chair in half circles looking out his office window. There are numbers and graphs constantly bleeping on the computer screen behind him and some flat-screen TVs hanging on his office wall are tuned in to different 24-hour business news channels on mute. He gets up, puts his hands in his pant pockets, and stares out the window at the building's brownish walls blending into the grays and blues down below. The view is so different from the one of the ocean merging into the sky that he has tried to stamp daily in his mind.

He picks up his phone from the desk and searches the contacts app looking for Jan's number. Since that painful "Hi" he's been wanting to communicate with Jan again. He texts her a message: "I want to see you again. I will fly anywhere. Can we meet?" He can't help himself.

Tim turns around to look at his computer screen. The purples, greens, and blues hue into each other as numbers scroll by lacing the bottom of his screen. Against his better judgment, he opens a web browser window and types her name in the search box: Jan Crawford. A string of lines materializes. A gallery of photos pops up as well. In some shots she is alone, he's seen those many times over the past few months. They look like photos you would put on a book jacket.

Tim notices there's a new photo, a more recent one. She's smiling, she has a new haircut. She is looking up from a table with a book in her hand, and a lady is standing across from her looking down at the book Jan is handing her. *A book signing!*

He clicks on the picture to get to the website. He reads the news article. She is signing books of her new book "*Broken Time*" in New York a couple of weeks ago. His face feels cold and wet, his heart races slightly. *She was here! I missed her. I could've seen her.* He closes his eyes. He reads more of the article and finds the publishing house's name. He looks up their website, continues searching for the tab on their authors, and clicks on that. Perhaps he can find Jan's book signing tour. *Will she be back in New York?* He slides the cursor down the screen and doesn't find any in New York. But this weekend she will be signing a book in Chicago. *Chicago? That could be doable.* He checks the date, the weekend.

Tim's hands are wet, and a bit shaky. He brings his hands up to his chin and rests his head on his thumbs. *This weekend is so soon. I can't make up a business trip. Should I surprise Mandy and Elsa with a trip to Chicago? To make up for our beach fiasco? No, no, no, that won't work.*

If I surprise Jan. Would she even talk to me? What excuse could I make? A client? He slaps his forehead with the palm of his hand, *What are you thinking?* He rubs his temple and closes his eyes. *That won't work.* He wouldn't visit a client for the weekend. He opens a new webpage on his browser. Airlines: Flights from New York to Chicago Friday night…return Saturday midday. His heart races a bit more. The possibilities create a flurry of emotions like electricity flowing through his fingers as he clicks on the airline flight. He almost clicks on the purchase button when he hears chatter behind his office door.

Tim looks up as the office door flies open, 'Tim, you're not gonna believe this!' Jeff Buckley walks into the office with an electronic pad and puts it on his desk. Jeff's excitement is a symptom of his young age. Barely over thirty years old, business successes still show on his face.

Another young woman walks in behind him, but she is unamused.

'What am I looking at?' Tim raises his head and looks at both of them. Jeff is still smiling, and Raquel Thompson seems pleased, but not as ecstatic as her coworker who is standing next to her with a smile from ear to ear. Raquel has her arms folded in front of her. Jeff bumps into her softly, 'Come on Raquel, this is exciting!' She shrugs.

'So, what is so exciting Jeff?'

'We got the deal. We got the account! Joshua called, the ink is barely dry.' He pats his tie onto his chest, still smiling, 'or should I say, the electronic signals are barely lit…the people at Centurion just gave us their account to manage all their employee's savings slash pension slash retirement funds.' Jeff circles with his index finger in the air, 'Thousands of employees, Tim, thousands.' Still, an ear-to-ear smile on his face.

Raquel continues to stand next to Jeff. She cleans an invisible spec of dust from her skirt, Tim replies, 'Well that is huge! Go, Joshua!'

'And there it is in literal black, and white.' Jeff points repeatedly at the electronic pad lying on the desk in front of Tim, 'The CEO just signed it, or clicked it, if you want to get technical. Josh says we have a lot of work to do now.'

Tim gets up and walks around the desk, 'Yes, we do Jeff. Raquel…' He nods at them as he walks by them and out of the office. Raquel and Jeff follow him to the floor. There are around five desks, each one with a computer screen flashing images and bleeps just like Tim's. There's an office at the end of the hall with the door shut. That is Joshua Fletcher's office. Tim lifts up his arms, 'Listen up everyone, we now have the Centurion account!' Everyone claps, and cheers, except for Raquel. Tim reads the room, and continues, 'So.' He looks at his watch, 'We will celebrate right now at five o'clock, have some bubbly, and go home.

Tomorrow is Friday so we have a lot of work to do.' He waves his arms encircling the room, 'Since we're three hours ahead of them, we will be in bright, and early, and on time, and get things rolling for when we have to get all the documentation and affairs from Centurion coming in I'd say around ten or eleven in the morning.' He slaps his hands.

He shakes Jeff's hand, 'Thanks Jeff for bringing me the good news.' he pats his arm, reaches out to Raquel, and shakes her hand, 'Thanks Raquel for all your hard work.' He smiles. She smiles back.

Chicago, IL

Sitting next to a large window at a small round table in a restaurant in Downtown Chicago, Jan digs a chunk of *flan* with her spoon as Dianne watches her sipping a *cafe con leche.* Diane got in last night from New York to join Jan during this leg of her book tour, which is about the book "*Broken Time*" but Dianne has been speaking non-stop about the publication of the new book, "*The Summer Rose.*"

Jan deletes Tim's text and puts down her cell phone on the table. The emerald and diamond ring she wears on her wedding finger glints as she moves her hand bringing her coffee up to her lips. When Jan lowers her cup, Dianne reaches for her hand and touches the ring. 'That's such a beautiful ring. Does it have a backstory?'

As a reflex, Jan pulls her hand, then shuts her eyes, 'Sorry, sorry.' She touches her mouth, 'I got this ring with George's things.' Her lips turn downward. 'He had it in a safe deposit box, I guess he was holding it to give it to me on some occasion.' She shrugs.

'Well, it's beautiful dear.' Dianne smiles sympathetically, 'But, I have to say, if you keep wearing it on your wedding finger you're giving the wrong impression.'

Jan laughs wholeheartedly, 'Bah, I'm not looking. Last summer was enough to teach me a lesson. I rather write about lovers than be one at this point. It's just too painful.'

'Girl, forget the sad talk.' Dianne waves her hand as if brushing off the mist of sadness in the air, 'In due time you will find someone who will cherish you as much as you will care for him.'

'Yeah, I'll wait.' Jan moves her head to look out the window at traffic rolling by.

'Well, let's get back to business.' Dianne spreads her hands on the table as if making some space, 'Missus Fairchild is confident the book will come out in the spring. They're trying to get it to print as quickly as possible, so it gets a boost from this launch. She expects this will be the best-selling beach novel next year. I'm so excited.' Dianne shivers as she talks.

Jan smiles as she takes another bite of her chocolate cheesecake. Dianne frowns, 'Why aren't you excited as I am? You used to be so happy when I gave you this type of news.'

Jan Ho-hums, 'This is a big change for me, so I'm not as thrilled as you are Dianne. I'm just not sure how it's going to turn out. Plus, we are on this other book's tour right now.' She points to "Broken Time" which is on the table.

'But I read it! It's a total switch for you, and it's excellent. Your readers are going to love Rose and Otto!' Dianne waves her hands and signals in the air as if cleaning an imaginary sign and says, "*Jan Crawford, more risqué, the romantic thriller.*" You are evolving, my friend. It's an awesome story.' The gold bangles on her wrist jingle as she pats Jan's hand on the table.

'Yeah, well, I'm glad you like it.' Jan turns down a side of her lip, 'As I said, I had some help with the research but it was painful.'

Dianne pulls back, 'Yeah, so you've told me…though not in detail. Care to share?'

Jan takes a sip of water, 'No, not really. I'll have to keep that to myself.'

Chapter 19

December 19, 2021
New Smyrna Beach, FL

Gouging a groove in the old pinewood bedroom floor, Buford pulls out the heavy dark mahogany box from under his bed ignoring the screech of wood against wood. This is where he keeps everything he's collected from the days he was with Cassandra.

He crouches down next to his bed to rummage through the box. His mouth turns down as he picks out the gold-wrapped gift he wasn't able to give her. That night he was willing to take her back, he would've done anything to get her back. That dreadful night, life shifted and the future would be meaningless, forever unraveling pain.

His hands search through the lavender and pastel colored sachets, dozens of message cards and brochures from Cassandra's shop, quartz stones, and tincture bottles he's saved as keepsakes to remember her by.

Picking up one of the sachets he's invaded by sorrow as he draws in the soft perfume of patchouli. He shuts his eyes and kisses it, trying to connect with her memory. Slowly opening his eyes again, Cassandra's smile stares back at him. Her photograph lays haphazardly on top of the tiny brownish amber-colored glass dropper bottles in the box. Running his fingers along the image of her long copper curls, her face, and the hand holding her head, Buford focuses on the ring. That diamond and emerald ring she never took off. *Jan! Why does Jan have that ring? She must've taken it from Cassandra that night. She has Cassandra's ring!*

The memories of that night again cascade back as he thinks back to that last birthday. Calling to mind how much he drank that night, he touches the gold-wrapped gift box. That night he needed courage, so much courage, to go see her. He wanted her to know how much he loved her, how he couldn't stand to be without her.

He opens the gift box. Laying on black velvet inside the box is a beautiful gold-reddish phoenix brooch, its tiny diamonds on the tips of its wings and tail make it seems as if it's in flight. As the pain creeps deeper into Buford's soul he takes the brooch out of the box and slides over to lean against his bed. He holds the brooch with both hands and cries as thoughts and feelings continue incessantly to flow through him like a torrent. *I'm so sorry Cassandra!* He moans. *It wasn't supposed to end like this. It wasn't my fault.*

But that night won't ease up in his head; the pain of not having Cassandra, the guilt he feels for what he's done, and the remorse he carries inside him for not getting justice for her death weigh so heavily in his heart. It's all his fault: his weakness. He could avenge her death, and yet his fear has kept him from getting Jan to pay for what she did.

That night four years ago runs clearly through his head like a movie.

> His heart sinks as he watches from the shadows behind the tall Podocarpus hedge column at the house next door to Cassandra's building. That "*good-for-nothing lazy kept man*" is kissing Cassandra at the front door of her shop. Buford looks down sadly at the gold-wrapped gift he has for her. It's her birthday after all, and he remembered. He's willing to take her back, he will do anything to get her back.
>
> Buford puts his hand in his pants pocket. His fingers feel the cold even surface of the tiny glass dropper bottle. Tonight, he's not the one captivated by Cassandra's beauty or the recipient of her love. She's sharing her inmost longings with a traitor, a cheater who has turned her into a mistress. She is so much more than that!
>
> Buford holds the tiny milkweed tincture drop bottle in his hand, inside his pocket. After Cassandra shuts the door, George starts walking away. Buford takes off after him, keeping a few feet

of distance between them. After around ten seconds, in the opposite direction of where George and Buford are headed, a man wearing dark sweatpants and a jacket gets out of a gray sedan parked a few houses ahead. He crosses the street toward Cassandra's door.

Several blocks away George enters the Honky-Tonk bar and walks right up to the bartender. He orders a beer. Buford goes into the bar from the side door and takes up a spot in the room where he can lean against a column and watch George.

Buford keeps his head down but raises it often eyeing George's back, who's sitting alone at one of the high tables looking around the room and nursing his beer. After a while, his beer glass is half empty. George gets up and walks over to the old jukebox on the other side of the room, leaving his beer on the table.

Buford decides this is his chance and pulls away from the wall walking quietly past the bar. He holds the dropper concealed by his hand. As he walks past where George's drink is he squeezes a few drops of the tincture into the beer glass. He quickly puts the dropper back in his pocket, heading out the front door into the night.

The bedroom seems to be spinning now, Buford's heartbeat races faster, and his mind rambles errantly aggravating him to the point he throws the brooch across the room. It crashes against the window leaving a spiderweb crack on the glass, falling onto the floor like a dead broken-winged bird.

Chapter 20

Monday, December 22, 2021
New York City, NY

Keeping up with the holidays, Mandy and Stacy are extremely busy at the antique boutique, to the point Mandy is bringing Elsa to work with her after school because they have so much to do.

Now, a few days before Christmas, with no school, and having to spend her days at the store, Elsa is poking around in the back of the warehouse where most boxes and some larger items are in storage. She throws a book to the side on the floor, and slouches her body down the armchair, her arms halfway hanging out when Mandy walks in, 'Elsa! That's not a good posture for a young girl! Sit up straight.'

'Mom, I'm bored.' She pouts.

Mandy walks over, and crouches down in front of her, 'Yes, dear, I know.' She cleans a spec of sugar from Elsa's mouth. Her soft fingers feel like silk on Elsa's face.

'I want to be with Daddy! Can I go to his work sometimes too?'

Mandy gets up, 'If this is boring, you should know Tim's office will also be super boring.' She turns around, 'Look, we'll be done in a little bit here. How about you and I go for hot chocolate after I'm done? I think I can wrap things up in about an hour. What do you say?'

Elsa stares at her mom and shrugs, 'Well, okay. I guess. I wish I could go to the beach.' she whispers with a soft sigh.

A torment of emotions confuses Mandy's thoughts. These past few months have been lonely because of Tim's absence. He works late and when he's home they hardly interact, it's as if she lived alone, only with Elsa. After their summer holiday, their relationship got worse. All this time she'd been thinking they could work out their differences, and light up the spark they once had. Last summer there seemed to be a spark but nothing she's tried since then has worked. She shuts her eyes briefly and doesn't say a word.

~

Tim is still at his office. Everyone at work has already gone home two hours ago, but he's still slumped at his desk. He pulls a glass from the credenza behind him and pours himself an inch of whisky. *It's the holidays*, he tells himself. The only light on the whole floor is coming from above his desk and the lit-up exit signs above the stairway and the elevator down the hall.

He takes a swig of the amber liquid and picks up the mouse next to his monitor. He makes the cursor travel across the screen clicking through a few tabs. He scrolls down the page on the search engine looking for the beach house rental website he used in the summer to book the house for their vacation. This time he knows where he's going, nothing to reinvent. That exhilarating time has carved a hole in him and he needs to fill it up. He clicks on the image of the house they stayed at last year. It's available for the same dates he had booked before. *I will have to ask Mandy if she wants to try again this year. Will Jan be there? Maybe I should reserve it now, that way Mandy won't be able to say no. A Christmas present.* He smiles.

~

Packing boxes of orders to be shipped, the next day Stacy and Mandy are trying to get the last-minute purchases ready to ship before New York City shuts down for the Christmas weekend.

'Well, I hope you enjoy your Friday before Christmas with your family, Stacy. I'm telling you, we're busy here today, and tomorrow I'm going to be bogged down preparing casseroles and desserts to take upstate to Tim's parents. No rest for the weary.'

'Well, I plan to just relax, watch some movies, and drink a lot of wine. I'm taking these days off, and just worrying about Christmas on Christmas. Thankfully my aunts and mom will take care of everything. All I gotta do is bring lots of presents.' She laughs as she scrolls some clear tape with the dispenser gun over the middle of a box she's packing, 'Yeah, lots of presents, for my Dominican aunts and mom, plus a couple of Puerto Rican uncles and brother-in-law, and of course the nephews and nieces.'

'Have you ever thought of getting married, Stacy?'

'Oh, hell no! I'm content and satisfied. I love my freedom. No ma'am, not me.' She wiggles her index finger.

'Sometimes I wonder what it would be like…to be alone. It can't be very different than how I live right now.' She looks around, leans her head back to look through the door toward the front, brings her hand to her chest, and shakes her head, 'Don't get me wrong. I love Elsa, she's my life. That's not what I mean. I wonder what it would be like if it's just her and me.'

Stacy moves in closer leaning over slightly, 'Baby, baby, what is going on? Is everything okay between you and Tim?'

Mandy lowers her head, and Stacy turns her head also looking over toward the door to see if anyone's approaching. 'Come, come.' She leads Mandy to the armchair near the table they were working at, 'Here, sit here, and tell me all about it. What is going on, mi niña?'

Mandy sits down, clutches the long silk bow hanging from her blouse, and breathes in a sigh, 'I don't know Stacy. It's been a while. It seems Tim and I aren't in sync anymore. He works late.' She reaches out for Stacy's hand, 'Last night he didn't get home until after nine o'clock. I barely see him. I try to create outings for us on the weekends, but he's usually tired or goes out alone. Sometimes he takes Elsa places, but it's not like it used to be, and there's this.' Mandy reaches for her purse, pulls out a Tarot card, and gives it to Stacy, 'What do you think this means?'

Stacy looks at the card, "*The lovers*" is written on it. 'That looks like a Tarot card. Where did you get it?'

'I found it in Tim's drawer. It's weird. I had never seen him be interested in things like this.'

'Hmmm, that is strange, I'd say. But what does that have to do with how you're feeling right now, Mandy?'

'It's just all so strange. Tim is not himself lately, then this. I wonder if he has someone else…It's like I don't even know him anymore. I've lost all sense of connection to him.'

'Did you think about asking him about it?'

'I'm not sure I want him to know I've been looking through his stuff.' She turns her head frowning. She shrugs, 'I'll just have to play it out and see what happens.'

Stacy's mouth frowns, 'I am so sorry Mandy. How is this affecting Elsa?' She swings her head around, then in a hushed voice, 'Maybe we should not talk a lot about this here. Elsa is bound to hear us.' She takes both of Mandy's hands in hers, and says, 'Look, once the holidays are over, let's talk about this some more. I get that this would be a big decision for you to make, you cannot make a decision like this in haste.'

Mandy shakes her head, 'I know, I know, but I don't know what to do anymore, and I am desperate,.' She sobs.

'All right, all right, I see that. But hang in there a bit more. Maybe Tim's just stressed out at work right now. Didn't you tell me he just got about three new large accounts? He must be so bogged down.'

'Yeah, I guess.' Mandy shrugs. Stacy gives her a hug and pulls her up from the chair, 'What do you say we finish packing these next couple of boxes and put them near the rear door so the driver can pick them up? Let me get Elsa to help us.' She moves away toward the door. 'Hey, Elsa! Do you want to come here, and help us a bit? Where are you?'

Mandy dries up her face with the back of her hand, and moves one of the boxes on the table, picks it up, and heads toward the rear. Elsa rushes in, 'Yes, yes, what can I do?'

Stacy points to the smaller lighter boxes, 'Look at those small boxes there, honey. Help me with that, and bring them over to where your Mommy's at. Great, great, you're doing good. Thanks, Elsa.'

Chapter 21

December 26, 2021
Saphire, NC

Christmas has come and gone, tiny specs of colored lights shine by the gate at the front of Jan's property. Inside her living room next to the fireplace the tall Christmas tree is dotted with blue, green, yellow, white, and red blinking lights. George liked the tree to have lights of different colors. With a cup of hot apple cider in her hands, Jan stands looking out the large living room window watching tiny flakes of snow fall over the already white hedges. It looks so clean, beautiful, and lovely but Jan knows how cold it is out there. She shivers and hugs herself in a gesture to feel the warmth from her soft gray cashmere shawl. She smiles thinking of her brother Max and his gift to her this Christmas. She brings the Cashmere shawl to her face, feeling its softness. *He's splurged this year. I'll have to ask him what he's up to.*

But it's Sunday, and Christmas is done. Sad, empty, cold, and lonely. Unlike Miami where Max lives. Jan wishes she could feel the warmth of Miami. These are lonely days for Jan and they will continue until she goes in a few months on yet another book tour. *I don't have it in me to write these days, waiting for the new year to waltz through. Maybe I should take a drive in the mountains tomorrow and see what I find.* She stares at the tall pine trees, the gray sky, and soon, the darkness.

~

New York City, NY

The door of the condo flies open hitting the wall as Mandy pushes the small suitcase with her foot. She stammers through and waits for Elsa at the end of the hallway, 'Come, Elsa, let's get you ready for bed.' She rolls her eyes at Tim who is walking through the door with two handbags and also pushing a carry-on suitcase into the living room.

'Mandy don't be that way, we need to talk about this like adults.'

Mandy and Elsa have already disappeared into the bedrooms. Tim accommodates the bags into a corner and follows. He hears the shower and the bathroom door is closed so he pulls away and goes back to the living room. The lights of the city cast shadows in the room so Tim decides to keep the lights off. He strolls over to the credenza and prepares a drink, settling into the side chair.

A few minutes later Mandy walks in and finds him holding the drink in both hands leaning forward in his chair. He looks up, 'Mandy, this was coming sooner or later. I knew it, you knew it.'

Mandy sits on the sofa across from him, her legs crossed. The truth is she knew this would happen. For a while she's known she's been losing Tim. However, she didn't expect him to approach the subject while they were staying with his parents. She turns her head toward Tim, 'It was Christmas for heaven's sake Tim! You couldn't wait until a better time to tell me you're filing for divorce? That was a cowardly move.'

Tim closes his eyes. Forgiveness? Could he be forgiven for anything? Should he even ask? A million reasons roam through his head at high speed as he tries to grab even one excuse to give Mandy as to why he did it now. Being at home with his parents suffocated him to the point he knew he had to make the decision. He closes his eyes recalling Christmas Day and his mother going through the motions of giving out gifts, showing some smiles but her heart not being in it. His dad is still present in the home when needed, out of habit, because it's what's comfortable for him. His dad never thought about what his affairs had done to his wife. His parents live together because it's convenient but there's no spark there. Tim can't remember when there ever was. Do they even talk to each other anymore?

The visit to his parents hit hard. He realizes he's emulating his father and he has to put an end to that. Right now there is no spark left in him either and he doesn't want to live like that. He doesn't want Mandy to become like his mother, devoid of affection, zest, and joie de vivre, and submerge into emptiness day after day. He doesn't want to become his father living a lie. Should he tell her? He doesn't.

'I'll move out tomorrow, Mandy. I'll sleep on the sofa tonight.' He gets up and goes to the bedroom to change clothes.

Chapter 22

Late February 2022
New York, NY

Excitement warmed the still chill of these corridors ten years ago. Today, the thermostat is probably at sixty degrees. Then Jan didn't notice it but today she feels the actual chill run up and down her body. She shakes her head, every time she visits Jan feels the cold creep into her bones.

The elevator doors open in front of her on the thirtieth floor. The sitting area is absolutely quiet. Just as she recalls, the walls continue to be absolutely white and utterly bare. Nothing has changed since the first time she walked through this door ten years ago for the first time. She swerves to her left toward the corridor and walks to the end of it where two large maple-colored doors await. She knows she will find Susan at her high desk on the other side. That is the receptionist at Hart & Fairchild Publishers. She opens the door and walks in.

Susan looks up and smiles. 'Miss Crawford.' There is brightness in her greeting. How does she manage to show so much warmth in this chilly environment? Jan doesn't understand. She smiles back.

'She is waiting for you. Go right ahead, you can walk right in. John will let you through.' Jan walks toward Mrs. Fairchild's office. Susan picks up her phone to dial John and announces her.

John is standing next to Miss Fairchild's office door when Jan arrives, 'Good morning John. How are you doing?'

Jan notices he's wearing a v-neck sweater under his jacket as he opens the door to the inner office, 'I'm well Miss Crawford, thanks so much. She's waiting for you.'

Jan walks in. Mrs. Fairchild's white curls bounce as she rises from her seat. Jan silently admires her white crepe blazer. She wonders, *How can she look so dashing in white? And look so young? Maybe the freezing cold keeps her ageless?*

Mrs. Fairchild reaches out to Jan, takes her hand, and places a peck on each cheek, 'Dear, dear Jan, how are you? How was your flight?' *How can her hands be so warm in here?* As Mrs. Fairchild gestures for her to take a seat she signals to John who hasn't left the room yet, 'John, please, can you get us some coffee?' She looks at Jan, 'Is coffee all right? Or would you prefer some juice or tea?'

Jan waves her hand, now seated, and smiles, 'Yes. Thanks, John, coffee would be great.' *Give me something hot!*

Mrs. Fairchild makes herself comfortable, she sits back at her desk across from Jan, and rests her elbows on the arms of her office chair, 'So, tell me, how have you been? Ready for the next flurry?'

Jan smiles, 'Well, not quite ready, but yes, I guess. A book tour is really what I need right now. I can't seem to get myself down to writing these days.'

'Well, that's wonderful. The book is already getting great reviews, and once you're out there meeting the readers again, and doing the interviews, and the radio shows and podcasts, I'm sure it will take off like a rocket!' She laughs. Her thick voice manages to convince Jan this will be a 'Great adventure, indeed.'

Jan nods, 'I am looking forward to it. Has the list of locations been decided yet for the tour?'

'Well.' Mrs. Fairchild moves some papers around on her desk and pulls one out from under a pile of others. She hands the sheet to Jan, 'I've been talking with Dianne about it, and I'm not sure how much she's told you because we just finished this list late last night, but we want to expand the tour, almost double it from the last one.'

Jan's eyes open wide. John walks in with a tray, and places coffee in front of each of them, they thank him.

'Oh, wow. I wasn't expecting this. But why?' She stares at the list.

'Dear Jan, the book has had so many reviews, and already so much response from your readers, we know we have to enjoy this advantage. This is going to be your best seller yet. You are going to have so much success with this title.'

'Okay, so where am I going, and for how long?'

'Well, the tour is set up to begin here in New York City with TV interviews on two National TV morning shows, and a cocktail party with booksellers, and bookstore owners, that's all we'll do in New York. Then you'll continue with podcasts, radio appearances, a few book signings in large bookstores, and local TV interviews in different parts of the country, starting with North Carolina, Florida, a few cities in the Midwest, Seattle, of course, California, and ending back in Chicago like we did last time.'

'This is going to be exhausting.'

'There, there, Jan. Think about a marathon. You're ready for this one. This is the one you were waiting for. Once you meet with your readers, that will energize you. I feel you are going to have so much fun you won't even notice, and the month will go by in a flash.' Mrs. Fairchild waves her arm across the table, then picks up her cup.

Jan raises her eyebrows. Inwardly she knows the book tours are the pinnacle of her work. It's where she puts the reader together with the book. It's a special bond, where the image she has created in her mind materializes. So she accepts the challenge, she lifts her shoulders, a half smile on her face.

Launching so close to "*Broken Time*" is going to be a push for this new title, since the summer is a market they had not taken advantage of before with Jan's books. At least that's what Mrs. Fairchild says. She is hopeful, 'I hope you have another thriller in you, dear because this is the path you're on now.'

~

The screen across from Tim is flashing its usual array of colors, a map pops up after he types an address in the search box. He moves his cursor over it and clicks on it, zooms in looking for a satellite view, there they are. Two houses. The beach, the sand, a line of houses running north, the North Environmental Park. He remembers them well. *Memories.* A pang of nostalgia still lingers in his chest, in his mind. He slides the map into street view. There, the driveways run into each other. His two-story rental, and on the other side, Jan's house. A one-story white cottage with a tiled roof and a light blue garage door. He checks the house number and types the address to Jan's rental to see if he can find its rental company online. *Has she booked the property yet? Will she return this year?* He is going back. Mandy received the 'Christmas gift' with lukewarm appreciation, but Elsa was elated. Mandy is not very happy about going to Florida again this summer, specially since they will be divorced by then. She only agreed so they could share a couple of weeks with Elsa as a "family." Elsa misses her dad these days, though she sees him almost every weekend.

Tim wants to make Elsa happy and hopes he can also reconnect with Jan. Only time will tell. *I hope she does visit this year. I think she will, she said she comes down every year. She has to!*

He can't find the address of Jan's cottage listed anywhere. None of the common house beach rental sites have that address available. He shuts off the screen in a huff and bursts out of his office chair.

A few miles away at home, Mandy pours wine into her glass. She lifts it up and stares at the burgundy liquid reaching almost to the rim. *I wonder what he's doing right now*. She drinks half of it in one gulp, squinting her eyes in the process, and walks over to the sofa. She turns on the TV and cozies under a fleece blanket. She mutes the TV. After a few minutes, she falls asleep.

Chapter 23

Sunday, April 17, 2022
New York City, NY

Lazy Sundays are a favorite for Mandy. She likes to take in the morning sun laying on the vintage chaise lounge sofa next to the long window at the end of their living room. Today she is reading a new novel she bought for her two-member book club.

Tim is visiting today. He and Elsa have teamed up to make breakfast, and all she can hear is giggling coming from the kitchen. She also hears some howls and squeals, and spraying? *They better not be making a mess in there.* She shakes her head but it doesn't bother her. Today she isn't interested in being alarmed by anything. In any case, it's Tim's turn to pick up the pieces if needed.

She pulls up the soft crocheted blanket to her chest and opens the dark blue covered book on page 57. She smiles at the memory of giving Stacy a copy of the book. Stacy couldn't believe Mandy had met the author on her last vacation, 'How cool is that?!' She'd exclaimed. Today she has to read as much as she can, maybe even get ahead of Stacy, so she doesn't spoil the story for her.

Mandy hears the clink of the silverware on the china. She doesn't want any of those calories, she's happy with her coffee brew. That's all she needs this morning.

After what seems like a few seconds, but was most likely fifteen minutes, Tim comes over. She looks up from her book wishing he'd nuzzle her neck, make her feel warm, and kiss her.

'What are you reading?'

Closing the book, Mandy shows him the title, 'It's quite interesting, actually.' She lifts herself up, 'Jan Crawford's newest book "*The Summer Rose.*" She passes the book to Tim.

Mandy doesn't notice as blood seeps away from his cheeks. He takes the book in his hands and comments, 'Ah, her new book. Is it any good?' He lowers his face and ruffles through a few pages so Mandy can't notice his complexion.

'It actually is.' She levels up and straightens on the sofa, Tim is sitting on the ottoman across from her, his head still bowed. He coughs and hands the book back to Mandy. She continues, 'I read one of her books while we were at the beach, but this is totally different. It's like she's taken another genre, another theme. It's still romance but with suspense and mystery, with some interesting plot twists. I can see why she goes to the beach to write. This story is set at the beach. Our beach.' She smiles, 'She's in New York this week. I believe tomorrow she's going to the morning TV shows. She's doing the book tour, you know? What authors do to promote their books.'

'Yes, that's great.' Tim busies his hands rubbing them on his lap. A stream of roiling up inside him. *New York! She's in New York! I will not let her get away. Not this time.* He gets up from the ottoman and heads to the kitchen.

Mandy closes her book and lays it on her chest, she wonders if Jan has decided to stay alone forever and what that would mean. These past few months have been hard for Mandy. Maybe Jan could tell her how she does it. Mandy opens up the book again and relaxes her head on the sofa, 'The book is great, by the way. I think you'd enjoy it. Would you like to read it when I'm finished?'

Tim leans over to the kitchen door and shrugs, 'Sure when you're done with it. Maybe I will. Let me know if it ends up fulfilling your expectations.'

'Okay. So what are you two doing today?'

'Later on we're planning on going out for lunch, and then to the park for a walk. Do you want to join us?'

'Sure, I'll read a little bit more, and I can meet you at the restaurant but just lunch. I have plans for tonight.' Of course, she's lying. She will stay home and watch TV.

Chapter 24

Monday, April 18, 2022
New York City, NY

The book tour begins. Jan is riding in her limo down the streets of downtown Manhattan. They're expecting her to appear on one of the morning TV shows. She's a bit nervous, it's the first time she does national television, or any television for that matter. She's quite comfortable in her library, at the beach house, or in small cozy rooms at different bookstores around the country. TV, she's never even fathomed what that is like.

Dianne called very early this morning to give her the usual pep talk, 'Now, Jan, just sit straight, think about your characters, think about the book, think about your process. That is all you need to do.'

'My process? What do you mean by my process?'

Dianne's smile translates into her words, 'Well, that's what those hot shot TV and radio people always ask, "*tell me about your process*," or something like that. I guess they mean, how you write, why you write, and where do the characters come from. You know… your process.'

'I'll try Dianne, I'm not even sure where anything comes from. Well, I gotta get going. I need to get ready and get some breakfast, I'll call you when I'm done.'

'Oh, I'll know when you're done.' Dianne winks at her own image in the bathroom mirror, 'Just one more thing, don't wear white, okay? I read somewhere white is a no-no on TV.' The line went silent.

'*Oookay.*' Jan stares at her cell phone, 'good thing I wasn't planning on wearing white.'

Back in the limo, Jan thinks about Tim. New York. The Big Apple. If this limo kept riding south she would be in the Financial District. *Would I see him?* She shakes her head. *There are millions of people in New York. There's no way I'd see him walking down the street. I wonder if he's read the book, or if he even knows about the book. What would he think? Would he think it's about him? About them? About us? Would he know?* She straightens up in the back seat, the driver announces they are almost at their destination.

~

It's 9:05 in the morning when Tim sits in front of his desk and clicks on his computer mouse. The screen lights up and he opens his email software. He sees one of his search alerts with the phrase 'Jan Crawford' in the subject and his heart starts pounding. He skims through the email looking over many different links about Jan. He clicks on one mentioning her calendar of events in New York. He scrolls through it.

~

Mrs. Fairchild had booked a beautiful meeting room with rooftop access overseeing the city even though it is still quite chilly in New York City at the end of April. It would probably not be on the rooftop in this weather, but the view from the top floor of the hotel is spectacular. Around two hundred guests mingle talking about publishing, marketing, distribution, and of course, social media, all trying to get a word in with the author as well. Everyone would love to speak to Jan Crawford or at the very least with the well-known and powerful publisher Martha Fairchild. Of course, Dianne is there as well, working the room, trying to get the right people to occupy Jan's time, the heavy hitter book distributors, for example.

Sifting through groups of people and a few waiters carrying Hors d'oeuvres and tall champagne glasses, Dianne walks over to Jan with Mister Samuel Chen at her arm, 'Hey Jan, let me introduce you to Mister Chen. He is very successful at marketing many best-sellers, and he has taken a liking to your book, my dear.'

Jan extends her hand to Mister Chen, and they shake hands, 'Pleased to meet you, Mister Chen.' She says with a smile.

'So happy to meet you Miss Crawford.' He replies with a warm and strong handshake.

Dianne excuses herself, 'Please, go right ahead, I'll leave you to it.' She pats Jan's back and takes tiny steps toward the front door.

Elevator doors open to a large carpeted corridor. Tim looks at the wall in front of him for a sign of where to go to find the Queensway Room. He turns right and sees a few ladies at a table outside of a larger room.

His hands are shaking, he fixes his tie and presses it against his chest, and walks toward the table.

'Good evening ladies. Is this Jan Crawford's event?'

Sheila looks up from talking to Colleen and runs her hand through her highlighted curls, a fake smile on her face. She's annoyed at the man interrupting her delicious gossip about last night. 'Yes, sir. Do you have an invitation?' Her voice is as steady as her finger points at a sheet on the table with a long list of names on it.

'Well, no, I don't.' He stammers as he puts his hands in his coat pockets.

'I am so sorry sir. But only people with invitations can go in. This is a private event.' Sheila says looking at Colleen as she nods for her approval. Colleen nods.

Dianne hears a man's agitated voice as she exits the large salon and walks onto the corridor. Tim's voice increases a few decibels, 'Yes, I understand. But look, I am a friend of Miss Crawford and I need to see her.' His face is flushed, 'It's very important!'

Sheila and Colleen stare blankly at Tim. Sheila lifts her chin and tilts her head comforted by the power she has over this person. Her red lips shine in a forced smile. Dianne walks passed them, behind Tim, and squints her eyes. As she tries to see if she can catch what he is saying, she realizes he is insisting to go inside and needs to speak to Jan Crawford. *Who is this guy?* She decides to turn back and walks behind the table, standing behind Sheila and Colleen.

Tim looks up and tries to convince Dianne to let him in. 'Ma'am, I'm Tim Evans, a friend of Jan Crawford's and I would like to have a minute of her time. Do you think that would be possible?'

'Hello, Mr. Evans.' She answers, 'I'm Dianne Taylor and nice to meet you but I'm very sorry. Miss Crawford can't come out right now. This is a business gathering and she is extremely busy. I will have to ask you to leave. Maybe you can call her and meet some other time?'

Tim lowers his head and looks at his business card which he already has in his hand. He takes a pen out of his jacket pocket and writes a short note on the back. 'Would you be so kind as to give her this? Thank you.' He gives Dianne the card. Forlorn, he turns and heads toward the elevator.

When he's out of earshot she says to the girls, 'If you ever need to call security, they're just down the hall.' She rushes off to the restroom. *For sure, I don't need an overly enthusiastic fan here at this moment!* She rolls her eyes and puts her well-manicured hand to her chest.

~

A couple of hours later, now in the limo, Jan and Dianne kick off their shoes. Dianne pours some champagne into a tall glass and offers it to Jan.

Jan shakes her head and puts out a hand, 'No, I can't drink anymore, I'm tapped out.'

Dianne shrugs, 'Suit yourself.' and takes a sip of the golden liquid, 'Mmm, I looove champagne. How can you pass up on this, girl?' She closes her eyes, and savors the flavor, 'Oh, I almost forgot!' Dianne puts the glass down, and searches through her hand purse, 'Here, here.' She hands the business card to Jan, 'someone left this note in the front for you. He didn't have an invitation, and the girls wouldn't let him through. I figured he was a fan or something.'

Jan takes the card and reads the back. Her face washes out, she looks like a ghost. Troubled, Dianne says, 'Jan, what is it? Who is that? I knew I shouldn't have given you that! I knew it, I knew it, I knew it!' She slaps her lap, and pokes her forehead, 'Dianne, why did you give her that note?!' She asks herself out loud. Jan remains quiet for a few more seconds, a tear rolls down her face. Dianne reaches to her, 'Oh my dear Jan, What happened? Who is he? Please tell me. Now I'm really freaking out.'

Looking at Dianne, tears roll down her face. Jan leans her head on her shoulder, 'That was Tim, Dianne. That was my neighbor at the beach in Florida. My lover, my experiment, my research.' She lifts her head, more tears, 'I thought I was done with it. I tried. I really tried. I made myself get over him, but I guess I'm not. Oh, I was so afraid of this, Dianne.'

Dianne pats her lap, 'My dear, it's ok. We all go through stuff, though, I have to be honest with you, you sure go through more than most!'

Now wiping tears off with a paper tissue, Jan laughs. They both laugh so forcefully that Jan starts coughing as Dianne hastily reaches over for one of the champagne glasses, 'Oh my, now we don't want to end up in a hospital, Jan. Take it easy. Breathe now, take a sip of this.' She hands her the glass, 'Come on, it'll do you good, just a sip.' Jan drinks some champagne.

Dianne continues, 'Now, we're going to head on over to your room, look.' She points to the window, 'We're almost there, and you're going to spill the whole story. I want it all. Now, let's go!'

~

Looking up from the TV, Mandy checks the time on the clock, and again it's past nine o'clock. This is the time Tim had been arriving home before he moved out. *I wonder what he's doing now.* Elsa has been in bed for a bit, maybe she's still awake. Mandy keeps on watching the show. *Maybe I should go and read her a bedtime story?*

She looks over to the TV screen at a couple of blond women with botox lips yelling profanities at each other wearing short cocktail dresses full of glitter. She rolls her eyes and gets off the sofa and turns the TV off. She throws the TV remote down and heads over to Elsa's bedroom. *Reality TV just isn't real.*

~

Opening the door to his condo Tim walks in and drops the keys in the bowl on the console table near the door. He takes off his coat and puts it in the closet.

The condo is dark and quiet. After leaving the hotel where he tried to see Jan he considered hanging around the lobby waiting for her to leave, but then rejected the idea. Instead, he went outside and walked in the park for an hour to think things over. If Elsa was here he'd be sitting here with her watching TV or reading her a book. He looks at his watch, *maybe I should just go to bed.*

~

'I know he's married.' Dianne raises her eyebrows at Jan, nibbling on some chocolate strawberries from the fruit platter they ordered when they got to the room. Jan picks a strawberry, 'That's why I left, Dianne. I would've been doing the same thing that was done to me.' She shakes her head, 'I couldn't.'

'Tell me about his wife. Does she know?' Dianne folds her legs in a yoga position on the bed.

Jan shrugs, 'Not that I know of. That's the reason I left before it got more complicated. I refuse to be a home wrecker. Both Elsa, their daughter, and Mandy are beautiful people.'

'And, what does he do?'

'He's a hotshot financial guy. I don't know. He lives here in New York.' She shivers, 'I'm glad I'm leaving tomorrow. I don't want to see him!'

Dianne shrivels her lips upwards, 'Mmm, I don't believe you. I bet you really want to see him.'

Jan closes her eyes, takes a deep breath, lets it out, winces, and pulls at her hair, 'I know, I know. I can't stand it!' She looks at Dianne widening her eyes, 'I need to find someone else! Maybe I can forget about Tim.'

'Geez, girl. You're in trouble.'

~

Slowly opening Tim's office door mid-morning the next day, Raquel steps into his office. Tim is reading through a spreadsheet laid out on his desk and doesn't look up, 'Yes?'

Someone is standing behind Raquel at the door, who says, 'Tim, there's a lady here to see you.'

He lifts his head. His face warms up with a soft smile on his face, 'Hello Jan.'

Raquel retreats leaving Jan at the threshold. Already standing near the door, Tim reaches for her. He takes her hand, and pulls her in, kissing her on the cheek. Jan's face heats up and she blushes, 'Hello Tim.' He closes the door and signals her to take a seat. He sits in the chair right across from her. He wants to reach out and hold her hands but stops himself, 'How are you Jan?'

Jan sits, shuts her eyes, and takes in a deep breath. Tim watches her and breaks the silence, 'I'm glad you're here.' Now he reaches for her hands and holds them.

Jan lifts her head, 'Tim, I'm so sorry about everything! I don't know what to do.' She looks into his eyes, 'All this time I've been lying to myself, avoiding you, shoving the thought of you away, but I can't anymore. I know that what I was feeling was going to get the best of me and I could not let myself be that woman.'

'I know, I know because I have not been able to stop thinking about you, either. Even after all this time.'

'That is one reason why I came today.' She looks at her hands being held in his, and a teardrop falls sliding down her hand unto his, 'Because I can't either, Tim.' She shrugs as he lifts a finger up to her cheek to wipe away a tear, 'I guess I don't care anymore.' She raises her head, 'What are we going to do?'

He takes her hand, 'Look, for now we can keep it quiet. The fact is Mandy and I are getting divorced.'

Jan's face pales and she places her hand on her chest, 'What? Why? When? Oh, Tim, I'm so sorry.'

'Please Jan, don't be. It was all unraveling even before I met you… It's still not final yet, but it will be in a few weeks.'

'How is Elsa taking your separation?'

'She's adapting. We try to support her in every way we can because she has also been struggling with school.'

Jan pulls away from Tim and turns her head, 'I'm glad both of you are supporting Elsa. Divorce is so difficult for children. I wouldn't want to add to the whole situation. Me coming here isn't going to help.'

Tim smiles, 'We just have to be smart about it. Nobody has to know. Mandy will eventually find out, but we can hold off for a while. But tell me, when are you leaving New York?'

'I should actually be on my way to the airport right now but I decided to stay one more day to come by. I wasn't sure how you'd receive me.'

'I have wanted to see you every day since you left the beach house. I've been tracking you for months. When I saw you were in New York I looked everywhere to see where you were staying or where you were going. I knew you'd be on TV yesterday morning. Mandy told me. I surfed the internet and found out about your business cocktail and tried to see you there.'

'Yes. I heard.' She says raising her eyebrows. She smiles, 'Dianne gave me your card, she's my agent.'

'Yes. I met her. Quite the personality.'

'Ha! Ha! Yes.' She wipes the tears from her face with the back of her hand. 'She is very defensive and very good at what she does. She's also a very good friend.'

'What do you say we go somewhere? Are you hungry?'

'I could eat, sure.'

'There. All right. We can talk more freely away from here. Let's go.'

~

'I knew it! I knew it!' Mandy cries out as she slams her book on the desk in their office. Stacy looks at her, smiling. Mandy isn't happy, 'I knew you'd jinx it for me!'

Stacy is now giggling a bit mischievously, 'Now, Mandy, I wouldn't do that. I just got a little bit ahead of you in the story. So, how do you like it up to now?'

'I think the story is great. Let's see, poor Rose. She loves Otto, or is it really love? What do you think, Stacy?'

'I'm not sure. I see Rose likes Otto, that's why she went to bed with him. But love him? I'm not so sure. I think she's trying to get back at him because he left her after they had that romance in college. I think this time it's more a passing sleepover for her.'

'A sleepover?' Mandy laughs, 'Hmmm, maybe you're right. But she seems to be very passionate about Otto. Though he is married. How is that a good thing?'

'Well, she did show up at their beach house, right next door. Was she stalking him?'

'That's what I mean! Whom do you consider provoked whom?'

'I think they both did it, in their own way, but he is guiltier because he is cheating.'

'Oh shit!' Mandy's face grows pale, her heartbeat quickens and she takes a seat on the chair next to her desk.

'What? What's wrong Mandy? Are you okay?'

'Oh, my God! I can't believe it!' She brings her hand up to cover her mouth, 'They actually did it.' She touches her face which feels hot and sweaty as it turns red.

'Yes, they did. Or, are you talking about something else?!' She stares at Mandy who is now pressing the back of her hand to her forehead, her eyes closed. Stacy prompts her, 'Mandy…Mandy, what's going on? Do you want a glass of water?' She pours a glass of water from the pitcher on the credenza and places it on the desk.

'No, no, it's okay, Stacy.' She looks up at Stacy, her face a tinge grayed, 'Rose and Otto and their romance in college! It's just like Tim's fling in college he had with a girl. He told me all about it and Jan used it in the story. She gave it a twist, though, to adapt it to her story, but how could she have known all the other details? The business Otto launches as a college student, the love affair?' Mandy's eyes are open wide staring at her friend, 'Stacy, Tim and Jan actually did it!' A tear falls down her face.

'What?! What did they do? I don't understand.'

'It all makes so much sense! Rose and Otto mirror Jan and Tim in too many ways. They were having an affair when we were at the beach last summer!'

~

Walking down the block after brunch, Jan takes his hand in hers and lifts it up running her finger along each one of the lines of his palm. He laughs, 'Palm reading? Are you reading my fortune?'

Jan withdraws embarrassed still holding onto his hand, she leans her head on his shoulder, 'Not really. Not at all. I was just thinking of all that's happened to me, to you. How you and Mandy aren't together anymore…'

They reach Jan's hotel lobby and walk in silence all the way to the sixth floor of her hotel. Reaching the door to her room, emotions, expectations, and energy converge inside her making it hard for her to pull out the key card from her purse. They rush into the bedroom, taking off each other's layers of clothing, one by one. Jan moves to turn the lights on but Tim stops her. He closes the door and wraps his arm around her shoulders bringing her face close to him. He slows her down as his lips passionately search for hers, he runs his fingers through her hair, and she wraps her arms around his neck. Their kiss lasts a long minute before they come up for air.

Though the room is dark, there's enough clarity for their eyes to meet. Without speaking a word they recognize what remoteness has meant these past few months, that what they feel may not be contained or temporary, that their desire for their bodies has grown stronger than they ever felt before. This time away has only enhanced the fire Tim feels for Jan, the pull probably more forceful today than their first time.

Jan's tan coat and Tim's black jacket lay on the floor near the doorway. Now Jan's fingers furiously unbutton Tim's shirt and he pulls her dress over her shoulders. Their lips continue to create an incessant urge to grasp the invisible desire their bodies long for as the rest of their clothes fall to the floor.

Naked and still standing, Tim softly runs his fingers along Jan's arms and over her back and front, touching every inch. Splashes of electricity run from her arms through the rest of her body. She reacts as she feels his manhood grow against her loins and she leans in searching for completeness. She kisses him as her hands run from his chest southward, fervently wanting more from him and giving more through every kiss, every brush of her fingers. They try to stay linked as they slowly stride toward her bed. Tim falls in first pulling her with him. Jan pulls up and kneels on the mattress watching him from above. She runs her fingers over his face and chest. She leans in and her lips cover his mouth. She softly travels down to his chest and further. Sensations flurry through him and he grabs Jan back to him. He wants to love her and provoke her body to respond to his love. She takes in the intense reactions her body is uncovering. She doesn't want him to stop.

Swerving into each other simultaneously, their bodies' attraction fuse into one. Tim enters her softly but their rhythm increases suddenly, steeply reaching for a tidal flow. Jan and Tim arrive together at their final peak.

~

Scrolling through images on the screen, Mandy sits with her phone in her hand. She has so many she's had to delete some and only keep the ones that bring her joy. One of Elsa riding a merry-go-round in the park a few years ago. She smiles as she sees a selfie of all three of them sitting on the deck at the beach house. Then another close-up at the beach last year where Elsa is scrunching her nose at the camera. A tear rolls down her cheek as she tries to define what her life will look like going forward. Even before Tim gave her the ultimatum of divorce the day after Christmas, she had a feeling the months of loneliness would translate into an actual breakup. Despair fills her with confusion, insecurity, remorse, and regrets. She's tried to overcome but she's not sure when or if she'll feel whole again. Now she needs to focus on the reason why she's in this predicament: Jan Crawford.

Since she made her discovery earlier today, Mandy has rummaged through dozens of websites looking for anything about Jan's life. She dives into everything she can find, comments on social media about her books, blogs about her career, her private life, maybe there's some lost post from a rival. What is out there is quite tantalizing. *How is it that there hasn't been a news outlet that's gotten a hold of her story? Her husband was a murderer? That's interesting.* It's open season. Time to hit back, show what she can do, and get Tim back. *Jan doesn't know who she's dealing with.* She opens the Contacts app on her phone and clicks on a phone number.

'Hello. Linda?'

'Yes. Hi Mandy! How are you?'

She puts her cell phone on speaker so she can look for her Journal on the desk, 'I'm calling because we're heading out there again this summer and I want to make sure you're still doing real estate. I want to look for a home at or near the beach.'

'Well, yes, I'm still doing real estate. I would be glad to show you around. If you want I can set up for you to get emails again on the properties coming onto the market. That way you get a feel for what's out there.'

'Yes, that's great. Also, maybe you can help me with something. What can you tell me about Jan Crawford's husband and that murder he was accused of a few years ago?'

Chapter 25

Friday, June 10, 2022
New Smyrna Beach, FL

Very few puffs of white clouds hang against the light blue sky. The ocean waves hit the shore and in the distance, the seagulls' mew blends into a song as a backdrop. Tim walks through the French doors of the same house they rented last year, he sees Elsa standing at the edge of the deck staring at the beach. She is wearing a two-piece flowery bathing suit and holding a colorful plastic bucket and shovel in her hands. The salty air prompts the memory of Jan. *I missed this!* He turns his head to the right toward the house Jan rented last year but the porch is empty. 'Hi there honey. How are you doing this morning?'

Elsa looks up at him with a smile, 'I'm great.'

'Where's your mom?'

'I think she's upstairs. Can I go to the beach Daddy?'

There are a couple of kids running in and out of the water near the shore. The brown-haired freckled boy is wearing bright green trunks. The girl is younger, close to Elsa's age, and wearing a red two-piece bathing suit. Her brown hair is tied up into two long braids draped over her shoulders.

Tim pokes Elsa's shoulder, 'Sure, go ahead. Look, there are some kids playing on the beach.' She nods. 'Go on, I'll watch from here if you like.'

Mandy rushes outside, 'Hold on, hold on.' She approaches with a tube in her hand, 'Elsa come on baby, let's get some sunscreen on you first.' Elsa winces her eyes and turns her lips into a pucker.

Mandy leans down, 'I know, I know…but you know us redheads have to be careful about the sun, Elsa.' She lathers Elsa's back with the cold liquid. Elsa shudders. Mandy touches Elsa's shoulder, 'There, now turn around, and let me put some on your nose.' Elsa turns, closes her eyes, and puckers her face again while her mother rubs some of the liquid onto her face. Mandy finishes, and says, 'Okay, now you can go.' Elsa runs off, her long red hair bouncing in the wind and on her shoulders.

Tim and Mandy watch as she joins the boy and girl at the beach. Mandy's standing with her arms crossed, 'How's the hotel?' Tim nods, 'It's ok.' Mandy walks back into the house, excited that a family is renting the property next door. *No room for that seducer!*

At that moment, Max Hayes walks out of the house next door. His medium-length layered hippie hairstyle with the accent of a mustache and close-cut facial hair doesn't look messy. In his mid-thirties, his style resembles more of a retired tennis player than a software developer, which means he wears it well. Max yells out to the children, 'Alex, Hannah, come on in, we're going to the store.' He waves them over. He turns to his left as he notices Tim standing on his deck, and waves, 'Hello there! Nice morning.'

'Yeah, sure is. Great time to be here!' Tim waves back.

Tim walks down the stairs of the deck toward the beach. Alex and Hannah run up toward their father. Elsa is standing at the beach with the bucket in her hand, a bit glum. Tim approaches. 'Hey there, honey. Don't worry, your friends have to go shopping. I'll be with you. Do you want to go into the water?'

Elsa drops the bucket and starts going closer to the shore. 'Wait up, let's put the bucket and shovel closer to the house, otherwise, they will be pulled into the ocean by the current.' He takes off his t-shirt as Elsa rushes up away from the water, and throws the toys onto the property, then rushes back to her dad. As Elsa jumps and they both splash in the water near the shore the spritz in the air caresses their faces.

~

Jan flinches and pulls her arm away once the suitcase is off the conveyer belt at the airport. She moves her arms in a rotating motion, trying to loosen up her muscles, and rubs her right arm. *I must've packed more than I thought.* She pulls the handle of her suitcase and her carry-on bag and waltzes through the Daytona Beach airport toward a rental car counter. She sees her cell phone light up with a message from Max: *Hoping you got in ok. Call when you get this. The kids can't wait to see you.*

Jan smiles and piles her handbag onto the counter to get her wallet out, the suitcase falls off the wheels and she ignores it. A young woman approaches her, 'How can I help you?'

'I have a reservation.' She pulls out her driver's license.

~

Sitting outside under the umbrella eating hotdogs and chips, Max and the children watch as Mandy and Elsa walk over onto their deck. Elsa is carrying a small basket in her hands covered with a tiny red and white checkered cloth. They walk toward the neighbors' house, go around the fence, and open the gate. Mandy says putting her hand over her eyes to cover the bright noon sunlight, 'Hello, neighbors. I hear Elsa met Alex and Hannah this morning at the beach.'

Both kids are chomping into their hotdog buns, Max looks at them sidewise, then nods and says, 'Yes, they did. How are you, Elsa?'

Elsa smiles, Mandy says as climbing up the steps, 'Well, hello, I'm Mandy, sorry to interrupt your lunch.' Mandy extends her hand to Max, 'Elsa made these sugar cookies, and wanted to share them with her new friends.' Elsa stretches both arms holding the basket, and hands it over to Hannah, 'Yes, I made them this morning.'

Hannah takes the basket smiling, 'Thank you, Elsa!'

Max adds, 'That is so nice of you Elsa.' He looks up at Mandy, and signals her to sit down at the table, 'Would you both care to join us?'

Mandy brings her hand up to her chest, 'Oh no. Thanks, we have lunch waiting for us at home.' She retreats a little, 'We want to invite you all over for dinner. What do you say?'

'Sure, that sounds great.' Max looks over to Alex, 'Maybe you guys can play some more later on at the beach when the sun isn't too hot, what do you think Alex?'

Alex nods. Elsa draws a long smile on her face. Mandy says, 'That would be nice. Well, have a great lunch, we have to get back, my husband's waiting.' She turns around to leave, eyes open wide. She still can't get over not being Tim's wife. She waves goodbye. Elsa waves and they head back to the house.

Fist-thumping the bowl trying to get the last morsels of potato chips, the kids look up to their father as he says, 'What nice people.' Their fists bump into each other and they laugh loudly. Max tries to quiet them down, 'All right, all right kids, take it easy, there are more chips in the kitchen.' Hannah jumps up, grabs the bowl, and runs through the sliding door toward the kitchen.

As the front door opens at the end of the hallway, Hannah yells, 'Aunt Jan! Daddy, Aunt Jan is here!' Jan laughs and walks in dragging her suitcase and carry-on bag. She props it against the wall as Max and Alex walk into the room to greet her. 'Hey there, Alex.' Jan rubs her hand over his head, 'Boy! You're getting so big!'

Hannah rushes over to her as well. Jan crouches down, 'You've also gotten so much taller since I saw you last summer, Hannah.' She gives her a hug, 'Here, come over here, I brought you something.'

The girl squeals with delight and starts jumping up and down toward the sofa where Jan sits down to rummage through her handbag. Jan hands her a light blue and pink unicorn plush toy and a candy bar. Alex stands next to them with anticipation. He smiles, and Jan looks in her handbag and pulls out a candy bar as well. Alex doesn't look impressed. Arms crossed, Max is standing behind them watching it all play out. Jan dives back into her handbag and pulls out a package containing a white ball the size of a golf ball. It has a tiny eye painted on it. The package says EYE-Bot in large letters. Alex takes the package, stares at it, quickly turns to

Max, and shows it to him, 'Look, Dad, look what Aunt Jan brought for me! Wow!, an EYE-bot!'

'He does have a phone, right?' Jan looks up at Max. Max nods. She adds, 'Phew, I'm glad I don't have to get him a phone to run the app for that thing!' She gets up and hugs her brother again, 'Good to see you brother. Looking good.' She caresses his 5-day beard, 'You look older with that beard, you know!'

He laughs, 'I think that's the point.' Jan walks over to the refrigerator in the kitchen, 'Anything good for a snack? I'm starving.'

'Yeah, there are some hot dogs, we just finished eating a minute before you got here.'

'Great. I'll make a hotdog then.' She opens the fridge, pulls out the buns, hot dogs, and condiments, and places them on the counter next to the stove. She sees a small basket, and pulls the cloth up to look inside, 'Oh those look good.' She grabs a cookie.

'Yeah, the neighbors brought them over. Alex and Hannah have a new friend, Elsa. She made them.'

Jan's face tinges a bit on the reddish side. She stares out the kitchen window toward the house next door. The deck is empty, and the French doors are closed. She closes her eyes as she puts a cookie in her mouth and savors it without chewing. She bounces back to reality, and cuts a line along the length of the hotdog, then places it flat on the frying pan, 'Oh good, great.' She tries to hide her face from Max. She pulls her cell phone out of her pocket to text Tim. She thinks better of it and puts the phone away. *Maybe later.* Max is now in the living room sitting on the sofa.

~

Walking through the door balancing her purse, keys, and paper bags full of groceries, Mandy uses her foot to shut the door. Tim looks up, 'Here, let me help you with that.' He grabs her bags and takes them to the kitchen counter.

'Oh, you're here? I thought you were going out with Elsa? Anyway, you're not going to believe what I just learned in town! Some people were gossiping about Jan, well, really about her husband.' Mandy doesn't elaborate that she was the one asking questions about it. She barely catches her breath and continues, 'I was telling the lady at the vegetable shop where I'm staying. She referenced it's next to where the famous author stays most summers.' She smiles as she takes out celery and carrots from the bags, 'and she went on about Jan's husband murdering that medium woman and their affair!' She turns to Tim with eyes wide, 'Can you believe that?! How did Jan come back here after that?'

Tim frowns, shrugs, and turns around, 'Yeah. It seems the cops say he did it.'

'What are you talking about? For real?! Why didn't you say anything?'

'I told you about the affair. I didn't want to give you the wrong impression about Jan, since you liked her so much. I don't know.' He shrugs.

'Why would that change my opinion about Jan? She didn't have anything to do with that! Did she?' She sounds disingenuous.

Tim tilts his head sideways and turns around to look at Mandy. She goes on, 'Really! How can we be sure about that, dear? Think about it.' Mandy brings out a cutting board and knife from the cabinet.

Tim heads over to the French doors to go out to the deck, 'Let me check on the kids and tell Max the time we're expecting them for dinner.'

~

As dinner time arrives, Max, Jan, and the children walk out of the cottage. Jan, leery about showing up unannounced to this dinner, tries to hold back, walking behind Max. He puts his arm across her shoulders and hauls her along. They cross the common driveway between their houses and ring the doorbell.

After a few moments, Mandy opens the door, and softly shrieks, 'Jan! Oh my gosh! What a surprise! So good to see you!' She reaches out to embrace her, a fake smile on her face, and gives her a long hug. Jan pulls away and hands Mandy a bottle of wine, 'Yes Mandy, so great to see you too! How have you all been this year? I can't believe it's been a year now! You look great!'

Mandy gestures to them to come inside, 'Come on, come on, hello Max, thanks so much for coming. I am so happy you all accepted the invitation.' She looks down at the children who are politely standing and smiling, 'Well Alex, Hannah, go ahead. Elsa is waiting for you, go right up to the bedroom, she has something to show you.' The children go up the stairs, and Jan and Max walk in following Mandy toward the living area. Tim is sitting watching a baseball game, an avid Yankees fan, and he's yelling at the TV. Max laughs.

Tim gets up and turns to greet the newcomers, 'Hey there.' His face flushes so he lowers his stare and puts down his beer on the coffee table.

Max looks at Tim, then at Jan who stands still trying to be expressionless. Max smiles, 'Hi there, good game?'

Exchanging looks again, Tim stares at Jan, then he walks up to them. He shakes Max's hand, then Jan's. He stutters a bit, 'You can say that if you're cheering for the other team.' Tim points to his chest, 'This here is a diehard Yankee fan, and we're not doing so well today.' His lips draw a straight line. 'Hello, Jan.'

'Hi, Tim.'

Mandy grabs Jan's arm and pulls her over toward the kitchen while Max and Tim continue talking about baseball. Mandy goes on excitedly, 'Jan, I have to say, congratulations. That latest book of yours is just fantastic!' She moves her shoulders upward, 'I just loved every minute of it.'

Jan smiles, 'Oh, wow, I'm so glad you liked it.'

'You're kidding! I felt like I was living it!' She softly slaps Jan's shoulder.

Jan wonders what she means by that, 'It was a bit out of my league there in the beginning, but I got it done, and it has had a great response from the readers. Thanks so much, Mandy.'

She waves her hand, 'Oh, don't think of it. My partner, Stacy, and I read the book, and we kept talking about it for weeks.' Mandy hasn't been able to get the book out of her head since she came to realize how much her life has changed since Jan came into her life. She tries to stay in the moment, 'You made us start a two-person book club.' She smiles.

'Really? Well, that's great. I love book clubs. I wish I had time to be a part of one, but my publisher keeps me on my toes.'

'Plus, the setting of the book brought back memories of our time here last year.' Mandy smirks, though Jan can't see her face.

Jan feels relief when Mandy mentions the beach. Not for being found out, but because that is probably what her earlier comment meant.

Mandy works her way around the kitchen and pulls out a platter of lasagna from the oven, Jan notices a cheesecake on the counter. Mandy goes on, 'Well, yeah, first we started with your book. She got all excited about it because I told her I'd met you! I told her I bet you were writing this book right when we met you last summer.' She walks toward the dining area and puts the lasagna on the table next to the salad bowl. Mandy straightens the salad dressing cruet, checks on the seating, and turns back toward the kitchen counter where the garlic bread is. Jan notices so she picks up the bread basket and hands it to her, 'Well, yes, I was writing the book last summer.' She smiles.

Raising her shoulders up and down excitedly, Mandy says, 'Stacy is going to get a kick out of that when I tell her.'

All of a sudden Mandy stops smiling, she touches Jan's arm, 'There's something I need to tell you.' She lowers her eyes, 'It's all over.'

The color drains from Jan's face, 'What do you mean? What's over?'

'Tim and I are divorced. We're here for Elsa. He's staying at the hotel on Main Street. I just thought you should know.' Shrugging, she turns around to pick some serving spoons from the counter, 'I don't know, though we're not married anymore, I'm still not over him, you know? I feel we could somehow get back together again.'

Jan's eyebrows shoot up in surprise. It's not often she is at a loss for words but today she's not quite sure what to say to Mandy, 'I'm so sorry to hear that, Mandy.' That's all she can come up with.

Still with a sad smile on her face, Mandy takes off her apron revealing a beautiful white summer ensemble, 'Okay, we're ready now. Go tell the guys to come to the table, and I'll go get the kids.' The stamped floral embroidery cascades down a very expensive designer-looking outfit draped around her slender body. It's like a bunch of red hibiscus flowers hugging Mandy's torso. She looks awesome.

Sitting at the table with lasagna and salad draping all their plates, the kids are chatting at one end of the table, the adults at the other. Tim and Jan steal loving glances here and there, hiding behind their wine glasses. Mandy keeps livening the conversation, either she is star-struck or nervous, Tim wonders why she is so loquacious tonight.

'So, tell me.' Mandy looks at Max, 'How long have you two been together?'

Jan and Max look questioningly at each other. Max points to Jan, and then himself, and laughs, 'Well, we've been together forever!'

Mandy's face looks confused and Tim lowers his gaze, trying very hard to hide a chuckle. As she is cutting into her lasagna with her fork Jan intervenes, 'What Max means to say is we're not a couple. He's my brother.' Jan takes a bite of her lasagna, 'Oh Mandy, I have to tell you, this has to be the best homemade lasagna I've ever tasted.'

Most in the room interpret Mandy's disappointed face as embarrassment but she is actually furious. The short-lived satisfaction she felt at Jan having a lover quickly changes over to dread and fury, which is just one short step away from the wave of revenge billowing up inside her.

After a few seconds of awkward silence, Mandy is back to smiling again, 'Oh well, I'm so sorry.' She brings her hand to her chest, and touches the napkin on her lap a couple of times, 'I thought you were a couple. Oh boy, silly me!' She brings her wine glass to her mouth. Tim doesn't say a word and is, in fact, staring at his food to avoid looking at Mandy.

The embarrassment eases and they continue discussing what's gone on during the past year. Max explains his wife, Esther, will be here tomorrow. She had to come up later because she's working on a big legal case down in Miami, where they live, so she can only be here for just a few days.

After dinner, Mandy suggests they all sit together to take a picture. She takes out her phone from her pocket and sets it up on the table with a timer. 'Come on, hurry, get together!' She riles everyone on the sofa and the cell phone camera clicks.

Max gets up, 'Hold on! Hold on, Do you mind if I post a picture in my stories on Instagram? I want Esther to see what she missed.' Everyone nods and smiles and Max makes a short video to upload in his "stories" with a few stickers and a message: '*Wish you were here!*'

The evening wears down and Hannah has dozed off on the sofa. Max picks her up. They all say their goodbyes. Jan tells Mandy to come over for coffee in the morning, and they can meet on her patio and catch up. Tim stares at Jan as they all exchange farewells, Jan nervously lowers her head. Max notices the exchange between them.

Alex is already at the door of their rental. As Max and Jan walk across the driveway Max says, 'Well, they're very nice. A nice family. Interesting that you guys meet up again right here at the same place. Isn't it?'

Jan shrugs, 'I guess. What do I know? I always rent this place every year. Maybe it's just a coincidence.' She walks in after Alex who is already down the hallway. Max follows her with Hannah in his arms.

~

The kitchen clock glowing emerald numbers show 1:14. Jan runs the faucet to catch some water in a glass and looks out the window. A bluish light simmers and blinks through the downstairs window next door. *Mandy must be having a hard time sleeping also.* She takes a sip of water and heads back to her bedroom dragging her feet on the cold tile floor.

Chapter 26

Saturday, June 11, 2022
New Smyrna Beach, FL

Dark gray skies are split by lines of orange hues. The round sphere of orange fire has not shown itself yet on the ocean's horizon. Sitting on the patio chair with her feet curled up, Jan's laptop is open but the screen is off, her eyes are still heavy from lack of sleep so she takes a chug of a very hot sweet latte she made and brings the mug up to her temple to soothe the soft headache she feels coming on.

This is going to be hard, pretending in front of Mandy. Perhaps I've been foolish coming back here this year. She takes another mouthful. Meanwhile, the sun paces itself, inch by inch rising above the line ahead, marking a bright path on the water Jan wishes she could walk on, and disappear from it all.

Out on the patio deck a couple of hours later, Alex and Hannah are eating cereal and fruit. Jan is typing away on her laptop. They hear cartoon music sounds coming from inside the cottage, and all of a sudden rush up from their seats and head inside. As Jan looks up, Mandy is walking out to her deck with a very large coffee mug in her hand, she crosses her yard and around the fence to Jan's cottage. Jan smiles, 'Good morning Mandy!'

Climbing the stairs at a slow pace, Mandy pulls up a chair and settles into it with caution. Jan asks, 'What's wrong? You look how I feel.'

Mandy puts the back of her hand to her forehead and manages a shy smile, 'I don't feel so good, I must've had too much wine last night. I don't know. I have a splitting headache.' She raises her mug, 'I was hoping this big sucker here, would help relieve that, but it's taking a while. So, how are you?'

'Even though I could barely sleep, I've been doing great, out here since before sunrise, so I've gotten a lot done.' She lowers the laptop screen.

Mandy reaches her arm out, 'Oh no. Don't stop working on my account. I can come some other time.' She closes her eyes. Jan thinks Mandy's going to pass out and gets up from her chair to try to help her. Mandy opens her eyes again, so she sits back down. Jan points to the kitchen, 'I have some pecan rolls, would you like one? Great breakfast treat.'

'I would love one, but I'm not sure I'd enjoy it with this headache. I really shouldn't eat anything. This coffee is as good as it gets. I just ran away from a heavy breakfast at home.' She raises her eyebrows and puts the warm cup up to her head, 'Waffles, berries, whipped cream. Not for me today.' She waves a hand.

Jan relaxes in her chair and smiles taking a sip of her coffee, 'Yes, I've heard about Elsa's favorite breakfast.' She looks out to the ocean.

Mandy straightens up, her cheeks redden but she tries to conceal her irritation. The chips are really falling into place. Mandy's thoughts whirl in her head a mile a minute crisscrossing like threads on a murder board. Her instincts have not been playing a game on her. Mandy feels she's onto something. The love of her life slipped away. The doubts, feelings, and suspicions she's been fighting during the past year have actually been escalating unpleasant samples of proof.

Running out the door and down the steps toward the beach, the children help Mandy recover and maybe Jan didn't notice her reaction. For the sake of her plans she needs to start setting them in motion, 'So, tell me all about your book tour. Where did you go? Did you meet anybody interesting? Was it exciting?'

Jan leans her head slightly, and focuses now on looking at Mandy, 'It was very interesting. I had fun sometimes.' Her mind wanders to that morning in her New York hotel with Tim, shrugging she quickly snaps out of that memory, 'Some others not, it was a long time away from home, and it does get quite tedious repeating my message over and over again.'

'I listened to one of the podcasts you were on. In fact, Stacy and I listened to it together at our store. We enjoyed it very much.'

'Ah yes, your store. Tell me more about that. How's it going?'

'It's going. We're growing a little bit at a time, and it's great because I can spend quality time with Elsa. My schedule is very flexible, and Stacy is wonderful about that. She doesn't have any kids.'

Jan leans back in her chair, 'Ah, I see. How long have you been in business?'

'Since before Elsa was born.' Mandy raises her eyebrows reminiscing on how long that's been, 'Stacy and I stayed in touch after college. We both liked antiques and being interior designers we decided to focus on that specialty. It's taken off. We sell anything 'old', and fashionable: furniture, lamps, house gadgets, dinnerware, and even appliances. This past week we sold a Sewing machine from the '60s. It was a beauty, in such great shape, well maintained, and it still works!' Stacy moves in her chair, 'But we really design spaces for our pieces.'

'Oh wow.'

Mandy winks, 'Yeah. I enjoy it. I'm always on the hunt.' She takes a sip from her large coffee mug, 'I want to visit that antique store on Main Street again. Last year I found a couple of vintage platters. I'm hoping to find some more, Anna has great sources. Do you want to join me? We could go shopping together!'

Jan is relieved when Max walks outside, ' Sure, sure, let me know when you want to go.'

They all look over toward the beach when they hear all types of giggling going on as Elsa, Alex, and Hannah now seem to be making sand castles and running around each other.

Mandy lifts her head, 'Oh, good morning Max, how are you today?'

'Very well, Mandy. Oh good, I see the kids are enjoying themselves. We'll have to ask them to come inside soon, the sun will get too strong in a couple of hours.'

Mandy turns her head to look at the kids, 'Yes, I guess you're right.' She switches back.

Max continues, 'So, how's Tim?'

'He's good. He's at the hotel. He'll come over later.'

Max looks confused and turns to Jan. She nods and winks at him. She mouths *I'll tell you later.*

Mandy turns back and gets out of her chair, 'Okay, Maybe I should go. Jan, I'll let you know when we'll go check out that antique store. I'm sorry I wasn't much good company today. Would you watch Elsa for me? Just have her go inside when you call the kids over.'

'Sure, don't worry about it. I'll be out here watching, and if not, Max will be here.' She points to Max.

Max answers, 'Sure thing.'

'Thanks, I really appreciate it.'

They smile and wave as Mandy leaves. Once Mandy is out of earshot Jan explains to Max what Mandy told her the night before about them being divorced. Tim is staying at the hotel on Main Street and comes over to be with Elsa during the day. Max lifts his eyebrows, 'Wow. That's steep.'

~

Mandy hears a soft beep tone as she walks inside the reception area. Officer Sharon Sutter is at the counter in the lobby, 'May I help you?'

Mandy puts her hands on the counter. she says nervously, 'Yes, I think you can.' She looks down the hall, then back at the policewoman, 'I would like to get a copy of a report on a murder. Is that possible?'

'An incident report.' The policewoman brings out a clipboard from under the counter and places it in front of Mandy, 'Here, fill out this form.' She looks up at Mandy and adds, 'There could be a cost, depending on how large the file is, or how long it takes to put it together for you.'

'Sure, sure.' Mandy stares at the gold name tag clipped above the left pocket of the officer's uniform, 'Officer Sutter, no problem.'

Officer Sutter reaches over for a pen to give Mandy, 'Once you fill it out I will pass this over to the Records Section and they will take care of it. It will take a few days, most likely.'

'Yes, I understand.' Mandy takes the form and pen and begins to walk over to a chair nearby to read the form. She turns around, 'Officer, maybe you can help me. I know the name of the killer but not the victim.'

'Is the perpetrator in custody?'

'Well, no. He's dead.' Her lip raises to one side as she leans her head, 'His name was George Crawford. I only know the deceased's first name was Cassandra.'

Officer Sutter smiles, 'Yes, a very well-known case in these parts, ma'am.' She points to the clipboard in Mandy's hand, 'You can write down the victim's name as Cassandra Davis.'

'Thanks, I appreciate it.' She turns again and heads over to sit in the chair.

~

Reaching for her, Tim pulls Jan to him and embraces her, 'Too long, it's been too long Jan!' They kiss, leaning on a picnic table in the North Environmental Park near the beach.

Resignedly, Jan smiles, 'This sneaking around is going to get the best of me. I'm having a hard time concentrating on my work as well.'

He smiles and winks, pouts his lips and kisses her neck, 'You came to work? I didn't think you'd have the time to work this time.' He wipes her hair from her face, She searches for his lips and they connect again, deeply, longer this time. 'I need more than this Jan. You should come to the hotel with me.'

Holding his face Jan looks into his eyes and smiles, 'Soon enough, Tim.' They get up from the picnic table and start to walk down the path. Jan takes his hand, 'Mandy told me yesterday that the divorce came through already. I didn't think she'd share that with me.'

Tim lowers his gaze and kicks some sand, 'Yes, it's all said and done now. She's been pretty decent about it all, though I'm taking care of them, of course. I haven't told her about you, though.'

Jan leans her head on his shoulder and wraps her arms around his waist, 'Might as well wait. But you should know she's still hung up on you. She seems invested in getting you back. As for us, we need to wait. There are too many people here now.' She looks up, 'Max's wife is coming tomorrow, and I'd hate to have a lot of drama around all of them.' Jan stops and turns around to face him, 'We have to be patient. We will figure something out.'

Crossing his fingers, 'I hope you're right, the sooner the better. I'm not sure how much longer I can wait. I want you to be with me without restrictions.' Tim pulls her in again, he looks into her eyes and reaches with both hands to hold her face. He softly brushes his lips against hers and the heat evolves provoking a deeper kiss, a will to abandon everything and everyone.

~

Shrieking softly, Elsa tries not to get the ice cream that is dripping down her arm on her pink shirt. Walking behind Elsa and Alex down the sidewalk from the ice cream parlor, Hannah laughs and Jan's noticed, to Alex's chagrin, that he has just poked Elsa in the ribs. 'Alex, be careful. Let's walk a bit faster so we can get you all cleaned up.' Elsa likes the attention and Alex can't help himself when he's around girls he likes. They are walking down Main Street and the summer heat has already melted a drip of ice cream down each of their arms.

They turn the corner and cross the street. As they arrive at the house, Esther is taking out a suitcase from the trunk of her car. Hannah screams, 'Mommy! Mommy!'

Esther pushes away, 'Oh no, you don't! You're not getting all that ice cream on my clothes!' Esther laughs, then leans in, 'But come here.' She points at her own cheek, 'Come give me a kiss. That'd be okay.'

Staring at the bright red sports car, Jan puts her hands on her waist,

'Hello, Esther! How was your drive up? I see you got to drive the fancy car!'

Esther smiles gleefully and winks at Jan, 'Yeah. The perks of driving up alone. The drive was uneventful, just the way I like it. I'm glad the week is over. I had to swing into the office this morning.' She reaches for her handbag, and starts walking toward the house, 'They don't pay me for all this trouble, believe me. But that's why I'm late. How have you all been and who is this young lady?'

'Hi, I'm Elsa.'

Alex chimes in as he points to the house next door, 'Yes, we met her when we got here. She is staying over there with her parents.'

Esther looks over to the house approvingly, 'Nice, very nice. Well, nice to meet you, Elsa.'

Elsa says, 'Nice to meet you too.' She takes a bite at the cone, all her ice cream has disappeared but her arms are sticky.

Esther turns around as she reaches the door, 'Say, kids, what if we go to the Water Park tomorrow? Would you like that? You too Elsa.'

All three children start hopping up and down shrieking with excitement, Jan and Esther watch them, 'That would be nice, right?' Jan adjusts her visor, 'You can all have some real fun there, for sure. Elsa can ask her parents if they want to also come. Right, Elsa?'

'Yes, yes!' Elsa is hopping up and down still, her sticky hands in the air. 'I'll go tell them now!'

Esther adjusts the handle of her suitcase so she can wheel it inside the house, 'Good. That would be great. Let us know Elsa. Okay kids, let's go tell Daddy.'

They all walk inside.

~

Getting out of her SUV, Mandy waves at Linda and walks over to her car. Linda, whose blonde curls and makeup seem to be fighting the Florida heat as she stands in the middle of the parking lot of the real estate office, waves back as she places her handbag over her shoulder and signals towards the dark blue sedan parked near her, 'Hello, Mandy. Great to see you again.' They shake hands, 'Did you see the list of homes I sent you?'

'Yes. They're beautiful. I can't wait.'

'Okay, I suggest we start with the one farthest away and work our way back here.' They reach Linda's car and she gestures for Mandy to get in after she clicks her remote to unlock it, 'It shouldn't take too long since we will only visit five homes.'

Mandy accommodates her handbag next to her in the car. Linda gives her a printed copy with homes for her to look at, 'We'll go to the one labeled number one first.' She maneuvers the car in reverse and they drive out of the parking lot.

After a few minutes, Mandy puts the sheet down and asks, 'Linda, would you mind telling me more about that murder I called you about?'

'What do you want to know? It was such a long time ago, in this town we just as soon as forget it. But, why are your so interested in that?'

Mandy shifts in her seat, 'I know. I'm sorry to be such a pest. The thing is, knowing Jan Crawford and staying right next door to her again this year, I really am curious about it.'

Linda takes in a deep breath, 'I don't like to talk about it because that situation was very close to home for me. My brother Buford had been Cassandra's boyfriend before she died.'

Raising her eyebrows, Mandy asks, 'Your brother was involved with Cassandra? Oh! I thought Jan's husband was her lover when she died?'

'Well, he was, but my brother was in love with Cassandra way before Jan's husband was having an affair with her.' Mandy nods as Linda turns a corner, 'My brother hasn't taken Cassandra's death very well. Even over the years, he still suffers because the love of his life was killed.'

Bringing her hand to her mouth, Mandy exclaims, 'Oh, Linda, I'm so sorry. I had no idea your brother was involved in all this. I wouldn't have called you about it if I knew. I wouldn't have asked.'

Linda stops at a red light, 'Don't worry about that. It's okay.'

Linda goes through the crossroad and they drive for a couple of blocks in silence. Now Mandy feels more embarrassed for using Linda to find out about that whole affair. Linda can't stop herself, though. She loves her brother and would rather have people get the real story from her, 'Well, if you should know, my brother doesn't think the cops got the right killer.'

Mandy's thoughts go back to what she heard at the market the other day but this is news to her, 'He doesn't? Why not? Who did it then?'

Linda shrugs, 'Though the cops say Jan Crawford's husband, George, the guy who's dead, killed her, my brother Buford says he didn't do it.'

'Oh, wow. How can he be so sure?'

'I don't know. I don't question him too much, though. He gets upset when he talks about Cassandra so I don't bring it up. He's a good man but his grief has made him depressed and maybe get into other stuff. He managed to lose a very good job and now he just cruises through life drinking and sulking about his Cassandra.' Linda parks her car in the driveway of a beautiful two-story Mediterranean-style home just off Atlantic Avenue. She keeps the engine running and turns to look at Mandy, 'Let me tell you about Cassandra…' Linda explains that when Cassandra arrived in New Smyrna, she didn't know anyone. She set up her shop just a few steps from the beach in a small commercial location Linda owns. She tells Mandy that one day she was too busy and asked Buford to take the rental contract to Cassandra to sign. After meeting her he'd make any excuse to see her. He'd go to her shop or to the small apartment in the rear to fix things. He never charged Linda for any work. She thinks he probably made up things just to go over and see Cassandra. One thing led to another and after a few months, they were an item. They seemed to be in love. When he was off work he would be at Cassandra's. It got to the point that he'd talk her ear off about Cassandra's products and herbs and rocks. One day he even brought her some herb sachets as gifts that he said he'd made himself. She guesses Cassandra showed him how to make them. Cassandra's business took off, she became very popular with the tourists and the locals. They seemed to be happy. They were together for a year or so.

Mandy takes a drink from her water bottle, 'Do you know why they broke up?'

Linda shakes her head, 'Buford has never wanted to tell me. He was crushed. He kept trying to get her back until one day he saw her kissing George on the beach and he almost lost it. He came to my place drunk, devastated.'

'That's when he became a drunk?'

'No, he was still okay then. He got drunk that night and passed out on my sofa. It wasn't until she died that he slowly became what he is today. He lost his job. A good job. He was managing a crew for one of the local builders here. He was getting somewhere. But when he deep dived into his depression he started skipping work, being unreliable, and lost everything. At least he has work right now, he gets gigs here and there.' Linda turns off the car, 'Let's go inside and see this beautiful home. I shouldn't bore you with all this.'

Mandy reaches her hand and touches Linda's arm, 'Don't worry. You don't bore me. I am so sorry for your brother. Just one more thing. You say your brother says Jan's husband didn't kill Cassandra. So who did it?'

Linda closes her eyes, 'Buford says Jan did it. He tells the cops, but they've cleared her. So now all he does is go about challenging Jan every time she visits, poor thing. She's very strong to put up with him.'

'He challenges Jan? How?'

'He leaves her mementos now and then. He places Tarot cards on the door of her cottage every time she stays at the beach house. She used to complain to Chris, my boyfriend who is a cop. But now, she just ignores it.'

'Oh wow. That is so strange.' Mandy looks out her window at the green lawn in front of the home. *That's what the Tarot card was all about!* Another peg in Jan's coffin. 'Is there any way I can talk with your brother?'

~

The beach is a few miles of uninterrupted sand. Jan can go either north or south if she wants to take a walk. She wants some solitude as well as privacy away from everyone staying at her cottage and definitely away from Mandy. She takes a walk on the beach until she reaches the hotel located about a mile south of her place. She needs to talk to Tim, alone.

Jan lifts up a fancy lemonade as she sees Tim walk into the tiny beachside hotel pool bar, 'I'm glad you came.'

'I'm glad you texted me.' He takes a seat on the high chair, 'But we're going to have to find a more private place. This isn't working for me.' He shakes his head.

Jan smiles and takes a sip of her drink, 'I wanted to see you, instead of texting you.' She touches his arm, 'I do Miss you, you know. Are you going to the water park tomorrow?'

He holds onto her hand, 'I'm trying to make sure Mandy goes but I'm dodging it. Maybe that way we can make a day for ourselves with everyone away.' He reaches closer to kiss her. Looking into her eyes, 'Jan, maybe we should just lay this all out in the open and get it over with.'

Jan's eyes open wide, 'For now, let's play it smart. Do you want a drink?'

Tim shakes his head. 'Let's just walk back. We can talk along the way.'

Jan nods, 'Okay. But, listen to me. Please, I beg you not to tell Mandy yet.'

~

Max and Esther are lounging on the deck basking in the sun's rays and watching all three kids running around with their colorful plastic buckets and shovels as they play in the sand. They throw water at each other, then dig some sand, and bring more water to fill up the 'moat' around their newly built castle. It is lost on them they built it too close to the shore and in a while, it will all disappear with the tide.

Mandy walks out to her deck and puts her hand over her eyes, 'Elsa! Elsa!'

Elsa looks up, 'Hi Mommy!'

Mandy's red locks wave in the wind as she turns her head toward Jan's cottage. She waves and smiles. Max and Esther wave back. Mandy watches them for a few seconds realizing this must be the kid's mom. She asks Elsa, 'Where's your dad?'

Elsa looks up and points south along the shore. In the distance, a couple of figures are walking back toward them. Mandy frowns, winks her eyes to hide it, and goes down the steps to cross over to Jan's home. When she gets to the porch she extends her hand to Esther, 'Hello, I'm Mandy, Elsa's mom. You must be Alex and Hanna's mother.'

'Yes, very nice to meet you, I'm Esther.'

Mandy continues, 'Thanks for inviting us to the water park tomorrow. It should be fun. Elsa's excited to go.'

Esther leans up from the chaise lounge, 'Yes, they've become fast friends. It's nice to see them get along so well.'

Tim and Jan reach the children and continue to walk to meet up with Max, Mandy, and Esther on the patio. Tim walks up the stairs, 'Hey there Mandy, how did the antique shopping go?'

Mandy looks at Jan, 'Ah… I didn't get to go, because Jan and I were going together. I did get some groceries. Where have you two been?'

Jan feels a bit of a chill run down her spine and she points south. She smiles, 'We just met on the shore, I was walking and bumped into Tim, the afternoon is lovely.'

Tim feels he should say something, 'Yeah, so we walked back along the shore.'

Mandy steps down, 'It is a very nice day for a walk. Nice meeting you Esther. We'll catch up later.' She walks toward the beach where the children are, she wipes off a tear threatening to roll down her cheek.

~

The sunset should be helping Jan feel better at the dinner table. They are sitting next to the large restaurant window with a view of the ocean. The ambiance, diners, many of them with small children, and the music blasting from the speakers are increasing Jan's irritation and negative vibes.

Alex and Hannah are excited and slurping their kid-sized drinks. Alex puts his drink down, 'We're all going to the water park. It's gonna be so cool!'

Max smiles, 'Yeah, I'm glad Mandy and Tim agreed to come with Elsa. We should have a lot of fun. Now, you have to remember, Alex, you have to take care of Hannah and Elsa, you are the oldest.'

Alex nods, 'Sure.' He draws on his straw.

Jan rolls her shoulders, trying to loosen her tense muscles, but she isn't feeling accomplished. The waitress arrives with their fish and chicken tender dishes and places them in front of everyone. Jan smiles but gets up and places her napkin on the table, 'Guys, I'm sorry. I'm not feeling very well. I think I'm going to go home. You stay and have a good time. I'll meet you at home. Okay?' She looks at Alex and Hanna's disappointed faces. Since Hannah is closer to her she gives her a kiss. 'Sorry Esther, we'll catch up later. I know you just got here.'

She waves her off and picks up her wine glass, 'Oh, don't worry about it, Jan. Go home and rest. We'll come later. You should take a walk back on the beach. That will relax you.' She smiles.

'That's my plan.' Jan picks up her purse, 'See you later guys.' She fist-pumps Max as she leaves.

Chapter 27

Sunday, June 12, 2022
New Smyrna Beach, FL

Walking out of her bedroom very early in the morning, Mandy puts on her navy blue hoodie and goes past Elsa's bedroom. She's still asleep. Tiptoeing down the stairs she looks out the floor-to-glass windows at the beach. A slither of sunlight is breaking on the horizon, she looks at her watch, *This should only take a few minutes.* She picks up the car keys and walks out the door.

Driving around for ten minutes she's following the directions her phone map app is telling her to follow. She'd put in the address Linda gave her. A bit edgy for having left Elsa alone at the house, she misses a turn trying to figure out what the app is telling her to do. Finally, after a few wrong turns she hears the voice on her phone say, 'You have arrived at your destination.'

She parks her car behind a long utility trailer hooked up to a black RAM pickup truck. She gets out of the driver's seat when she sees Buford approaching the trailer and placing a landscaping edger in the back. She waves, 'Hello. Sir! Sir!'

Buford looks at her questioningly and she extends her hand, then pulls it back as she notices Buford wearing large dirty gloves, 'Buford, right? Hi, I'm Mandy. Your sister Linda told me how to find you.'

'Hi, what do you want? I can't take on any more clients.' He packs the edger onto the trailer and picks up a pair of hedge shears, 'I'm busy.'

'Yes, yes, I see that. And it's not about work. Sorry for barging in so early on a Sunday, but I needed to contact you. Linda told me where you live and I want to talk to you about Cassandra.'

Buford stalls in mid-step, he pokes the ground with a pruning pole and holds onto it. 'What about her? That was a long time ago.'

'I know you loved her very much. Don't you think her murderer is still out there?'

'What's it to you?'

'It's everything to me.' Mandy leans one elbow against his truck, 'You see, you and I have something in common Mr. Buford.'

He pauses, then eyes her sidewise, 'And what would that be?'

'There's this woman who destroyed my marriage. I believe she's the same woman you believe had something to do with Cassandra's death. I think we both can get what we want if we team up. I think Jan Crawford killed her. Don't you?'

Buford looks at her, winking one eye shut, 'The police don't think so. Why do you?'

'Well, essentially, because you do. But, yes, I think she did it. There has to be a good reason why you think so. Still after all these years you must believe it.'

'Why are you telling me this?' He moves his other elbow onto the pruning pole to continue to lean on it.

Mandy pauses a few seconds, 'I think you should go to the police. Go and tell them what you think.'

He turns around and walks toward the side of his detached garage, 'I already told them George didn't kill her. Now, I've got work to do, go away.'

Mandy watches him from the sidewalk, 'Look. I won't bother you, but you should go. If you change your mind, you can find me at the two-story house next to where Jan Crawford lives.' She waves and turns back toward her SUV.

~

Tim's motives are clear and he needs to get out of this water park trip. He knocks on Mandy's door. No answer. He knocks again.

'What! What?' The door opens abruptly, 'Oh, it's you.' She turns around and leaves the door open. Tim walks in and closes the door behind him. Mandy walks to the kitchen to tend to the skillet on the stove. Tim walks out to the deck.

After a few minutes Mandy walks outside to ask Tim if he wants breakfast but he's on the phone. He looks frustrated as he ends his call. Immediately he looks at his phone and begins texting.

Mandy leans on the glass door, 'Everything okay?'

'Ah, yes, maybe.' Tim looks up at her. 'I'm dealing with a few things with Joshua.' He shrugs and looks back at his phone. Until today he had not really focused on work at all. Tim types in a few more texts. 'Are you ready for the water park?' he asks trying to hide his motives.

'Yeah, we're all packed. I'm going to get some breakfast for Elsa and was wondering if you wanted some. Are you ready?'

He raises from the chair, 'I'm not sure I'll be able to come. It seems I have to concentrate on some issues that have come up. I'd rather stay and get it taken care of. I don't know how long this will take and the trip will be too distracting.' His phone vibrates and rings.

Mandy's back at the kitchen counter. She hollers back at him, 'But today is Sunday! Why are you doing work stuff?'

'Joshua is in China and as you know they are thirteen hours ahead of us. He has a very important meeting in the morning and needs me to coordinate a few things for him here.'

Mandy huffs and frowns. She punches the snack pack and yanks it off the counter. She puts it on the dining room table with the other bags and walks out to the deck where Tim is. Mandy mumbles, 'This trip was supposed to be your time with Elsa, Tim.'

Tim doesn't answer. He is looking at his phone. He gets a positive reply from Jeff telling him that everything is well and not to worry, he will take care of the documents Joshua needs. He looks at Mandy, 'I'm really sorry.' He raises the phone in his hand, 'This is going to take a while.' He gets up and walks down toward the beach.

Mandy stands in the threshold of the French doors, a frown on her face.

~

A while later the group is on their way. Traffic seems steady as Max drives through the town's main road to get to the Interstate highway. Esther turns around in the front seat of their van to speak to Mandy who's been quiet since they left.

'Mandy, how do you like New Smyrna Beach so far?'

Mandy looks over, still pensive, and shrugs, 'I'm not sure. At first, I loved it. I was thinking it would be a great opportunity to buy a summer home here but now, I'm not so sure.'

'Aww. What's changed your mind?'

Mandy looks out the window to what feels like speeding palm trees racing down the highway, 'This may not end up being the spot where I'd come every year.' She shrugs.

'Sorry to hear that. We like it and try to come as often as possible.'

Mandy crosses her arms and brings her index finger to her chin, 'By the way, I would like to know more about that murder Jan's husband was accused of. What do you think about that?'

Esther looks at Max widening her eyes. She pats her lap, 'Oh, wow. Let's see. I don't think he did it. But how do you prove it when he's dead? I guess they pinned it on him and that's that.' She shrugs.

Still looking out the window, Mandy says, 'But did he have an affair with the victim, that psychic?'

Max momentarily closes his eyes, but stays the course, now driving on the interstate. Esther bites her lips, 'Yes, that much was proven.'

Mandy turns her head to look at Esther. 'As an attorney, would you have defended him? I mean, if he were alive?'

'I'm not that type of attorney. I work in corporate law. But, yes. I knew George. I think he was incapable of murdering someone. Cheating on someone doesn't make you a murderer.'

'I'm almost sure as well.' Mandy leans back to take a look at the kids. Each one of them has a tablet and is watching some cartoon or playing a game, 'I've been reading the articles on the internet. I wish I could get a copy of the police report, though. I think someone else did it.'

Esther looks at Max from the side of her eye, and she finds him eyeing her. She points to the highway so he pays attention to his driving, 'You're into true crime?'

'I guess you could say that.' Mandy looks out the window.

Esther steals a silent glance in Max's direction as she knows how uncomfortable this conversation is for him.

~

Jan and Tim first met with an impossible love affair. Now, they could be free to love each other but will their love ever be whole? Are these feelings enough to carry them through? Is the price of the pain they will inflict too high? During the past few months since she made the choice of reconnecting with Tim, love has hurt more. Like a woodpecker hammering on the bark of a tree, Jan's conscience drums guilt and remorse, even though Tim insists he would've eventually left Mandy if she had not come into his life. He filed for divorce and didn't know if he'd see her again. Distance and separation found a way to create friction in their hearts and longing in their souls. Despite it all, the longing is what has kept Jan going day after day. The hurt is also swarming inside both of them, trying to escape, looking for the oxygen of their reunion to tinge itself with their passion and then be able to become fulfillment.

Tim softly turns the knob on the front door and enters Jan's cottage. He can hear the sound of the ocean and seagulls sifting through the sliding door as he walks down the hallway. He reaches behind Jan, who is sitting at the dining room table and kisses her neck. She feels a string of warmth dance through her body, and reaches for him, 'Tim! What are we doing?'

He helps her get up and embraces her. His kiss is feverish, his grasp of her firm. They can finally let go. She feels his kiss burn as it awakens her lips, and the sensation travels along her chest down to her loins. They both succumb to the heat and her fears recede with every kiss, with each embrace. They rest their heads on each other's shoulders for a while.

Jan lifts her head and Tim grabs her hand and guides her to the sofa, they sit facing each other. Tim runs his fingers through her hair, 'We need to figure this out, the sooner the better.' His touch and his words provoke a teardrop to roll down her cheek.

~

Buford lays the plant runners on the ground. He cleans the sweat from his forehead and puts his fingers in his shirt pocket. He pulls out a card and glances at the image: The three of coins. He rolls the card through his fingers and proceeds to pull out another one, the King of Swords. He picks up his pruner and other tools laying around the garden and walks toward his truck.

~

A strange kind of energy ignites when Jan and Tim's sadness mixes with the tension their bodies exude as they move under the soft cotton sheets in the darkened bedroom. They pull each other in as their blood enlivens their skin. Tim's lips cascade kisses down Jan's neck and his fingers softly graze her breasts, enticing flashes of pleasure she has yearned for since they last met in New York. Emotions entwine as their body's senses create a rhythm that rushes them through unexpected levels of elation, passion, and pleasure.

The forbidden lust runs up Tim's loins as Jan traces her fingers along his thighs touching inches of skin that draw out desire in both of them and anticipation for much more. Their passion beats the rhythm of their bodies into unison when she invites him to deepen and slide into her and create the staccato sensations her body finally succumbs to.

~

Lazying on a couple of chaise lounges drinking fruity drinks, Mandy and Esther are watching Max and the children enjoy their afternoon at the water park. Hannah slides down the water chute into Max's arms, wiggling her feet and splashing water all around. As soon as he puts Hannah to the side, Elsa does the same, shrieking with excitement. At the top of the taller slide, Alex yells, 'Hey Dad, watch!' As he gestures at Max to get out of the way. He's a big boy, he doesn't need catching. Mandy and Esther laugh.

~

An intimate encounter in the morning and some lunch, and now after another try at lovemaking, Jan combs her wet hair in front of the bathroom mirror. Tim walks over behind her and wraps his arms around her waist. Jan leans her head back laying it on his shoulder. Tim whispers in her ear, 'The whole world fades away when I'm with you.' Jan closes her eyes, she wants to stop time, breathe in sweet memories, and trap the feeling of now, to make it last forever.

Tim disrupts the moment, 'Last year, why did you leave without saying goodbye?'

She turns around and puts her hand on his chest, 'I couldn't bear watching you leave and I didn't want to stay behind alone. The day I left was the anniversary of the day George died and when I found out he was unfaithful. That, you leaving, and what we had embarked on, was just too much. I needed to figure things out for myself. I was getting in too deep and I couldn't continue lying to myself.' Jan places her finger on his lips, 'because I was falling in love and because I was not supposed to love you.'

Tim kisses her finger and whispers, 'Sometimes you just can't rule your heart, my love.' He kisses her, then puts his finger under her chin and raises her face to look into her eyes, 'Another thing, we didn't address the Buford issue. You said you'd file a report.'

The color drains from her cheeks and Jan pulls away from him, 'I know. But, if I left, what use was it to file a report? That man has suffered enough as it is.'

'He almost assaulted you Jan! He was harassing you. I'm surprised he hasn't come around yet.'

Jan frowns her lips, 'He probably doesn't know I'm here. Just like Mandy, he doesn't know Max very well.' She laughs.

Tim shakes his head, 'And you wouldn't answer my calls. I would've followed you anywhere.' He kisses her again, 'I have to tell you something.' He explains that he did go to the police station and gave Chris the cards but the police couldn't do anything unless she filed a report.

Jan figured as much. Tim pulls away looking at his watch, 'Well, you need to get some work done, so I'll head over to the hotel. Look, as soon as your brother goes back to Miami, I want you to come over and stay with me, you hear?'

Jan nods, she leans in again for a kiss, 'Yes. I will. Now go before they all come and find you here.' She chases him out of the bedroom and down the hall.

'I wish they would just show up and find me here.' Tim opens the front door and leans back in to kiss her. Jan waves him off and laughs, and closes the door behind him. Halfway down the driveway, Tim turns around to go back. As he lifts his hand to knock on the door, his hand stops mid-air as he sees two Tarot cards stuck on the door. He pulls them off and examines them. *Two cards this time!* He puts the cards in his pocket, turns around, and crosses over to the street. *I'm going to have to do something about this.*

Chapter 28

Monday Morning, June 13, 2022
New Smyrna Beach, FL

It's deja vu all over again. Mandy takes a peek at her bed. How she wishes Tim was lying there. She walks out of the bedroom to check on Elsa. She's still sleeping. She walks out of the house

Trying to pull the SUV out of the driveway avoiding the cars parked in Jan's driveway, she rolls out onto the street. Driving up on Main Street she doesn't notice Tim walking out of the coffee shop across from his hotel. He sees Mandy drive by. *Where is she going? Is Elsa with her?* He dials Mandy's phone. She doesn't answer.

Mandy drives down a few more streets to reach Buford's house. She rolls down her window but notices his truck isn't there. The morning is misty and humid, a wet kind of heat sticks to her skin as well as to her thoughts. Mandy decides to run around the area to see if she can find him. After running through several blocks around the neighborhood, she crosses Main Street to the other side. She drives down a few more blocks leaning her head forward in search of Buford's truck. She turns the corner, then up and down a few more streets. She finally sees a truck that looks like Buford's parked on the curb next to a flat-roof lime-colored home with a low white picket fence located in the middle of the block. She waits until she sees him walk out of the rear of the house and then gets out of her vehicle.

Reaching Buford who is getting stuff out of his truck, Mandy approaches, 'Buford, hello. Good morning,'

'What do you want? I told you to leave me alone.'

'Look, did you give any thought to what I talked to you about?'

'No. I just want you to leave me alone.'

'Look, Buford, we can pair up and get some results here. You say George didn't do it. How are you so sure?'

'Because I know!' Buford leans over the truck looking for a tool, 'I already told the cops. I told you. Why don't you just leave me alone? They're not going to do anything.'

'There must be something you know that you haven't told them, otherwise, they would've done something about it, about Jan.'

Buford waves his arms, 'I don't need this, lady! Just go! They say he did it and that's that. She has to turn herself in and confess!'

Mandy pulls her head back, 'Confess? Do you think she's gonna confess? You have to be kidding. Buford, George was your girlfriend's lover and it's like you're defending him. You've got to tell the cops what you know.'

Buford shrugs. Mandy places her hand on her hip in frustration, 'Look, Buford, I am getting a copy of the report. I am sure there are many things in there that will make you change your mind. You need to go to them. I believe the killer is running loose and so do you. She needs to be put away! Buford, I have a plan.'

~

Always the protector, Jan was always available to shield Max from the bullies, hear his complaints about his teachers, and give him tips on how to make more friends as they navigated the years of elementary and middle school; that is, until high school. Jan was two years older, so once she went to high school, Max was on his own. Those last two years of middle school were tough on Max, and he realized how much he had relied on her. He never thought he would be the one to ever give her advice, to counsel her on life's shortcomings or challenges. This time though, it's taken him a few days to muster the courage, he feels he needs to switch roles.

Max is sitting on the sofa in the living room drinking coffee. The lights are out, the whole house is quiet. He hears footsteps coming down the hallway, he knows it's Jan. Her footsteps are very familiar, she's got a fast pace to her step, even in the mornings.

Stepping into the kitchen she is surprised to smell delicious espresso coffee. The stove feels warm. She turns around in the kitchen and looks toward the dining and living area. She catches Max slumped on the sofa, holding a mug between his legs, staring back at her. She smiles. He doesn't smile back.

Jan frowns and puckers her lips. She walks over to him, dragging her feet now, her arms hanging. She whispers, 'Well, good morning there. What's going on? Is everything okay?'

Max looks down at his half-empty mug, then looks up at Jan who is now sitting next to him. He raises and slants his head, a mixture of doubt and wariness on his face, 'You tell me, is it?'

'What do you mean, Max? You're upset about something. What is it?'

'Jan, what's going on between you and Tim?'

She shivers, her limbs feel weak, and she feels the blood draining from her face. She knows she can't hide things from Max. Her reaction shows him he doesn't need words to know he's on the right track. She lowers her head, 'It's a long story.'

'Try me, we've got all day.'

She looks at him, her expression is between a bit shy, a bit ashamed, and a bit resigned. She shrugs and holds her hands together and all these years of bitterness, betrayal, loss, humiliation, and yearning begin to pour out. After giving him a few brushstrokes on losing herself these past years and her new love affair, she remarks, 'Oh Max, let's get dressed and take a walk. I'll tell you everything.'

~

Tim sits at the dining room table in the chair that faces directly at the front door, his takeout coffee cup on the table right in front of him. This time he's drinking it black, no sugar, no cream, just straight. Relying on it to liven up his nerves, he wishes he could pour a shot of bourbon or something stronger in it. The house is quiet since Elsa is still asleep. He hears keys jingling on the other side of the door, Mandy walks in a few seconds later. He stares at her.

Mandy almost drops her keys on the floor, 'Oh. Good morning.' She walks over to Tim and places the keys on the holder on the wall near the kitchen divider.

'Where were you, Mandy? You left Elsa here all alone. What is wrong with you?'

She pats her hair down, a bit moist from the humidity, 'I was just out getting something I needed.'

'I don't see you carrying anything Mandy. What are you up to?'

She doesn't answer and walks to the kitchen. She pulls a mug out of the cupboard. Lying is not Mandy's strong suit so she decides not to say anything. Tim wishes he could just come clean and tell her everything and get it over with, but he's promised Jan not to do that yet.

She sits down at the table across from him, 'So, how is work handling things? Everything okay there now?'

Tim's expression is still dismal, he says curtly, 'Yeah. Everything's all right.'

Elsa walks down the stairs carrying Molly, the stuffed doll Tim gave her last year, and rubbing her eyes. 'Well, hello pumpkin.' Mandy is grateful for small miracles, the last thing she wants is to have to continue this conversation, 'You're up kind of early today, do you want some breakfast?'

Without saying a word Tim gets up and walks out to the deck. He takes off his tennis shoes and walks toward the shore.

Buford suddenly pulls behind a Sea Grape bush on the side of the house. He's checking on Mandy's story. Is she who she says she is? Unnoticed, he turns to look over toward the French doors. He sees Mandy staring out. He pulls away and heads to his truck to wait for her and find a way to talk to her again. She's not alone, so he'll have to follow her somewhere if he has to.

Looking out the French doors, Mandy wonders if Tim's going over to meet with Jan somewhere. She stands with her arms crossed watching him head north leaving footprints in the sand.

~

Sitting in his truck, Buford wishes he had a drink. All this conversation about Cassandra is wearing down on him. Pain makes him angry and this lady is bringing up gushes of it to the surface again. With his eyes set on Mandy's driveway from a parking lot across the house, he thinks back to those days, specifically to the day he met her and his life changed.

> He recalls how upset he was with Linda for using him as a messenger boy because that afternoon she had to meet a very important client and she also needed to get a rental contract for her new tenant. Buford wasn't necessarily tenderhearted or a perfect brother. He knew he owed her a lot. After all, had been living rent-free in her home. So, he did the decent thing and took the contract to his sister's client.
>
> As he hurriedly walked into the small storefront property Linda owned he felt he'd walked into a different dimension. There, standing by a table in the middle of the room was the most beautiful creature he had ever seen. Her brown curls flowed over her shoulders. The beads of her three-stranded necklace gleamed with glints of amber and aqua hues. Her eyes matched her emerald dress. She smiled at him and just like that, he'd been at a loss for words. Those penetrating green eyes reached out to him leaving him speechless. He walked up to her and handed her the papers. She smiled and extended her hand, 'Hi, I'm Cassandra.'

Buford doesn't remember much of what happened next. He knows she signed the contract and that he showed her the place, again. She'd already seen it before with Linda. As they went from room to room he searched for issues with the property that he promised he'd come back to fix, anything to have an excuse to return. Over the following weeks, excuses became abundant and he never even charged Linda for the work. All he wanted was to see Cassandra.

Again his mind wanders:

> Cassandra didn't know many people in New Smyrna Beach. She met Linda and Buford, and a few people at the food stores and such. She moved in and set up her psychic shop. Behind the consulting room, she'd organized a small workshop where she prepared her products. He visited her often in the evenings and she'd always be working in the workshop, cataloging stones, crystals, and quartzes, or pounding herbs with a mortar and pestle. She also prepared tinctures, which she put in tiny amber-colored glass dropper bottles. She made other products as well, such as pouches with healing herbs, scented and perfumed sachets. He learned to make many of these products and loved helping her.
>
> He was happy, he liked when she read the Tarot cards to him. Those readings were always positive news. The cards promised their love will last forever.
>
> When Cassandra hadn't been able to keep up with the demand, Buford had found a way to always offer to help her after work. He had found himself preparing concoctions and pouches, and sometimes soaps and oils, late into the night. You can say, lust and love had been bound to happen.

Buford stares now across the street, but there's no movement in the driveway. He talks to himself, *That woman wants me to deal with Cassandra's murder? Well, she's going to have to help me, then.*

~

The southern portion of the beach is still pretty empty. Beachgoers don't usually venture this early out to swim, though some folks are walking in both directions in scant numbers. Three and four-story condos frame the beach to the right. Walking on the wet sand near the shore, Max and Jan go over old stories from their childhood and their recent years. 'Why didn't you tell me this was hitting you so hard, Jan?'

Looking up at the sky, some clouds hovering over them, Jan's eyes are damp, 'I just couldn't get it together, you know. It took me a while to accept George had been with Cassandra and then that he was considered a murderer. It was a lot to take in.'

'After a while, I thought you were okay. You were writing and working, I didn't think you needed help. I'm sorry.'

Jan wraps an arm around Max's waist and leans against his shoulder, 'I guess I wanted to be okay and I thought to a certain extent I was, but yeah. I dove into my work so I didn't have to think about it. Then I decided to still come here every year, sort of as a penance or as therapy, or both.' She laughs, 'I'm not sure which. Afterward, I had the incredible idea of putting it all in my novel.' She hits her forehead with the palm of her hand, 'What the hell was I thinking?'

His curly hair bouncing in the wind, Max smiles, 'Well, I'm glad you've overcome most of it, but having an affair with Tim! That's a bit extreme, I'd say.'

She shrugs and puts her hand in her pockets, 'Yeah, I guess. It all unravelled when we met last year. I resisted him at first until I couldn't. I filed under having a "weekend affair, a one-night stand." I got carried away, I know. Then, I left and I didn't talk to him again.' She touches her chest, 'Now, they're divorced. We got together again after the divorce. I feel sad for Elsa, her home is broken now. But Mandy and Tim are trying to make the situation as amicable as possible for her sake.'

Max puts his hands in his pockets, 'Does Mandy know? Even if they're not together I don't see how she won't think you wrecked her home.'

Jan's shoulders fall, 'But I didn't. I know how this looks…and even when he told me he was leaving Mandy, it wasn't really an excuse. They were still together. It was supposed to be only one night.'

'And…'

'Well, at first for me it was only that. Feeling again. Then, one time led to another, and then a few more.' Jan shrugs, 'Back then I told myself it was research.'

'Research? What do you mean by research? You were involved in an affair as research? Jan!'

'Well, I was stuck and needed to feel some things so I could get my characters to come alive in my book last year. So, here comes this guy, very handsome, and we hit it off. One thing led to another, and I wrote my book and got entangled in a love affair in the process.' She raises a hand, 'Though I have to admit, I did cut it off, I promise. I went away. I felt terrible. So I left without saying goodbye.'

Max waves his hands, 'How is it then that he is here again? Divorced, mind you, but you are also here again. It seems as if you two are more entangled than ever.'

'We need to head back, it's getting late and I have to go to the antique shop with Mandy in a little while. I will fill you in on our way back, but that's it. I don't want to talk about this in front of the others.'

~

There are many stores near the beach such as restaurants, surf shops, cafés, and other voguish establishments. Currently, the beach town does not have a resident psychic or card reader quite like Cassandra. Maybe, there will never be. Among the different categories of businesses a beach town population can take on is that of antiques. Anna's store is a path down memory lane with a mixture of old Florida and the old South which you probably won't find anywhere else. Mandy finds it fascinating because of its quaint environment, and colorful and authentic pieces.

Esther, Jan, and Mandy walk in the door and Mandy rushes over to Anna who is near the register, 'Anna, let me introduce you to Jan and Esther. We are neighbors.'

Anna smiles, 'Hello Jan. We've met, and welcome Esther, a pleasure to meet you.' Anna extends her hand, 'Feel free to walk around the store. Mandy, I have many new pieces you may find interesting, come, come, let me show you. Wait for me at the counter while I bring some things I just got that are in the storeroom.' Mandy follows Anna while Esther and Jan stay behind.

Esther looks at a brass lamp sitting on a side table near the counter, 'I didn't know you liked antiques, Jan.'

Jan shakes her head, 'I don't think I do.' She laughs, 'I'm here to accompany Mandy and to learn about what she does. And I wouldn't be able to buy anything because this time I didn't drive.'

'You could always ship it.' They look around for a few minutes and Esther finds something she likes. She lifts up the lamp. 'This is a lovely lamp. It will go very nicely in my family room.' She takes it to the counter and Jan follows.

Jan raises her eyebrows, 'There you go. I'm glad you found something, that means the trip has been productive.' She leans her neck looking for Mandy, 'Let me check to see if Mandy found something.' Jan walks down the aisle between some shelves, then back to the counter and looks out a side glass door at the rear of the store. She notices some movement. Mandy is outside speaking to someone she can't see. Mandy seems agitated. Someone follows her as she turns to walk back inside. Buford! Jan frowns and quickly moves toward the other end of the room and starts looking at some crafted wooden boxes. She hears the ding of the door when Mandy stomps back into the store.

~

'Hey, Sharon. How are you?' Chris Gwynn adjusts his jacket over his shoulders as he walks through the security door out to the lobby from the detectives' offices in the rear. Officer Sutter looks up and smiles, 'Hello there Chris. I'm doing well, thanks for asking.'

Chris leans on the counter, 'So, I saw you pulled a report on the Cassandra Davis murder. May I ask why?'

'Sure. A lady came by requesting the report and I needed to pull up the case record number.' She looks down at her desk in search of her clipboard, 'Mmm, a lady by the name of Mandy Evans, here…' She hands him the copy of the request form, 'She's a visitor to New Smyrna Beach. She already picked it up.'

He scratches his chin, 'Evans. Did she say why she wanted it?'

'No, she didn't. I figure she was just curious about the murder. You know how it is these days.' She smiles and widens her eyes, 'People and true crime, it entices the people's weirdest curiosity. Maybe she's a wannabe detective?' She shrugs.

Chris frowns. 'That case is cleared, so no detective is needed. In any case, thanks. I'll keep an eye open if anything pops up, let me know. Also, do you have the address where she's staying?'

'It should be right there in the request form.'

She hands him a piece of paper and a pen. He writes down the information and returns the copy of the request back to her, 'Thanks, Sharon.'

As Chris heads to the exit, Sharon adds, 'Oh, Chris, by the way, Buford Hall was here earlier looking for you.'

Chris' eyebrows raise up, 'Did he say what he wanted?'

Sharon shakes her head, 'No he didn't but he was pretty agitated.'

Chris shrugs, 'Well, I'll check it out. Maybe it's more of the same.' His eyes open wide as a corner of his lips frowns downward.

~

Anna has made her sales of the day at the Antique shop. Mandy walks out satisfied with her purchases. She adds to her inventory more antique platters and a few beautiful sets of vintage red lampshades that remind Jan of the Gilded Age. Earlier Mandy also gushed over a French Antique Louis XVI Marble Sideboard which she arranged for Anna to have everything shipped to New York in a few weeks. Esther did purchase the brass lamp but Jan didn't get anything. They place Esther's lamp in the SUV and Jan suggests they go to the smoothie shop next to the beach before heading back.

Jan is still somewhat absent-minded trying to figure out what was going on between Mandy and Buford. She hopes Mandy and Esther don't notice her apprehension. Now sitting at a tiny light blue table, Esther is spooning thick chunks of pineapple out of her smoothie cup which is very compatible with the current warm sunny weather. Mandy and Jan are happy with berries and mango. Esther squeezes her eyes shut as the cold travels to her head. As the sensation dissipates she says, 'So, Mandy, how long have you had your Antique Store?'

Mandy smiles, 'It isn't an antique store. We buy these pieces because we get commissioned to decorate homes, offices, and meeting spaces. We store some furniture and items to have things on hand. But, to answer your question, I've had the business for almost nine years now.'

Jan raises her eyebrows and Esther replies, 'Ah, that seems quite interesting.'

Mandy looks at Esther, 'And what about you? Do you have any exciting cases you're working on now?'

Esther chuckles and waves her hand, 'No, not really. My law work is just corporate. Very boring stuff.'

Mandy sinks her spoon in her tall styrofoam cup, 'Wouldn't criminal law be more exciting? What do you think about defense attorneys?'

Esther raises her eyebrows and slightly frowns, 'I think defense attorneys are much needed, especially if one is in legal hardship. But criminal law is not my interest at all. I like the boring. It's comfortable.'

Mandy looks at Jan, 'I really liked your latest novel. It seemed so familiar.'

'I'm glad you liked it. It was a little challenging but I was able to get it done when the publisher asked. Familiar? Why do you say that?'

'Well, the murder, the characters, parts of the story. I was telling my partner Stacy that Rose and Otto, it's like I knew them.' Mandy stares into Jan's eyes trying to read her reaction.

'That's great.' Jan moves her gaze away unsure of the vibe she's receiving right now from Mandy.

'What do you think Jan? Yesterday I was asking Esther if she thought your husband George murdered that girl. What about you, do you think he's innocent?'

Esther watches Jan's face turn paper white. Jan feels a chill and a thin layer of dampness shroud her cheeks and upper lip. She puts her cup on the table, 'I've always thought George was innocent. He would not be able to kill anyone.'

'But then who do you think did it?' Mandy stares at Jan and quickly lowers her gaze to her smoothie.

Esther watches embarrassed. Jan tries to control her tone but her words carry some irritation, 'Mandy, I'd rather not talk about it, if you don't mind.'

'But really? Don't you want to clear your husband's name?'

Jan quickly raises from her chair, 'I'm going to head back now. I can walk from here since you have the car to drive back. Esther, I'll meet you at the house.' Jan picks her handbag off the chair, and walks away, 'See you later.'

Mandy's mouth falls open, she wasn't expecting her prey to take flight. She watches in disbelief as Jan pulls away from the table. Esther tries to conceal a giggle by sucking on her straw.

~

Linda has worked from home for two years now. Of course, she does go into the office now and then, but since the pandemic, she realized her work can be done anywhere, and what better place than home? Her home office consists of a small antique cherry wood desk with a hutch she purchased from Anna a few years back. It's placed between her living room and dining area and it accents her furniture quite well. Linda could completely avoid having a brick-and-mortar office since she became an independent broker, but she rather works under another broker to avoid many responsibilities and accountabilities. This arrangement allows her to still pretty much act as her 'own boss.'

Sitting at her desk, she tries to catch up with bills. She sifts through her mail, separating what she needs to pay attention to by stacking some envelopes to her right, and placing to her left those to send to the trash, 'Why do I get so much junk mail?!'

Chris walks in the front door, 'It's not like you don't send a bunch of junk mail yourself, Linda. I get a lot of junk mail from real estate agents.'

'I'm not doing that much anymore, Chris.' She raises her head to accept his kiss. 'I market myself on social media more than anything. That's where I spend most of my marketing dollars these days. Plus, a lot of it is free advertising.'

Chris winks at her, 'So, what are you up to?'

'Just trying to get things done. I'll be setting up a home for sale and also have to see which houses I will show another buyer I've lined up. How about you?'

'Well, I'm here to see you of course.' He touches his chest, 'But also I'm looking for Buford. Is he around?'

Linda frowns, 'Buford? He doesn't live here anymore, you know. What do you need him for?'

Chris lines his lips and tilts his head, 'He went to my office looking for me, and I know he doesn't live here anymore but he's always hanging around here. I suppose it's about the usual.'

'But that case is closed. Why do you want to rile that whole thing up again? You know how Buford gets.'

'Don't worry, I'm sure it's nothing much, Linda.' Chris folds his arms and leans on the arm of the sofa just across from Linda's desk. 'I'm just following up, plus I get to see you.' He winks, a soft smile on his face.

She swerves her head, 'Yeah, that's what you want me to believe. I just wish Buford would forget about that darn case.'

'Maybe it has nothing to do with Cassandra. At any rate, it seems like that case doesn't want to stay closed. It's crazy how it keeps popping up all the time.'

'What do you mean?'

'A couple of days ago some lady who is staying here in New Smyrna was asking about it at the precinct.'

'Asking about it? That's odd.' Linda squints her eyes. *Could it be Mandy.*

'Well, she asked for a copy of the report. I'm curious as to why she would want it. Sharon thinks she may be one of those people interested in true crime, you know, like those podcasters and wannabe journalists.'

Linda nods, 'Yeah, maybe that's it.'

Buford walks into the room from the kitchen and Chris lifts up his head, 'There he is. Hey Buford. How you doing?'

'I'm all right.' His face is serious and Chris can't tell his mood. He looks angry, but he always does. Chris continues, 'I'm glad you're here. Can we talk in the back?' He stares at Linda and lifts his eyebrows.

'Sure, sure.' Buford straightens his shoulders, 'Yeah, let's go out to the gazebo.'

Linda shrugs, her face showing confusion.

~

As Jan walks up from the beach to the house, Max smiles sitting on the chaise lounge. Now opening the sliding door she asks, 'Where are the kids?'

'They're inside playing some board game.'

Walking into the house Jan drops her bag on the dining room table. She goes to her bedroom and changes into shorts and a sleeveless shirt. She walks back outside, 'I'm taking a walk, do you want to come?'

'Nah! I'm fine right here. I thought you were with Esther.'

'Ah, yes, she should be back soon. I left her and Mandy at the smoothie shop. They're driving back.'

As she walks down the path to the gate she pulls out her cell phone to text Tim. She thinks better of it and puts the phone back in her pocket. *I'm going to be doing it alone right now.* She walks past Mandy's house where Tim is with Elsa, and heads north. The sand is cold and wet. She needs time to think. *Are you something I can't have? Should I let you go? This arrangement isn't working.* With Max and Esther leaving tomorrow, it is going to be hard to continue without hurting Elsa. She thinks she should probably leave and pick up the relationship with Tim later. Maybe, in New York?

After ten minutes she feels someone approach from behind, 'Hey! Hey!' Tim jogs next to Jan, 'What happened? Why didn't you let me know you were going out? I thought we said we'd meet up. I wanted to come with you.'

Jan continues walking at a fast pace, 'Tim. We can't do this now, at least for now.'

Slowing down his pace, Tim adjusts the cap on his head, 'Jan, what's going on? We have just found each other again.'

She puts her hands in her pockets, 'I have to be alone for a while. I don't think I can do it. We're going through all this commotion again. Last year is happening all over again.'

Softly pulling her arm to stop her from walking., Tim puts his hands on her shoulders and murmurs, 'Why? I need to be here for you. I need you to be here for me.' Tim straightens up and looks into her eyes, 'We are together and at first, it will be a little difficult because we have to lay low. I'm not giving up on us, Jan.'

Jan lowers her gaze, 'I'm not asking you to give up. I'm just not the type to hide. I want you but for now Mandy doesn't deserve this. Maybe we can pick up later on.' She stares at the wet sand between her toes. Tim lifts her chin and looks into her eyes, 'What happened Jan?'

'Mandy knows. She's been prodding. I think she feels something's going on. I don't want to be involved in a storm of emotions. I just can't.' Jan shakes her arms, 'Look, we can hold off until all your stuff is sorted. I can wait.'

Pulling her in again, Tim tries to search in her eyes for connection, 'Jan, listen. Look at me, we can do this, I know we can. I don't want to wait for you anymore. You're right here with me and that's all I want. This week when things settle a bit, I will talk with Mandy. We just have to be patient. It'll be better soon. Trust me.'

'Do you really want me, Tim? Do you really think so? How do I know this isn't temporary anyway. That you'll tire of me and go on to someone else. That's usually what happens. I know. I write about this stuff!'

Tim embraces her and pulls her in, he whispers in her ear, 'I don't want to lose you. Tell me what to do, but don't ask me to let you go. I won't let you go.'

'Tim, for now, we have to take a break.' She pulls away and looks at him, 'Let's just live our separate lives for a while.' She puts her hands on his chest, 'I promise we will pick up after the summer, I just can't concentrate on Mandy right now. I can't do us while Mandy and Elsa are here, It's too hard.'

Tim leans in and kisses her. She gasps and a shiver runs through her. He feels the world crumbling around him. He holds her tightly, and she also clings to him. Tim looks into her eyes, 'I'm in love with you, Jan Crawford.'

Mandy approaches in the distance. She watches them embrace and kiss. A tear rolls down her face and she abruptly turns to avoid the pain. She walks up the beach ramp over to the street. This is going to be a dreadful vacation.

Chapter 29

Tuesday Morning, June 14, 2022
New Smyrna Beach, FL

The goodbyes are bittersweet. Jan always feels at a loss when Max leaves and this time she's unsure of her standing in his eyes. Driving his sports car, Max sits next to Alex, his co-pilot. Esther is driving the van with Hannah sitting behind her. Putting her arms through Hanna's window, Elsa gives her a parting gift, handing her Miss Molly, the rag doll. She makes Hannah promise she'll bring the doll back next year when they meet again. Taking the doll, Hannah reaches around her seat looking for something. She pulls out her light blue and pink unicorn and hands it over to Elsa. They both smile and wave at each other. Jan's heart breaks, she can barely disguise her sadness. She feels sorrow for Elsa, for her own relationship with Max, and for her love for Tim.

Mandy is in the doorway watching the caravan of goodbyes. She waves as Esther's van pulls out of the driveway followed by Max and Alex in the car.

~

After a few hours, the sound of the waves mingles with Jan's emotions as she lays down strings of thoughts through her fingers onto the keyboard on her laptop and they materialize on the screen. Sitting outside on the porch watching the ocean and feeling the breeze helps her brainstorm and take hold of inspiration. The scene of her story unravels keystroke by keystroke as if flowing from the ether. Right now she is trying to nail the right narrative for the moment the victim in her story unexpectedly feels extreme pain in her chest from a bullet impacting her from out of nowhere, and she types what comes to mind, every letter and every word she thinks of. There will be time to edit it later on.

Watching from the corner of her eye, Jan sees a couple of people walking outside the fenced area of her yard. They're not scantily dressed like they're heading to the beach. As they approach, she realizes it's Chris Gwynn, his detective badge hanging on his chest, and a uniformed police officer. Her heart skips a beat as she has a flashback to the night George died. She waits. At the fence, Chris reaches for the gate. He sees Jan on the porch and says, 'May we come in?' Jan nods and waves her hand for them to approach.

She suspects this is official, not a friendly visit, 'Hello there, Chris. How can I help you?' She nods, 'Officer?' She lowers the screen of her laptop as Chris and Officer Duncan climb up the wooden steps.

Chris presses his lips tightly, he's already regretting this, 'Miss Crawford. Jan. We need you to come with us to the precinct.'

Jan leans her head and frowns, 'What's this about, Chris?'

'I'm not at liberty to say, ma'am. You need to come with us.'

'Am I under arrest?'

Chris shuffles his feet and lowers his gaze as officer Duncan watches poised with his thumbs hooked into his duty belt, 'No, you're not, but it would be great for you to come with us. We have some questions regarding the murder of Cassandra Davis.'

Jan narrows her eyes as lines form between her eyebrows. She disentangles her legs from a lotus position, gets up and picks up the laptop heading inside the house, 'Well, let me change into more suitable clothes, then. Come inside.'

'Okay, but don't take too long Jan.' All three of them walk inside the house. Next door, Tim is sitting under the umbrella outside on the deck watching the scene go down. He reaches for his phone and dials Jan's phone number. She answers the call in her bedroom as she is trying to put her arms through the sleeves of a polo shirt, 'Hey, Tim I'm busy, I can't talk now. Why are you calling?'

'What are those cops doing at your place?'

'It's nothing, really. I have to go to the station to talk to them.'

'What about? What do they want with you?'

'It's about the murder of my husband's mistress.'

'Are you sure they are your friends? Look, I've dealt with cops before and I don't trust them.'

'I've talked to them before. It's no big deal. Chris and I go way back. I'll be alright.'

Tim scratches his day-old beard 'Look, Jan, be careful. Just contact me if you need anything. Okay? Especially if you need a lawyer.'

'Don't worry, calm down.' Jan wiggles into a pair of denim capri pants, 'I'm sure I'll be back after lunch. In any case, I know attorneys. Don't worry. Bye, I have to go.' She shuts off her phone.

Running through his head all he knows about the years-old-murder, Tim ponders over why this has come up now since the police had pinned it on the dead man. He concludes it most likely has to do with Buford. He's never let up on Cassandra. Sifting his fingers through his hair, Tim then pulls out the most recent Tarot cards he took from Jan's front door from his shirt pocket, and stares at them. He frowns.

Tim hears TV sounds seeping from the house as the French doors open. Mandy walks out and sits in one of the lounge chairs. Pacing on the deck, Tim debates whether he should rush to the front to watch when Jan leaves but Mandy says, 'Tim, I need to talk to you.'

Walking to the end of the deck to look around the corner of the house, Tim tries to view the driveway in the front through the alleyway between their two houses. He sees the patrol car pull out of the driveway. Too late.

'Tim, what are you doing? I have to talk to you.'

Sitting back down, he studies Mandy, 'What is it?'

'What's going on between you and Jan?'

'Nothing, Mandy, okay? Just nothing.'

Sitting in the deck chair, Tim puts his elbows on his knees and sifts through the two cards in his hands. Mandy crosses her arms and stares at his hands, 'Don't lie to me Tim, I saw you two at the beach yesterday and that wasn't nothing. Do you know she could be a murderer, Tim? Did you fall for a woman who murdered her husband's lover?' She grabs the cards from his hands.

Getting up from his chair, eyes wide open, 'What are you even saying, Mandy? What gave you that idea?' He tries to walk away heading into the living room. He sees Elsa on the sofa. He doesn't want to argue with Mandy in front of Elsa, not about this. He looks up the stairs as if trying to escape as Mandy follows close behind, 'Don't you walk away from me!'

Watching cartoons on the sofa, Elsa feels a chill run through her spine and jumps at her mother's tone. Tim goes back outside to the deck. Mandy is close behind, shaking her arms with the cards in her hand, 'Tim, I know that girl who was murdered was a gypsy or a medium, or whatever! Do these Tarot cards have anything to do with her?'

Tim closes the French doors to try and avoid Elsa's ears. He tries to lower his voice so beachgoers and neighbors can't hear, 'What do you know about her? Why do you want to know?'

Mandy's face muscles tense up and her voice fluctuates, 'Before you moved out I found Tarot cards in the pocket of your shirt. The woman who died was Jan's husband's mistress. Were these her cards? Where did you get them? I'm certain Jan murdered that woman.' Holding the cards in her hands, Mandy shakes them in front of Tim, 'What do these have to do with you?' Mandy points at the cards, 'Do you know what they mean? Why are you carrying those stupid cards around? Who knows what you bring onto yourself or us.'

'What are you talking about? Don't be ridiculous, plus that case was closed years ago.'

'And why are you so interested in it, Tim? What's this about? You think I wouldn't find out?'

Looking closely at Mandy, he sees her agitation glimmering through, 'Find out what, Mandy?'

Her face flares up more, 'I know you cheated on me.' She loosens up, 'You and Jan have been having an affair since last year. What you don't understand is you are wasting your time with her. I am certain she murdered that woman. She's going to destroy you.' Walking over to the edge of the deck, Mandy crosses her arms and stares out to the ocean in the distance, 'For all I know she'll go after me next, isn't that how it goes?'

Tim puts his face in his hands. 'Oh, my God! What are you even saying?! What even gave you that idea?'

Mandy continues trying to convince Tim that Cassandra's murder and George's death will haunt them as well because he's lost all sense of reality by falling for Jan, 'Tim, open your eyes, her husband had a lover, and she wound up dead. She gets a lover, what do you think will happen next?' She folds her arms still watching the waves come and go. 'You've fallen for a murderer. I'm glad the cops are on to her, it's about time. My plan worked.'

'Mandy! What the hell have you done?!'

'Me?' She points at her chest in rapid motions, 'I just let things take their course. I did my research. I opened people's eyes to reality. That's what I did. She's a murderer, Tim.' Mandy puts her index finger up to her forehead and starts pacing, 'I don't understand why you can't see that. Who else could've done it? She murdered Cassandra. Buford's right.'

Tim shakes his head. Mandy tells him again she saw them kissing on the beach yesterday and throws the Tarot cards on the table. Between sobs she faces Tim, 'It's all in the book. All of it. You should read it, you know.' Turning around, 'She's betrayed you. She put your whole affair in the damn book, Tim. Just get out! I don't want you here!' She rushes into the house and slams the door.

After a few minutes, Walking into the living room, Tim finds the house silent, the cartoons are off. He walks around the living room, and peeks into the kitchen. 'Elsa? Mandy? Where are you?' Elsa and Mandy are nowhere to be found. Picking up what is left of his honor and dignity, he walks out the front door. Jan's rental car is in the driveway and all is quiet. Tim looks up to the sky, puts on a baseball cap, and puts his hands in his jeans pockets, stepping onto the sidewalk he walks toward Main Street.

~

Meanwhile, in the interrogation room at the police station, Jan takes a sip of water and places the bottle on the metal table. Looking around the stale room, she recalls what it felt like being here before. All the sadness and despair she thought she'd conquered are trying to reach for her and pull her in all over again. She shuts her eyes and thinks about her favorite place. Right now the beach is out of the question, so she floats her thoughts to the mountains behind her home. The tall pine trees near Sapphire, North Carolina, the smell of freshness, the different shades of green blending into each other, the crunchy sounds of her boots walking up the trails, the blue skies and spongy bright white clouds, the crisp air of early spring. It doesn't last, of course, Chris walks in with a folder in his hand and she is sucked out right back to reality.

The room's gray walls contrast the bright yellow color in the reception area. That's the point, to depress you. The room is chilly. She rubs her hands over her arms. 'Like in the movies, huh?' Chris sits in front of her, 'or in your book. Ever write about murder? Police interrogations?' He sifts through the reports in front of him looking for a specific page.

'Yes, you should read my recent one.'

Chris looks up, 'Why? Am I in it?'

Jan cracks up, then smiles, 'Ha! No. I don't think I put you in the book, no. Maybe in my next one?'

'The way this is looking maybe you won't want to put me in your book. Look Jan, we've known each other for many years. I know what you've been through, but there are questions here concerning Cassandra Davis' death. It doesn't fit anymore with George having done it.' He moves the folder toward her, 'or at least him having done it alone. We have gone through the file and believe someone else did it, or that he might've had help.'

Staring at the page Chris has put in front of her, Jan lowers her eyes to read it, 'What am I looking at, Chris?'

'George was in the bar at nine o'clock.' He points at the report, 'We had not put it together before, but he died at…' he sifts through the paperwork to find George's time of death. Jan is holding her hands as if in prayer on the desk, 'Nine twelve. He died at 9:12.'

Looking up, 'Yes, yes, nine twelve.' Chris rubs his chin a bit embarrassed, 'Cassandra's time of death was ten o'clock, give or take minutes either way. Cassandra's house is a fifteen-minute walk from the bar. We figured he was at Cassandra's before the bar. Or, maybe I should say… we know he was at Cassandra's before he went to the bar. In any case, we have his time of death. So, now we think George didn't do it.' He pulls out Cassandra's autopsy and points to the top of the autopsy where it says: T.O.D. between 10:00 and 11:00 pm.

Jan's lip turns up, 'That doesn't really exonerate him, does it? Time of death could be wrong.' She pulls back into the chair and folds her arms, 'And, what does this have to do with me?'

'No, it doesn't totally exonerate him, but we're now pretty sure he didn't do it. Your prints were on the hammer, same as George's.'

'You already told me the hammer was not the murder weapon. She did have trauma to her head, but she was strangled.'

'Your prints were on the hammer…'

Startled by the higher tone in her own voice, Jan responds, 'Of course they were. It was George's hammer. It was one of his tools, which was in the house, in his car, wherever. My prints were bound to be on it. That doesn't prove anything!'

'Okay, let's change the pace.' Chris pulls out a plastic evidence bag containing an open card like those celebratory cards you buy at a grocery store or drug store to attach to a gift, an ordinary birthday card. He shows Jan the front portion first. It has a large "21" printed on the front surrounded by a lot of flowers with only two words: HAPPY BIRTHDAY! He turns it over. The date is handwritten, *6/9/2013,* and with the same handwriting, a message: "*You're a big girl now. This is yours to keep. Happy Birthday. I love you, Mom.*" Below the message in block letters are written a bank name, a bank account number, and a password.

Chris hands her another plastic bag containing an envelope. It is the same size as the card. The envelope is addressed to Cassandra at the address where her body was found. The remittance is from Denise Davis with an address in Cassadaga, Florida.

'Do you know what this is Miss Crawford?'

Jan shakes her head.

Chris points to the envelope in the bag, 'Do you know who Denise Davis is?'

'No, I have never met her. No idea. Like I hadn't met Cassandra Davis, either, Chris!'

'Then, I guess you never will. She's also dead.'

Jan cringes. Chris shuffles through some pages, 'What I just showed you is an old birthday card Cassandra had. It was stashed with all her product recipes and other papers.'

Jan shrugs. Chris continues, 'Now, that card relates to what you're going to see now.' He flips a sheet of paper showing what looks like a bank account statement. He puts it in front of Jan. She leans in with her elbows on the table. She reads the statement and recognizes the bank name as the same written on the birthday card. She reads the names of the account holders: Denise Davis and Cassandra Davis. She scrolls down the lines of descriptions and dollar amounts, some are debited and some are credited to the account. There are a couple of yellow highlighter marks across some of the lines. 'What am I looking at?' She pulls back.

Chris points to the highlighted line, tapping on one of the highlighted lines with the amount of ten thousand dollars. 'There, ten thousand dollars credited to the account, and then another ten thousand. Also, look down here how both amounts are debited.'

Jan shrugs, 'And?'

'What was your inheritance from George after his passing?'

'What? What does that have to do with anything?'

'Bear with me...did you get access to ten to twenty thousand dollars after George died?'

'Maybe. There were many things that reverted to me when George died. Our house, for one. Our joint bank accounts, some heirlooms. This doesn't prove anything Chris!'

'Did you get money from a specific bank account with exactly that amount?'

'After probate, yes.' She lowers her gaze. 'The courts got involved because he didn't have a will. Since all he had was what an old aunt left him, the courts turned over money from a bank account that had about twenty thousand dollars in it.' She stares at the emerald and diamond ring on her wedding finger. She rolls it around her finger, and a soft tear begins to form. She wipes it off before it falls. '...and this ring.' She suddenly looks up at Chris.

~

Shortly after lunch, outside his hotel, Tim gets into a ride-share car. Noticing Elsa walking out of the ice cream shop a couple of doors across from the hotel, as well as Mandy and Linda Hall walking out behind her, Tim rides by them as the car crosses by heading west. *What are they doing together? What is Mandy up to?* The car is already crossing over the Causeway bridge onto the mainland. After a five-minute ride, Tim arrives at police headquarters.

Once he is inside the lobby, he asks Officer Sutter if there is an opportunity for him to see Jan Crawford. She looks at him, 'Are you her attorney?'

Tim shakes his head, 'No, no.' He pulls back startled, 'Does she need an attorney?' *Shit, shit. Do I have Max's phone number?* He runs his fingers through his hair and starts scrolling through his phone. He runs through his contact list. *Damn! Why didn't I get their number?* 'Okay, I'm not her attorney. Can I speak to Chris?'

'Officer Chris Gwynn?' She asks. Tim nods. Officer Sutter picks up the phone and dials it. She talks to someone on the phone, then turns her head toward Tim and he says, 'Tim Evans, tell him Tim Evans is here.' She hangs up. 'Wait over there.' She points to a line of chairs, 'Someone will let him know you're looking for him.'

~

'Elsa, go ahead if you want to play in the sand. I'll watch you from here, go on honey.' Elsa rubs her arms after her mom stops putting that gooey stuff on her and runs out to the beach. Mandy wants to pursue the rest of the steps of her plan to bring down her nemesis and famous writer Jan Crawford. Cleaning her hands with a towel, she picks up her phone. She opens her contact list app and presses a phone number. Stacy answers.

'Hey there Stacy, I need you to do me a favor. Guess what? Jan Crawford's been arrested?'

'Arrested?! What for?'

'Well, I'm guessing it has to do with that murder her husband was involved in.'

'You don't say! Wow. That's awful.'

'Well, she's not what we thought, Stacy, not at all. She and Tim are having an affair.' She waves her hands in the air.

'An affair?! For real Mandy? Are you sure? I know you had your doubts about Tim…'

'Yes, Stacy. I saw them. Tim has been cheating on me. Since last year.'

'Oh Mandy, I'm so sorry.'

'Anyway, my favor. I need you to call that journalist friend of yours who works at that web news site, you know? The one that carries all that famous people gossip?'

'Sure, you mean Tipper. Why do you want me to call him?'

'Well, girl, give him the scoop! Jan was picked up by the police just a while ago. I saw it with my own eyes.'

'Really, Mandy, you want this to be out there? What if it's nothing?'

'Stacy, what if it's something? Believe me, I have a feeling this is a big story.'

'You really don't like Jan anymore, do you?'

'Stacy, she messed with my family. No, you can say I don't like her.'

'Okay, I'll call Tipper. Can I give him your number if he decides to run with it?'

'Of course! Give him my number.'

~

Waiting in the lobby now over an hour now, Tim has watched many people walk through the only door leading to the rear of the building. Suddenly, Chris walks into the reception lobby from the rear offices, and walks over to Tim, 'Hello Tim, how are you? How can I help you?'

Tim tries to have Chris let him speak with Jan or at least to tell him why she is here. Chris explains Jan is here only to answer questions and she is here willingly. Chris won't give Tim any details on the investigation but he confirms it's about Cassandra Davis' murder.

'Does she need a lawyer?'

Pressing his lips, Chris replies, 'She hasn't asked for one.'

'Can I see her? I would like to speak with her.'

Chris extends one arm intercepting Tim's advance, 'Not right now. Maybe later or tomorrow. But right now she can't talk to you. We're still busy with her.'

'Tomorrow? Has she been arrested?'

'No, she has not. But she is cooperating.'

'So, she could walk out at any moment, if she wants to.'

'Yes, she could, but we are now speaking with her and she has not decided to leave. We have a lot to go over with her, so, go home. She'll be all right. Go there and wait for her.'

'C'mon Chris, this is ridiculous!' Tim turns and slaps his hands on his legs.

'Tim, go home. Some questions have come up and we need to clear them up. Just go. I'm sure Jan will call you in due time if she needs you.' Chris turns around and exits the lobby.

~

Hugging herself, Jan is getting used to the hoodie Chris brought for her. Her stomach is rumbling a bit, her mouth feels dry. She shrugs and moves her head in a circle trying to loosen up her shoulder muscles. Chris stares at her, then down at the open folder laying on the table. Jan sees there are stacks of papers and the points sticking out of what seems like photos, paper thicker than normal paper. *Probably crime scene photos he doesn't want me to see.*

Pulling out the bank statement again, Chris also puts another bank statement from "First Citizens Bank" on the table in front of Jan, 'Do you know this bank? This bank account?'

'I know there is a local bank in Sapphire, North Carolina called First Citizens Bank. I don't recall that bank account, no.'

Pointing to the date of the withdrawal, Chris' finger taps on a date, 'Look at them. Read the dates. This is Cassandra's bank account, there, August 29, 2016. Now look at the date of the deposit.' He points to the First Citizens Bank statement, 'There, August 30, 2016.' He pulls back in his chair, 'You see, from Cassandra's account to his account, two withdrawals here, two deposits there, only a day's difference, and you're going to tell me you didn't know about this?'

'I didn't know!'

'This is one of the main reasons we pinned the murder on George, Jan. "*Follow the Money*" as they say.'

Picking up the statement from First Citizens Bank, Jan stares at it for a moment.

Chris smirks, 'It's all there in black and white, it's Cassandra's money, and it's the only money in the First Citizens Bank account.'

Her heart beats faster but all she feels is her veins chill inside her chest. Looking at the names on the statement in the North Carolina bank account, Jan reads, *George Crawford and/or Cassandra Davis.*

~

Elsa hears knocking and opens the door of Tim's hotel door, Mandy is at the door smiling, 'Hey honey, are you ready to come home? I came to pick you up. Did you have dinner?' Without answering, Elsa turns around and walks into the hotel bedroom leaving the door ajar.

'Ah, hi there. I'm coming with you. Hold on.' Tim puts the brush on the bathroom counter and walks out adjusting the buttons on his sleeve.

'And, where do you think you're going?'

Widening his eyes at her trying to avoid Elsa seeing his expression, 'Forget it, Mandy. We'll talk later. I need a ride, that's all. I'm riding with you to the beach.'

'Oh, okay.' Mandy adjusts her purse to her arm and waits in the hallway, 'That's okay then, we can give you a ride to the beach.' She turns and starts walking down the corridor. Elsa and Tim walk out of the room and follow.

~

Laying down a large colored 8 x 10 photo on the table, Chris shows Jan a photo that displays a portion of a room with a large bookcase running from the floor to the ceiling along a wall. A few of the books are missing, others are strewn around on the floor. One of the shelves seems to be missing, an unpainted shadow line where the wood should've been. There's a colorful scarf with gold, orange, brown, and green tones lying on top of some of the books and the floor. Jan picks up the photo from the table to take a closer look at the bookcase. She doesn't recognize many of the titles, but some words stand out, such as *Awakening, Mediumship, Empath.* Some titles stand out, "*Modern Medium,*" "*Calls from Heaven,*" "*Tarot Readings through the Ages.*" She looks over the different books and her eyes fall on a shoebox-sized chest with the lid open. *I wonder what was in there.* Chris hands her another photo.

Chris lays another photo on the table. This one shows a small round table next to a loveseat with two empty wine glasses. One of them has lipstick residue on the rim, the other one is knocked over next to it. The pillows on the chair are in disarray. Jan takes a deep breath. Chris pulls out two other photographs from the folder face down. Watching Jan's reaction closely, he slowly turns them over at the same time. In one image she briefly sees bright crimson-red stains smudged on the handle and face of a hammer. On the other, caked clumps of brown hair cover portions of a woman's ashen face. There are also bruises on her neck. Flinching, Jan turns the photos upside down on the table. Chris puts his hand on Jan's and turns the photo over again. 'Look at it.' She doesn't open her eyes. He repeats, 'Jan, look at it!'

Her eyes are still shut, 'No, I don't need to see it. Why should I look at it?'

'Because you killed her.'

'I didn't. No, I didn't!' Getting out of her chair, she turns away from the table, 'I don't want to see anymore. This is horrible.'

Chris doesn't want her to get too defensive, so he decides to back down a bit. If he presses too hard, she may shut down and ask for a lawyer. He is curious as to why she hasn't asked for one yet. He is accusing her of killing Cassandra. Wait until he lays out more evidence. 'Okay, Jan. All right. I will put the photographs away. Now, turn around. I put them in the folder. Come sit here. I have a question, do you know where this is?'

'I can guess, but no, I have no idea. I've never seen this place before.'

'What's your best guess, then?'

'Since you're showing these to me, I assume that is where Cassandra lived.'

'Your guess is good. So, you're telling me you've never been to Cassandra's apartment?' He points at the photos with the bookcase and the loveseat and glasses, 'This was her living room.'

'No. I have never been in Cassandra's apartment. I didn't know about her until George died, until you guys started questioning me back when they both died.'

'You had never met Cassandra? You had never gone to her office or shop, or whatever?'

'No, I had never met her. I'd seen her in town, or on the beach, of course. She was beautiful, attractive, eccentric if you want. But we'd never been introduced.'

'You didn't know that George knew her?'

'No. I didn't.'

'Did you ever visit her shop? Even out of curiosity? I figure authors like to find out about everything.'

'No! I'm telling you.' She pulls at her hair and rubs her hands on her face, 'I never met or talked to Cassandra! Ever! I'm thirsty. I need some water.'

The fact is Jan only knew Cassandra from seeing her at the beach speaking with beachgoers and walking past her shop when she took afternoon walks or went shopping. She didn't know George had a mistress until he died and everything came up because of the murder investigation and his own death. The day George died and the days that followed were a tumult of emotions and realizations for Jan. Not only did she have to face George's betrayal, she had to conquer the affront of being humiliated, oblivious to the status of her own relationship. Her world fell apart.

The evening is heading into double digits shortly. Chris continues, 'Okay, let's go back to the beginning.' Slowly he puts his hands on the folder, Jan pulls back a bit, and he lifts up both hands, 'Don't worry, don't worry, I won't bring out that picture again. But there are a couple of photos I want you to see and tell me what you think.' He pulls out an 8 x 10 color photograph of a woman with dark brown curls framing an oval face. The pose is like those business poses photographers like to get of models, real estate agents or authors. Cassandra's a natural, with a smile that is larger than life, her face posed resting on her hands, she looks like a model in a magazine. Chris watches as Jan takes in the elements in the photo, as the color drains from her face. He doesn't flinch as she stares at Cassandra's headshot. He knows she's going to have a hard time explaining this one.

Jan doesn't move an inch but she raises her eyes to Chris who is staring at her without moving a muscle. She brings her hands up and in a rush takes the ring off her finger and throws it on the table. The ring lands on top of Cassandra's photo. Jan rubs her ring finger then covers her face. She shakes her head. She cries out, 'Oh my God!'

Chris raises his voice, 'Are you sure you want to stick to your story? Do you think I'm going to believe you didn't kill her now?'

Jan's face deepens with shock as she covers her mouth with her hands. It feels like the air leaving her lungs and liquid scraping inside her stomach, she feels sick. Chris takes the ring from the table and rolls it in his hand looking at it and emphasizing its significance. Jan puts her hands between her legs and closes her eyes. Now this place feels so cold.

Chris puts a photograph on the table and yells, 'Open your eyes!'

Jan shakes her head, her eyes still closed.

'Jan, I don't have much patience left. I'm going to tell you what I think you did. You went to Cassandra's after George left. You hit her with the hammer until she was unconscious. Once she was on the floor you strangled her. Then you took her ring out of spite, hurt, or vindictiveness. You wanted a reminder of George's deceit. I will ask you again. Did you do kill Cassandra Davis?'

Jan's shakes her head back and forth. He places another photograph on the table. He pounds on the color photograph with his index finger, 'Look at it Jan.' This one shows a large glass vase broken on the floor, some red Roses are strewn around near the broken vase and there's a puddle of water. Then he places another photograph next to it with a closer view of some of the Roses. 'Open your eyes…Jan, look at it!'

Jan opens her eyes slowly. One soft teardrop rolls onto Jan's cheek, she lifts up the cuff of her hoodie's sleeve to clean up her runny nose, she sniffs. She shakes her head, 'How many Roses?'

Chris watches her reaction and frowns, *What does that matter?* He shakes his head.

She asks again, 'How many Roses were there?'

'Twelve.'

After she cleans some more tears from her face she says, 'It was her birthday.' Jan shuts her eyes and more tears roll down. That was not a question.

'Yes, it was.'

'He didn't kill her.'

'We know.'

~

Shutting drawers as fast as he's opening them, Tim is trying not to leave a mess in Jan's kitchen. *Don't people use Address Books anymore?* Looking around he moves over to the dining room table where he finds Jan's laptop and some papers set in different piles. He shuffles through them, going through them as quickly as possible, but also trying to read what's written on them. They seem to be printed drafts of text, page after page. He lifts up his hands and places them on his hips. Standing in the middle of the room, he looks across through the sliding doors out to the dark black sky and waves glimmering under the moonlight in the distance. Staring toward the living room then turns around to look down the hallway. He pulls at this hair, 'Argh!'

Taking a seat at the dining room table, he lifts the laptop's screen. Maybe her contacts are on her computer. The screen lights up and requests a password, 'Aaah! Jan! Why now?! A freaking password!' He types the word *George123*, but the password widget just shakes without changing screens. *That's not gonna work.* He presses the palm of his hand on his forehead.

Walking into Jan's bedroom, a flash of recognition hits him as he smells the scent of her cologne and he is transported to their last encounter in this room. He looks at the drawer, opens the top one, and runs his hands through the contents. Not there. He looks at the bed, rushes to the nightstand, and pulls out the drawer, sifting through the contents. Nothing there as well. Sliding across the bed trying to reach the other nightstand, he sees some pieces of paper lying on top. He opens the drawer but there is nothing there. *Think, Tim, think!* He hits his forehead with his index finger. *How can you find Max or Esther?! Think!* His phone pings. It's a text from the office. Raquel Thompson is texting him a link to an Instagram account. Her text reads, "We're getting up there in the world if clients are posting about us on Instagram." There are two emojis, a thumbs-up and a smiley face.

What? I don't have time for emojis Raquel! But he clicks on the link anyway and it goes to a 'story' by one of his clients boasting of how happy he is now that his accounts are being handled by Tim's company and yada-yada-yada.

'Instagram! Right! Max has Instagram!' Tim quickly scrolls through his Instagram feed, clicking on some of the icons, not knowing how any of this works, he finds "followers and following." Max started to follow him the night they had dinner together. He clicks Max's account and then to message him. His finger tips run as fast as he can make them go on the screen, "Max, this is Tim. It is urgent you call me. Jan is in trouble. Call me now!" He types his phone number and hits send.

After a few minutes, a 312 area code pops up on Tim's phone. He doesn't have this number in his contacts list but he answers. It could be Max. 'Hello?'

'Hello? Is this Tim Evans?' Tim hears a vaguely familiar female voice but it's not Esther.

'Yes, how can I help you?'

'Hello, Tim. I need to contact Jan and I have not been able to get through to her. I know you are staying next door and I would like you to go over there and put some sense into that girl. Tell her she needs to return my calls. Specially this call, and I mean pronto!'

'And you are?'

'Oh, sorry, so sorry. We've met but you probably don't remember me. I'm Dianne Taylor, Jan's agent…and friend.'

'Yes, yes, I remember you. If it were under other circumstances I'd probably hang up on you. In any case, right now I can't help you.'

'Why not?! Jan is just next door to you. What's so difficult about that, sir?'

'I can't help you because Jan is with the police, at the police station.'

Dianne stays quiet for a few seconds, 'So it's true? She's been arrested?'

'Wait, How do you know she's at the police station?'

'It's all over the damn internet! Someone got wind of her being "arrested."' She makes fake quotes in the air, 'And it's gone pretty much viral. I don't know how this is going to affect her books and all, but this is a disaster, Tim.'

'Wait. What?! She hasn't been arrested, so I really hope that's not what they published on the internet.'

'Well, I don't know, arrested, at the police station, it's all the same. People publish anything on the web! It's about optics, Tim, optics. What is she doing at the police station?'

'They won't say. They can't tell me. I already went over there to find out. All they say is they're investigating that murder. You know, the one they accused her dead husband of committing.'

'She should've stayed away from that. I'm telling you. When she said she wanted to put some tidbits from that murder in the novel, I told her not to do it. She should've stayed away from that beach!'

'What do you mean staying away from the story? Was she writing about the murder?'

'Maybe. I don't know. She mentioned something about using part of it as a backdrop to her next thriller since her last book based at the Beach was such a success.'

Tim looks at his phone because it's beeping in another call, 'I have to let you go, Dianne. Call me back. I have to talk to Jan's brother. Bye.' He switches to Max's call, 'Max, is that you?'

'Yes, hi Tim, what's going on? Is Jan all right?'

Chapter 30

Wednesday, June 15, 2022
New Smyrna Beach, FL

Rolling her shoulders and looking at her face in the precinct's bathroom mirror, Jan ruffles her disarrayed hair., rubs her eyes, and splashes some water on her face. She looks at her watch, seven a.m. She feels so disheveled, maybe some coffee will help. Walking out, she zips the hoodie trying to get more warmth out of it but it doesn't help much.

Chris is standing at the interrogation room door down the hall, waiting for her. He slants his head toward the door, signaling to go back inside. She steps in and he follows. There's a woman sitting at the table on the side Jan had spent most of yesterday afternoon and evening sitting in. She gets up when they walk in. There's an empty chair next to the woman. Jan's chair.

The woman seems to be in her mid-thirties. She has curly medium short hair and a brown complexion. Jan thinks she looks of Indian descent, but as far as she remembers, Indian people don't have curly hair. The woman, who is wearing a gray tailored suit, extends her hand to Jan, 'Hello, I am Indra Lakhani, your attorney.' They shake hands.

Jan looks at Chris, then at Indra, 'I didn't call an attorney? Why are you here?'

'I am a friend of Esther's. She called me to come help and represent you. That is why I am here, as your attorney.'

'All right.' Jan sits in the seat next to Indra and looks at her, 'Thanks. Thank you for coming.' Indra sits down in her chair.

Chris takes a seat on the other side of the table and places the folder on the table. He starts shuffling through the folder like he did the previous night. Indra watches and after a few seconds as he is about to pull out a piece of paper she says, 'Officer Gwynn.' She extends her hand over in a gesture to have him stop pulling out the sheet of paper, 'Is my client under arrest?'

'No, she has decided to cooperate with us on the matter of Cassandra Davis' murder…' He still pulls out the paper from the folder, and lays it on the table, 'And she has been very forthcoming.'

'If my client is not under arrest I must then interrupt your questioning. You have not been accommodating to my client. You had her spend the night here under very dire conditions and this is unacceptable. Miss Crawford will now leave and get some rest, and we will take under advisement if she will return to answer your questions. However, that may not be forthcoming. I expect to have a full report available, on paper or digitally, for our review.' Indra raises from her chair and puts her briefcase-looking handbag over her arm, 'In the meantime, we are leaving now.' She looks down at Jan and signals her to get up. Jan looks up at Indra, her mouth open but not speaking, then at Chris. She shrugs and gets up. Chris raises from his chair and watches as they walk out the door.

~

The early morning breeze hits Tim's face as he walks over wet sand. The gray daybreak is slowly shaping the skies along the quiet beach. Seagulls fly above and sandpipers run in and out of the rushing water and away from the sea foam on the shore. Tim looks ahead as he approaches Jan's home. *Should I go inside?* The house is empty, nothing to look for there. He watches the rear of the home where Elsa and Mandy are, a light is on in *his* bedroom, Mandy's bedroom. He decides to walk back to the hotel instead and get some breakfast, and then go see Elsa. Looking at his phone, he decides it's too early to call Max to find out any news. He reaches the beach ramp and heads up to Main Street continuing his pace toward the hotel.

~

'Would you like some coffee?' Setting up a stovetop espresso coffee pot, she then opens a cupboard and pulls out a couple of mugs. Indra lays her handbag on the sofa and takes a seat, 'Sure. Just sugar is okay.'

'Thanks again for coming. Orlando is not very far, but also not close. Plus, it's very early. I'm glad Esther sent you.' Jan leans against the kitchen counter, her hands inside her hoodie's pockets.

'Yes. Esther is a great friend of mine. We were in law school together.' She nods reminiscing, 'Many sleepless nights we shared, hahaha.'

Jan smiles forlornly, she smells the aroma of coffee spouting out from the pot. Indra asks, 'Why did you stay there so long? You know they didn't have to hold you.'

Jan shrugs, 'I don't know. I guess I wanted to know what it is they wanted from me, why they're accusing me of killing Cassandra.'

'If they had proof you did it, they would've arrested you.'

Walking over to the living room with two mugs, a sugar bowl, and spoons on a tray, Jan extends it over to Indra who takes one. Indra continues, 'They seem to have driven away from thinking George did it, but they don't have anything on you, at least not anything I could see from what you shared with me. I am going to swing by there to pick up the investigation report and list of evidence but I may not get it yet. Since you haven't been indicted all I can hope for is an incident report of sorts.' She looks up at her phone to check the time.

Jan points toward the sliding doors, 'Well, before you go, let's go out to the porch and enjoy the beach while we drink our coffee.'

Indra follows her, 'Good, and you can tell me about all the evidence they showed you.'

~

Sitting at the dining room table eating cereal from a bowl, Elsa smiles at her father. Tim is sitting next to her. Mandy walks down the stairs, 'Hello, Tim. What are you doing here?'

'I came to see Elsa, Mandy.' He takes a sip from a cup as Mandy walks around the kitchen counter toward the coffee maker. Getting up from the chair, he walks behind Mandy and quietly whispers in her ear, 'We need to talk. Alone.'

Mandy takes her cup of coffee and turns around to face him, she brings the coffee to her lips, staring into his eyes, 'What about, Tim?'

'You know what it's about, and I'm not leaving until we clear up a few things.'

Pulling out from Tim's physical space, Mandy walks out of the kitchen toward the dining area, 'Well, look at you. You want to talk. I'm the one who should be asking you to explain things to me. But, yes, let's talk.' She opens the French doors and walks out to the deck. He follows her outside and shuts the doors so Elsa doesn't hear them arguing, which is most likely what will happen.

Noticing Jan sitting on her patio talking with some lady, Mandy stops in her tracks, her body held erect. She almost drops her coffee mug. Tim looks over as well, pain on his face, but also relief. *Jan is home now.* He waves. Jan waves back. Mandy turns around in a puff and rushes back into the house and up the stairs to her bedroom, slamming the door.

Tim follows her and reaches the bedroom door and goes inside, 'Mandy, let's talk about this.'

She purses her lips, 'Tell me, when did it all start? Since when did you and Jan hit the sack behind my back?'

He turns toward the window and watches Jan on her porch downstairs, 'Mandy. It's not her fault, it's all me. It was going to be a one-night thing, that's it, just an adventure.' He turns to look at Mandy who is holding a hairbrush in her hand, tears rolling down her face. She sits down on the bed, defeated. He continues, 'You and I have been broken for some time Mandy, you know it.' He sits down next to her, 'You know, we haven't been ourselves in a long time.' He shrugs, 'Do you remember why we came here last year in the first place?' She nods. He continues, 'I thought we could get back what we had during our early years. That maybe we could make it work. But the fact is I felt empty. I thought I could fill it up with work, and I worked long hard hours. I thought Elsa was enough to keep us together.' He points at her, 'You felt emptiness also. You know you did. You thought you could fill the gap we had with your business.' He takes one of her hands in his, 'Did we succeed?'

She wipes off tears from her cheeks, 'Yes, we did. Our businesses prospered, we had Elsa, and look what a beautiful young girl she's become!'

'Yes, Elsa is our greatest achievement but we don't have what we had any more. Elsa is wonderful, but she's not the reason for us to have stayed together, Mandy.' He points at her and himself.

'But why Jan? Why does it have to be Jan?'

Tim stays silent staring at his feet, at the floor. Mandy speaks again, 'She's a murderer, Tim! You have to believe me.'

'Why do you say that? You don't know that. You don't have any proof of that!'

'She is, I've seen the file. I also went to talk to the officer in charge of the investigation. Plus, Buford also thinks she did it.'

Tim's face turns red, 'Buford is an idiot! What are you doing talking to Buford? He's just a poor bum who's made bad choices and ended up where he is. What does he know?'

'Well, he told me George didn't do it, he assured me he knows George didn't do it.'

'Well, if the cops didn't believe him back then, why should you believe him now?'

'He never told the cops.'

'So how does he know?'

'Because…' She pauses and gets up from the bed, 'Because he followed George that night after he left that girl's house. He saw them kissing. He knows she was alive when George left, right before he died.'

Chapter 31

Thursday, June 16, 2022
Orlando, FL

Indra welcomes Jan and Tim as they walk into her office, 'Good afternoon, please have a seat, I'm glad you could make it.'

The office is spacious, the view is spectacular. Indra's office is on the twentieth floor of a building in downtown Orlando. It feels as if they're floating above the city. The office's exterior walls are floor-to-ceiling glass so the northern part of the city unfolds before them as far as the eye can see. The office decor is simple with touches of gray, green, and blue on the walls and furniture.

Tim and Jan sit on a sofa in the corner of Indra's office. Indra walks over with some folders in her hand and sits across from them.

Eyeing the folders in Indra's hands, Jan settles in, 'It's the least we could do.'

Indra picks up a few sheets from one of the folders and places them face-up on the coffee table, 'I had to go back and forth with Detective Gwynn but he finally provided the mysterious fingerprints. So, my investigator was able to run them, and he found a match.'

Tim and Jan look at each other, Jan says, 'What?! Why? The cops didn't run them before?'

Indra is about to explain but Tim interrupts, 'Prints from what? Where did they find the prints?'

Indra says, 'Well, Cassandra's cause of death was strangulation. She was hit with a hammer, but that didn't kill her.'

'Yes.' Jan closes her eyes and lowers her head, 'I knew that. I saw a picture of the hammer. It was George's hammer. It had my prints and his, and a thumbprint belonging to someone else.'

Indra nods, 'Yes, well, that was not the cause of death but I am guessing that because of the prints on the hammer and the deal with the money in George's account, they wanted a quick close of the case and decided that it was best if he had killed her. Easy close. In any case, the police found a couple of fingerprints on Cassandra's skin as well, on her neck to be exact. Those weren't George's, in fact, they couldn't determine whose they were back then. The unknown print on the hammer and those on her neck were from the same person.'

'What about Buford?' Tim asks shaking his head. 'Could it have been him?'

'No, he was discarded years ago.' Indra then leans in as she passes the report to Jan, 'My investigator called in a favor with an F.B.I. agent he knows and they ran the prints in a national database. They got a hit.'

'That's good news! Right?' Tim's face lights up, 'That's great. But why are we doing the police's job? They should've gone into that.'

'Perhaps they were focusing more on local people. Maybe they didn't run a national search, who knows?' Indra waves her hand, 'Now that Buford came clean on George leaving while she was still alive, maybe they will expand the search of those prints.'

Jan lowers her head, Tim had already told her what Mandy said about Buford going to the cops, 'That's why they're focusing on me. That, and the ring.'

Tim touches Jan's knee, 'Don't worry about that. So, what did your investigator find?'

'Okay, so here goes…' Indra hands them the mugshot of a middle-aged man. Typed on the bottom of the sheet are the words "LAKE HELEN POLICE DEPARTMENT" with a name under the photo: Joseph Kingston. 'This is the man whose fingerprints were found on Cassandra's neck and the one unknown print on the hammer.'

Jan's mouth falls open, 'So, he did it?!' She brings her hand to her chest, 'He killed Cassandra! Do the cops know?!'

Tim holds the photo in his hand, 'This is a mugshot, is this guy in jail?'

Indra nods, 'Yes, he is at the Union Correctional Institution, a prison here in Florida. He's there for murder.'

'Murder?' Jan frowns and looks over at Tim.

'Yes, he was convicted of murdering a woman a few years ago.' Indra picks one sheet from the table and passes it over to them.

Jan's face turns grey, and her cheeks and forehead suddenly feel damp. She rises abruptly from the sofa and walks quickly to the door. She is feeling claustrophobic and she rubs her hands, 'Ah, is there a bathroom? I need to go to the restroom.'

Indra gets up and heads to the door, 'Sure, sure, come I'll show you.' She points down the hall outside the office, 'There to the left.'

Jan practically runs down the hall.

Looking confused, Tim's phone starts vibrating in his pocket. He's already up from his seat staring at where Jan disappeared but succumbs to the phone's jolting insistence. It's Elsa. 'Daddy, Daddy.' He can feel the anxiety in her voice, 'I can't find Mom. Daddy, I'm scared.'

'Where are you?'

'I'm at the house. Mommy isn't here. She was outside reading a book, but I can't find her!'

'Okay, okay.' Tim looks over at Indra pleadingly, 'Elsa, honey, stay there. I'm in Orlando but I will be right there.' He takes a breath, 'I'm going to have a friend of mine go over to be with you until I get there, okay? Call me when they get there.'

Whimpering Elsa nods, 'Okay, Daddy, come soon.'

'I will be right there, honey. Don't worry.' He hangs up and turns to Indra, 'I have to run back, can you please check on Jan so we can go? We'll come back as soon as we can, but I have to go, my daughter's at home alone.'

Indra rushes over to the restroom. She finds Jan splashing water on her face, 'Jan, Jan? Is everything okay?' Indra touches her back, 'Are you okay? What happened back there?'

Jan looks at Indra through the mirror, 'Denise Davis, that woman who was murdered in Cassadaga…that was Cassandra's mom.'

Indra covers her mouth.

Chapter 32

Afternoon
New Smyrna Beach, FL

Laying on top of the table on the beach house deck, Mandy's cell phone rings and rings. It goes to voicemail, 'Where are you, Mandy? I'm heading over there now, call me if you get this.' Tim hangs up and takes Jan's hand for comfort. Storm clouds are hovering over them and about to break open.

'Jan, once Mandy shows up, we have to tell Chris about this guy.'

Jan nods. 'I think Indra is probably doing that right now, so don't worry.' She looks at Tim sideways, 'Poor Elsa, she must be so nervous. The most important thing is to find Mandy.' Jan tightens her grip on the seatbelt as Tim speeds up to take the New Smyrna exit off of Interstate 4, large and heavy raindrops start knocking on the windshield.

~

'Buuuford! You need to untie me, Buford!' Mandy's wrists are sore and reddened. The zip ties have burned her skin causing tiny cuts. She feels wetness rub between her skin and the plastic as she wiggles her arms behind her back. Her ankles are also tied together with rope. She can hardly keep herself on the chair. She blows her hair away from her face.

'Shut up! This wouldn't have happened if you would have done what I told you to do! But no, you had to go to the cops again. I told you I had a plan!'

Mandy wiggles in her seat, 'Ouch! Buford this hurts! You need to untie me now!'

'No, you are staying here until I get her back in jail. They let her out and it's all because of you! You talk too much. You're going to ruin everything.'

'Buford, they let her out until they get more evidence. They're most likely working on it, she has a lawyer. Now the cops are back on track.' She extends her legs because they're getting cramped. 'You have to know you and I are on the same side. Untie me!' She tries to stand up but Buford walks behind her and forcefully sits her back down in the chair again.

Buford moves around to face her and starts pointing as he yells, 'You will just continue to butt yourself in and pester the cops. I have a plan and you will ruin it. So you're staying here until I'm done.' He starts pacing around the garage and looks at the shelves above the counter where he keeps some of his tools. There are rows of tiny bottles and jars on a few lines of racks on the wall. He has to get Chris out of the way so maybe other cops will take him seriously. What worked with George may work with Chris. He just has to make sure he uses a less concentrated solution, just to scare him off and disable him for a few weeks.

Mandy closes her eyes. Tears and sweat smudge her face with dirt and dust, 'I need to go back to my daughter! Let me gooooo!'

Buford rushes over to her with a roll of duct tape in his hands. He tears off a piece and tapes it across her mouth. 'There. Stop yelling!' He brings his fists up to the side of his head.

'Mmmmph, mmmmm.' Marcy squirms in the chair to the point she falls off onto the floor. She tries to crouch in the fetal position but not an easy task since her arms are tied behind her back and there's rope around her ankles.

Buford approaches her and kneels down on one knee. He caresses her hair, 'You are pretty. Just like my Cassandra.' He caresses her cheek, 'But you're not going to ruin my plan!'

Mandy's eyes open wide. She panics and feels like she is starting to hyperventilate. She wiggles some more on the floor. She moves her head left and right to avoid his contact. Buford reaches behind her and puts his arms under her armpits. 'There, come on.' He rises her up from the floor back onto the chair. 'Now, stay still. I have to think! I'll be back later.'

~

Linda has seen her share of beautiful kitchen designs, from modern to quaint, but she feels more at home with a country style though she did avoid the roosters. She prefers garden motifs and rustic finishings. The light green tablecloth on the table in the side nook blends well with the light grayish-blue of the walls and the white cabinets. Chris is sitting on the windowsill bench watching Linda roam around the kitchen. 'Someone's with the girl, then?' Linda picks up the teakettle from the stovetop.

Suddenly Buford opens the kitchen door, and rain splashes from outside onto the mat. Linda scolds him, 'Close the door, hurry!' Buford lowers his head and runs his hands through his wet hair, his gruffness showing more than ever.

'Hello there Buford.' Chris says as Buford walks past them. Buford doesn't answer, he strides with lowered shoulders through the kitchen to the front of the house.

'Take off your shoes Buford! You're going to get the whole house wet!' Linda rolls her eyes and turns around with the kettle in her hands. She walks to the table, 'Sometimes he's going to get the best of me! I tell you!'

Chris turns his empty teacup over. He watches her pour some hot water, 'Yeah, Child Services were able to go over and take care of her until Tim gets back.' He moves his teabag in the saucer, 'You say you haven't heard from her? I thought you were going to show her some homes.'

'We made plans but she stood me up.' She waves one hand as she sets the tea kettle back on the stove, 'I'm used to that. Buyers do that all the time and forget to call you to tell you their plans changed.' She rolls her eyes and shrugs, 'I waited for half an hour, then it started to rain, so I came back home.'

'What a nightmare. Where could the mother be?'

'I can't imagine.'

'She came by to the police station the other day. Actually, I've been seeing a lot of her lately. She's really taken an interest in Cassandra's murder.'

'Really? What did she say?'

'I can't tell you that, yet. It's being investigated, but I'll let you know as soon as we can.' He gets up and goes to the bathroom.

Moving over to the stove, Linda has her back to the kitchen nook. She feels Buford pacing behind her, 'Buford, do you want some tea?' she turns around, again holding the kettle, and she sees Buford removing his hand from near Chris' teacup and putting something in his pants pocket. 'What was that? What are you doing Buford?!'

'Nothing.' He keeps his hand in his pocket. Linda promptly puts the kettle on the hot pad on the table and reaches for him but he tries to pull away. She tightens her hold and yells, 'Give me that! What is it?!' Buford yanks away but Linda tries to embrace him to get her hand in his pocket. He pulls back again and shoves her to the side. Chris walks in from the hallway. Linda yells at him, 'Chris, don't drink that tea. Buford, give me that! What is it?'

Now standing next to the kitchen door, Buford is about to bolt out. Linda yells, 'Grab him! Chris, don't let him go!' Buford twists the door handle but Chris grabs him from behind. Chris steadies him holding his arms behind his back. Linda digs into his right pants pocket and takes out a tiny dark brown bottle with a dropper cap. She looks at it, it's half full of liquid, 'Chris, you're going to have to get this tested. I would also get your tea checked.'

'Come over here Buford.' Chris drags Buford over to a chair, 'I'm going to let you go and you promise you will stay still.'

Buford nods though he tries to loosen Chris' grip on his arms. Linda takes the teacup away from the table and places it on the kitchen counter. Chris sits next to Buford on the bench, 'Now, tell me, what is this all about?'

Holding his hands together between his knees, Buford tighten's his lips doesn't say anything. With her arms crossed, Linda is leaning against the counter watching them. 'Buford, talk to him! What's going on?!' Buford shakes his head. Like usual, his mustache and beard hide all emotions from his face.

~

Hurriedly walking through the front door, Tim and Jan throw their jacket and coat on the sofa and Tim rushes to Elsa who is sitting at the edge. A tightly coiffed haired lady wearing a tan suit gets up. Miss Kerry looks at Jan then at Tim and Elsa, 'She's all right. She's a great kid.' She smiles.

'Honey!' Tim hugs her, 'Are you okay?'

'Yes, Daddy.' Some tears wet her eyes, and she hugs her dad.

Bringing her to his chest, Tim tightens his embrace, 'I'm here now. Don't worry. We'll find Mommy soon, very soon.' Elsa nods. Tim looks up at Miss Kerry. She explains, 'The policewoman who brought me over said she will contact me as soon as they have more on Mrs. Evans' whereabouts. Right now all we know is she disappeared from the deck in the back. Her car is here and we found her cell phone outside. Would you know where she could've gone?'

Tim looks at Elsa who shakes her head. Running his fingers through his hair, Tim approaches Ms. Kerry, 'I have no idea, but I know she wouldn't just leave Elsa alone. You see the car is outside.' Elsa gets up and walks over to Jan who embraces her.

Ms. Kerry looks at both Tim and Jan, 'Could you go around the house and see if there is anything missing? If she took her handbag? Clothes? Would she have gone to the beach?'

Tim turns over to Elsa, 'Did Mommy say if she was going to the beach?' Elsa shakes her head, 'Was she wearing a bathing suit?' Elsa shakes her head. Tim turns to Ms. Kerry, 'She doesn't even like to swim.'

Jan asks Elsa, 'What was she wearing, honey?'

'She was wearing her white blouse and shorts, she was sitting outside and I was watching cartoons. She was talking on the phone with Stacy, then I don't know after that.'

Tim walks upstairs to the bedroom. Jan looks at Ms. Kerry and suggests, 'Should we look around the beach?'

Picking up her handbag, Ms. Kerry shrugs, 'That could be an idea, maybe she went out to walk. But, she left a long time ago, from what I surmise, it's been at least two hours or more already. She would've been back by now.'

'Yes, I guess you're right.'

Walking down the stairs from the bedroom, Tim is carrying Mandy's handbag, 'This is her handbag. Everything is here, including the car keys. She didn't leave on purpose. There aren't any clothes missing, her suitcases are in the bedroom.'

As Ms. Kerry says goodbye she reminds Elsa to call her if she needs anything. Jan follows her to the door, and Tim and Elsa head out to the deck holding hands.

~

Walking down a long corridor at the precinct, Chris notices it's eerily quiet, as usual, on this side of the building. A glass window slides open as he approaches. David, the evidence clerk, puts out his hand, 'Hello Chris, what you got for me?'

Chris sets a couple of plastic evidence bags on the counter. One of them has the ceramic cup he brought from Linda's home. The other one has a dark brown dropper bottle inside. He also has a small bottle containing the tea he didn't drink, 'Can you get these to the FDLE Crime Lab for me? I need to know what's in it.'

'Sure.' Pulling out a clipboard with a form, David starts filling it out with the data written on the bags and jar Chris just handed over.

'When do you think I could get an answer?'

'Hard to say, but I can put a rush on it.'

'Could ya?' Chris puts a slip of paper on the counter with a file number written on it, 'Here, the top number is this case's file number. The second one is the file on the Cassandra Davis murder. I'm gonna need you to make a search for the fingerprints we don't have a match for, can you run them again? Make sure you widen the range to the whole state. If that doesn't bring a match, see if the FBI can help track it down.'

David raises his eyebrows, 'Oh, really? I thought that case was closed?'

'It was. "Was" being the operative word here.'

~

Trying to move her tongue inside her mouth, Mandy bites on it, but it feels a bit numb. She tries not to gag. Her lips feel drier and cracked, probably caused by the duct tape. Clumps of greasy hair fall over her eyes, she tries to shake her head. Tears roll down her cheeks. Her eyelashes feel heavy. *Elsa! Oh, Elsa!* She fears Elsa must be so scared.

Opening her eyes, Mandy moves her head around to see what's in the room. Earlier she was too busy trying to figure out a way to convince Buford to let her go. Now, it's been quiet for so long, half an hour? An hour? She has lost track of time. Where did he go? What is this place? The room is small, with wooden walls, one door, and two windows, a large garage door up front. She can see a couple of palm trees outside the window. *I must be in his garage.* There's a counter and cabinets under one of the windows. All sorts of garden tools hang from one of the walls, pruners, hedge shears, shovels, electric edgers, blowers, and other contraptions Mandy doesn't recognize. There are a few racks with lots of small bottles above the counter, *Spices? That's weird.*

Standing up from the chair, her wrists are hurting more than ever from the plastic ties; the cuts are getting deeper, and her skin is burning. Because her ankles are tied up, she can't move around so she hops from the middle of the room to the counter. *I'm thirsty.* She looks around for water, a faucet, something. *How am I going to drink anything with duct tape over my mouth?* She doesn't see anything. Shaking her head continuously, she tries to yell but all she can manage is for tears of frustration to roll down her face.

~

Sitting in the same room and on the same chair as when he interrogated Jan, Chris is now across from a person with creases on his face. His blond hair is still damp and his facial hair is more disheveled than usual.

With arms folded and leaning back in his chair, Chris doesn't seem to have much patience for him, 'I'm not going to ask you again Buford. What was in that tea? Look, we've been here for over an hour now, and I need answers!'

Lifting his head up, Buford narrows his blue eyes to stare at Chris, 'Answers? You want answers? Why did you let her go, huh?'

Looking a bit confused, Chris winks one eye shut and moves his head sideways. He leans forward and puts his left elbow on the table, resting his chin on his hand, 'Okay, I'll humor you. What are you talking about?'

'You let her go! Jan Crawford.' Buford moves his arm outward, 'She's out there! Free! She killed Cassandra and you let her go.'

Chris stares at Buford for a few seconds. Buford continues, 'She did it! Look, you see the ring she wears? I already told you the emerald ring was Cassandra's. Where did she get that? She probably took it as a souvenir the night she killed Cassandra. She killed her! She hated Cassandra because she was having an affair with her husband. She did it.'

Pulling back into the chair, Chris relaxes and crosses his arms across his chest, 'Look Buford, I can't give you information. The case has been opened again and I guess we have to thank you for that. That is as far as I go. Now, I have to keep you here until I figure out what's in that tea. Do you understand?'

'You're crazy Chris, you know? She did it. You hold me here and just let her walk. I told you she was alive when George left her house. He didn't do it.'

'Which brings up another question I can't answer. Why did you wait so long to tell us what you saw? Why did you let us pin the murder on George if you knew he didn't do it?'

'I can't tell you that.'

'There's a lot you don't want to tell me, Buford, you are maddening.' Chris gets out of his chair and walks out of the room shaking his head. Stepping into the common office, he approaches Sharon near the photocopier, 'Hey Sharon, can you put in a request for a warrant to search Buford's house?'

'What are we serving it for? You know Judge Taylor is very picky about blanket warrants. Any rooms in particular?'

Chris rolls his eyes, 'Gosh, how will I be able to find anything? I'm looking for poisons. Where do you think he'd store poisons? I don't know, the kitchen? Where he keeps his landscaping chemicals and tools? Make it for the garage, the kitchen.'

'All right. Coming up. By the way, Miss Crawford's attorney wants you to call her back.'

'Well, that's the least of my worries right now. I'll get back to her later. Get me that warrant. Once you have it, give it to some of the guys on patrol to go check it out. Buford is going to be here in holding so the house should be quiet.'

Chris feels his phone vibrate in his pants pocket. He takes it out and answers, 'Hey Linda, what's up?'

'Chris! Chris! You need to come to Buford's house right now!'

Chapter 33

Afternoon
New Smyrna Beach, FL

Hanging up the phone, Chris rushes over to Sharon, 'Forget the warrant. Put Buford in a holding cell. Nobody is to talk to him. He's not going anywhere. I have a feeling he's going to get a whole set of other charges thrown at him before I come back.' He turns around, 'And send a patrol car to Buford's address right away. That's where I'm headed.'

Chris talks under his breath, 'Buford, what the hell are you up to?'

~

Parking the SUV close to the Emergency room of the hospital, Tim turns around in his seat and looks at Jan and Elsa, 'Are you ready, Elsa? Are you sure you want to go in to see Mommy? She's okay but she's going to look a little out of sorts.'

Elsa nods quickly, 'Yes, I want to see Mommy.'

'Okay, then. Let's go. Jan? Are you coming?'

Jan shakes her head, 'No. I'll just wait here for you. Go ahead. Go to Mandy.'

'Okay. C'mon Elsa.' They get out of the car. Jan watches them as they take each other's hands and walk toward the Emergency Room doors.

~

Sitting in a patio chair in the rear of Buford's property, Linda watches as Chris walks out of the rear of the garage and approaches her, 'The techs are taking pictures and bagging a bunch of small bottles and things that look like herbs they found in the room. Do you have any idea why he would have Mrs. Evans tied up in there?'

Shaking her head, Linda frowns, 'I don't know other than what Mandy told me.' She covers her face with her hands, 'She had been challenging Buford to go to the police about Cassandra's murder. She said she knew George was not the murderer and that he had to get the cops to investigate Jan, instead.'

'Well, that's what he told me when I came to see him at your place the other day. That's why we brought Jan in for questioning. I'm a bit puzzled about why he'd kidnap Mrs. Evans or doctor my tea, though I have an idea why. But why kidnap Mrs. Evans… I don't get it.'

'Do you think he's lost it? That Cassandra's obsession has made him go mad?'

Chris shrugs, 'Perhaps. Who knows? We now know George didn't do it, and it most likely wasn't Jan either. So, why would he do all these things?' He touches her knee, 'Are you gonna be all right?'

Nodding, Linda smiles. Chris kisses her softly, 'Okay, I'm going to head back to the station now.'

'Okay.' Linda looks up as he raises from his chair, 'Chris, be careful.' Chris nods. Linda takes his hand and squeezes it, 'I love you.'

~

'What is she doing here!?'

It feels muggy in the dark open parking lot just outside the emergency room of the hospital. Holding onto Tim's arm, Mandy is yelling as they approach the car. Elsa is startled and jumps.

Jan is leaning against the car looking at her cell phone.

Putting his arm around Mandy, Tim explains, 'Calm down, Mandy, calm down. Jan has been helping us, she took care of Elsa when you disappeared.'

'I don't want to see her! Go away!' She turns around to look at Tim, 'She's a murderer, don't you understand Tim?' She points at Jan, 'She murdered that woman!'

It seems like they forgot all about Elsa who is beside herself and runs to the car, crying. Jan reaches over to hug her.

Hitting his forehead with the palm of his hand, Tim turns, 'Mandy! Stop it!' He rushes over to Elsa and puts his arm around her as well, 'Don't worry honey, please don't cry.' Crouching down to Elsa's level, he holds both her arms, 'Look, Jan did not kill that woman. Mom is wrong, we already know who did it. Please don't cry.' Loosening from Tim's hold, Elsa opens the door and sits in the rear, hiding, weeping.

In the middle of the parking lot, pointing and yelling at Jan, Mandy starts sobbing, 'Look at her Tim! She did it. She is a writer. She writes about this stuff all the time! She could've plotted this whole thing to get away with murder! She did it perfectly!'

Tim's shoulders fall, 'No, Mandy. No.' He reaches for her and guides her to the front seat of the car, 'Here. Get in the car. We'll talk about this at the house.' He helps her get in.

Reaching for Jan, her face is white as snow, her mouth is wide open, Tim tries to hold her hand. 'Look, I'll take you home, go ahead and ride in the back with Elsa.'

Jan shakes her head. Tim goes on, 'Come on Jan, don't do this.' He looks over to Mandy who has a clenched jaw and crazed eyes. Turning his face back to Jan, 'I think the pain meds are probably doing a number on her. She is not herself.'

'I know. Don't worry Tim. I get it. She's been through a lot. Let's not worry tonight. Go home. I'll get a ride-share and will get home in no time.'

Kissing her, Tim looks into her eyes, 'Let's pick up in the morning, okay?'

Jan nods, 'Okay, go take care of your family. See you tomorrow.'

~

The past day has been disconcerting for everyone. Having pulled the blinds down on every window and the vertical blinds across the sliding door to the patio, Jan sits in her darkened living room. It is dark inside and out but her eyes adjust slowly to the ambiance, not that it's helping much.

Touching her face, she taps the puffiness under her eyes with her fingers. She has drained all her tears and her eyes feel gritty. Even though she's already had two cups of very strong espresso coffee, she has a splitting headache. Not ready to go to bed, not that she would be with all the caffeine she's ingested, she throws herself on the sofa and lets her arm hang out and touch the floor. Arching her other arm over her forehead, Jan tries to relax by closing her eyes and letting her thoughts float through the past few years since the day George died. This is going to be a long, long night.

Next door at Mandy's home, Elsa is in her bedroom upstairs. In the living room, Mandy continues to try to convince Tim of Jan's guilt. Tim paces in front of the TV, 'Mandy, you're not being fair. Nor logical for that matter. Jan did not murder that woman.'

'You keep saying that, but Buford told me he saw George leave her house and she was alive when they left.'

'So? Why does it mean Jan killed her?'

'Because she did. Who else would want to kill her? She was having an affair with Jan's husband. Plus Jan has Cassandra's ring.' She touches her ring finger, 'You see that emerald ring on Jan's ring finger? That's Cassandra's ring. Buford told me.'

Sitting across from Mandy on the coffee table, Tim takes her hands into his, 'Look, Mandy, there has to be an explanation for that. Jan did not kill her and the police probably have the proof now that someone else did it. You need to drop it. For your own sanity.' He looks upstairs, 'For Elsa. Mandy, please drop it.'

Mandy pouts and lowers her head. She rubs her wrists feeling the coarse and fragile burned skin caused by the plastic ties. A tear falls down her cheek and Tim lifts her chin slowly. She says, 'What am I going to do? I thought we could be together again but you don't want me anymore. What am I going to do?'

Tim comforts her, 'Mandy, Mandy, you have so much ahead of you. You have Elsa and your business. You will be just fine. I know it hasn't worked out for us, but you will be okay.'

'Just go!' She pulls her hands away, 'Just go, okay! I want to be alone.'

Chapter 34

Friday, June 17, 2022
Raiford, FL

Drops of recent rain drip off of the metal security grille protecting the window of the room where Chris is at the Union Correctional Institution waiting for Joseph Kingston to walk through the door.

Opposite where Chris is sitting, the door opens. Dressed in a blue jumpsuit, Kingston has deep furrows on his forehead and salt and pepper hair. With a chain around his waist and shackles with a chain around his wrists, he is followed by a prison guard. 'Sit!' The guard shoves Kingston to the empty plastic chair across from Chris. Kingston sits and wrangles his shoulders so the guard moves away. The guard walks over and stands next to the door they came through. Chris signals the guard to go out to the hallway.

Chris studies Kingston.

Kingston stares back.

Leaning toward the table, Chris begins, 'Mr. Kingston, my name is Chris Gwynn. I'm a detective from the New Smyrna Police Department and I'm here to ask you a few questions.'

'Aren't you kinda far away from your jurisdiction?'

Taking out a slender digital audio recorder from his left shirt pocket, Chris places it on the table between himself and Kingston and clicks on a red button, 'For your information, I am going to record this conversation. So, let's begin. How long have you been in prison, sir?'

'Look it up. You already know how long I've been in this dump. What do you want? Why do I have to talk to you?'

'Have you ever been to New Smyrna Beach?'

Kingston shrugs, 'Maybe. I don't know one beach from the other. I'm not from these parts.'

'Where were you the night of June 9, 2017?'

'How am I supposed to remember that?'

Chris opens a folder he has on the table and runs his eyes through the report, 'It says here you murdered a woman by the name of Denise Davis on June 9, 2017, in Cassadaga. So, do you remember the date now?'

Kingston shrugs his shoulders, 'So, what if I do?'

'Where were you the night you had the encounter with Denise Davis?'

'Why should I tell you anything?'

'All right, then. Let's go back to the murder we know about. Why did you go to Cassadaga to see Denise Davis?'

'Do you want to know why that bitch died? I went there looking for what was mine; for what IS mine. She stole my money; money I did time for up in New Jersey. She ran away down to Florida with my money and my ring. She was a fucking double-crosser. Hell, she's a triple-crosser. That ring, that's a very expensive ring, I have to tell you. I had that ring to give to her. Do you know I loved that bitch? That I wanted to marry her?' He nods earnestly, 'She left me in jail to rot and ran away. Well, she thought I wouldn't find her. She was very wrong.' His lips form a gruesome smile as he points vigorously to his chest, the veins on his neck thickening as he screams, 'But I did. I sure found that bitch!' He throws himself leaning back into the chair.

Staying still Chris enunciates slowly, 'So, after you "killed that bitch," where did you go, Mister Kingston?'

'I was…enjoying myself.'

Chris pulls out an 8 x 10 photo of Cassandra, her curls framing her smiling face and wearing the emerald ring Jan identified before. He puts it in front of Kingston, 'Do you know this woman?'

Looking at it, Kingston shakes his head and pouts his mouth.

'Look, we can go the easy route or the difficult route, it's up to you. We have your fingerprints and your DNA in our evidence room over in New Smyrna Beach, so what's it gonna be Kingston?'

Kingston's nostrils flare up as he breathes out, 'That's Denise's daughter, Cassandra. She had the ring. I knew it. That's the engagement ring I gave Denise that bitch is wearing.'

'Were you in New Smyrna Beach the night of June 9, 2017?'

Kingston nods. Chris pulls out another photo, this time it's the closeup of Cassandra's corpse showing bruises around her neck, 'Did you do this Mister Kingston? Did you kill Cassandra Davis after you killed her mother Denise Davis?'

'She wouldn't give me the money. I knew she had it because her mother told me she had it. I looked everywhere in her house but she tried to stop me. I should've found the ring, at least. You have no proof that I killed her.' He crosses his arms.

'What a waste. About that proof, just wait and see. Wasn't one murder enough for you?'

'That bitch, it was all her fault. Like daughter like mother. They were trying to fool me. That Denise took my money and ran off with someone else. We were gonna get married and everything. I stole that money for us, but she figured she could enjoy it all herself. For all I know Denise had the money hidden somewhere in that creepy wooden house of hers where she talked with all her ghosts. They both got what they deserved.'

Chris feels acid surging from his stomach. What he wouldn't give for an antacid. Taking a chug from a bottle of water he brought, he resigns to a little relief but it doesn't help his acid reflux. Disgruntled and impatient, Chris gets up from his chair, 'Mister Kingston, I will be pressing charges against you for the murder of Cassandra Davis as soon as I get back to my precinct.' Chris nods at the guard, 'You can take him back.'

'Don't I get a lawyer?'

'I don't care what you do.' Chris turns around and walks over to knock on the other door behind him.

~

This morning splashing water on her face, Jan softly presses her finger on the saggy darkened bags under her eyes and blinks. She brings her arms above her head and tries to massage her scalp. Her head is still pounding. Hearing a faint ringtone coming from her cell phone in another room, she closes her eyes. The ringing stops.

She drags herself to the kitchen when she hears pounding on the front door. Still dragging her feet as she walks to the front, she looks into the peephole. Tim. She opens the door, he embraces her as soon as he sees her. 'What happened?' He pulls away and looks at her face, 'What's wrong? You look…'

Almost without energy, Jan hangs onto him, 'Yeah, say it, I look like shit.'

Tim smiles and kisses her, 'Well, that's not what I was going to say, but you look awful. Are you okay?'

Turning around, Tim follows her as she walks over to the sofa. Raising his eyebrows, Tim takes in the disarray of a sheet and a blanket strewn about and a pillow lying on the floor. He helps her sink into the sofa, 'Here, take a seat. Let me get you something warm. Tea?'

Jan smiles at him, she likes it when he takes care of her. It's been a long time since somebody looked after her. She closes her eyes. 'I'd better have some coffee.'

Rushing to the kitchen, Tim grabs the coffee percolator from the cupboard. He looks around for the coffee and mugs. Once he's prepared the pot and placed it on the stove he goes over and leans in next to Jan to give her the news. Mandy is returning to New York today. She'll fly out this afternoon and Elsa will stay here with him for a few more days. 'But we'll be stranded here without a car.'

Jan laughs softly.

~

Lifting her head, Sharon Sutter watches Chris walk into the precinct lobby. 'Sarge wants to see you. It seems the Commander does too. I think they're waiting for you.'

Nodding, Chris figured as much, 'Thanks, Sharon.' He walks through the secure door and down the hall to the Operations Division Commanding Officer's office. Tapping on the door, he hears 'Come in!'

Chris takes the chair in front of the commander's desk, 'Morning, Sir. So, he definitely did it. We need to charge Joe Kingston with the murder of Cassandra Davis.'

Lifting his phone handset, Commander Nilsson punches three numbers, still looking at Chris, 'How did you get him to confess?' A few seconds later, Nilsson says 'Come to my office, Gwynn's back.' He hangs up.

Adjusting in the chair, Chris puts a folder on the commander's desk, 'Well, it wasn't a "full confession."' He makes air quotes with his fingers. At that moment, Sergeant Diaz walks into the office. Chris continues, 'On its own, the recording would be weak in court if that's all we got but he definitely did it. He squirmed a bit but I told him we have his fingerprints and DNA on the scene of the crime, and…'

Sergeant Diaz interrupts, 'But we don't have his DNA.'

Chris looks at Diaz, 'Who says we don't? We haven't tested it, but there was unknown DNA under Cassandra's fingernails and on her neck.' Chris shakes his head and waves his arm, 'But that doesn't matter because he told me why he did it, so we just run the tests and there will be more proof and we will probably not even need to go to trial.'

'Would we want to go to a trial?' Commander Nilsson asks.

Chris is unnerved, 'He murdered Cassandra Davis, sir. If he pleads not guilty we should probably put him on trial.'

Commander Nilsson sets back in his chair, 'Mmm, I don't know. Why waste all those tax dollars on a trial? He's already in prison for life.'

Sergeant Diaz interjects, 'Let the attorney general worry about that. Chris, how airtight is this?'

'I just got the fingerprints back and his fingerprints are on the hammer and on some other things in the victim's house. His thumbprint matches the one on her neck as well. Of course, DNA takes longer, but I'm sure that will be a slam dunk. In any case, we have time. He's not going anywhere anytime soon.'

'Why did he do it?' Commander Nilsson leans in.

'Why do they always do it?' Chris purses his lips. 'For the money, of course.' He shakes his head.

Chapter 35

Tuesday, June 21, 2022
The first day of summer
New Smyrna Beach, FL

It seems as if the Sanderling Sandpipers' tiny legs move as quickly as hummingbirds' wings. Their beaks clip into the sand but the tide rises and the waves roll in so the tiny birds run away to the drier sand.

Walking on the beach, Linda and Chris watch the flock of small birds sway back and forth in a choreographed dance. Chris takes Linda's hand, 'I know this is hard for you darling, but Buford is going to have to do the time. He did kidnap Mrs. Evans.'

'I know, plus he tried to poison you.'

'Yes, he did, but I don't think it would've killed me. The toxin wasn't enough to kill. Maybe I would've had palpitations or something. Maybe he wanted to send me a message?'

'Chris, he didn't put enough in your tea because I stopped him. What if it had been more?'

'Well, then that…' Chris stops walking. He turns and stares at the horizon, the sea is calm, white clouds hover in the distance, and three pelicans fly over the ocean. Seawater washes over their feet and Linda turns to look at the ocean, then at Chris, 'What is it?'

Chris frowns his lips, 'What if George Crawford didn't die of natural causes?'

'What are you saying?'

Chris puts his hands in his pockets and shrugs, 'I'll be darned! That's why he didn't tell me before that Cassandra was alive when George left her house. I won't be able to prove it, but what if Buford poisoned George and that's how he had the heart attack?.'

The blood drains from Linda's face, and she puts her hand over her mouth, 'Oh no!'

~

Blowing from the east, a soft breeze carries a bit of salty mist. Jan pours wine into her glass and places the bottle on the table between them. Taking a sip from a beer bottle, Tim lounges next to Jan on the porch of her beach cottage. They watch Elsa play in the sand near the shore. A glint of light bounces off Jan's emerald and diamond ring as she brings the glass to her lips. Tim looks at it and then at Jan, 'So Chris gave you back the ring? What are you going to do with it?'

Jan frowns her mouth and lifts her hand to look at the ring in the sunlight, 'Mmm, I haven't decided yet.' She moves her fingers to make make it sparkle, 'It's a beautiful ring. I don't feel it's mine, but I haven't decided what to do with it. You know what I decided I will keep, though?'

Tim winks as he watches her, 'I suspect I do.' He smiles.

Jan stretches on the chaise lounge, 'Yeah, I bet you do. Guess what?'

Tim turns his head to look at Jan curiously. She continues, '"*The Summer Rose*" made it to second place on the Best Seller's list!' She lifts her glass, Tim lifts up his beer bottle, and they salute.

'Congratulations! I know you're onto great things Jan!'

'I'm so happy. Dianne says they're also monitoring numbers from the other novels. It seems "*Broken Time*" and even "*The Blooming Sun*" are also climbing in the charts because "*The Summer Rose*" is getting people interested in my other books.

'Maybe all the news around you has to do with that as well. I guess we have Mandy to thank for that.' Tim winks at her. 'Well, I have to tell you, my love. Life is looking brighter than ever.' He turns his head to look at her, 'My love is very successful. My daughter is okay and I know she will be happy. My business is fine, so I'm content.'

Jan turns her head to look at him, 'Tim, I never thought I'd get a chance to love again. Life is a journey in which we try to figure ourselves out. I learned I've mostly hurt myself with my misgivings and fears. Finding and having you, I've gotten a second chance. But I have to warn you, I'm still learning to love.'

Tim sits on the side of the chair, 'None of that matters. What matters is…

I'm never letting you go.'

Epilogue

Spring 2024
Lake Helen, FL

Walking over in the Lake Helen Police Department parking lot to the police car parked next to hers, Jan Crawford holds the car door open for the pregnant woman emerging from it. Holding onto the car's doorframe to keep her balance, Charlie Wallace pulls out, her blond long ponytail wrapping around her left shoulder. Smiling, she stands at Jan's level and says, 'Thank you.'

As both of them walk to the front door of the building. Charlie asks, 'Is there anything I can help you with?' Jan opens the door for her.

Looking at a piece of paper she has in her hand, Jan walks into the lobby, 'Yes, I have an appointment with Sergeant Charlie Wallace. We're supposed to meet here this morning.'

Charlie extends her hand, 'Welcome to Lake Helen Miss Crawford?'

Smiling now Jan sees the nameplate on Charlie's uniform "Wallace" and shakes her hand, 'Nice to meet you, Sergeant Wallace.'

As she opens the door behind the information desk, Charlie tells the young police officer who's at the desk, 'Officer Brown, good morning. Can you please give Miss Crawford a visitors badge?' She signals for Jan to follow her through the door.

Now both seated in Charlie's office, Jan explains the reason for her visit. She is researching Denise Davis' murder from six years ago.

Accommodating her larger frame in her chair, Charlie relaxes, 'Are you researching this murder for one of your books?'

Jan leans back, 'Yes, I am interested in the murder as research for a book but I also have a personal stake in all of this. Are you aware of Denise's daughter's murder in new Smyrna Beach?'

Holding her hands across her belly, Charlie nods, 'Yes, I found out about that dreadful situation last year when they brought the charges against Kingston for her murder. What a waste of life.' She shakes her head.

'So, I was wrongfully accused by her ex-boyfriend at one point of murdering Cassandra. I am very interested in all the details concerning her life and, of course, of that of her mother.' Jan bows her head for a few seconds, 'My husband, who is also deceased, was Cassandra's lover before they both died.'

Charlie's eyes open wide. Staring at Jan for a few seconds, she then points at her, 'Now, that, I didn't know.' Getting out of her chair, 'Wait here a moment.' She walks out of the office.

Sergeant Wallace arranges with Officer Brown to show Jan around Lake Helen, the outskirts where Denise Davis lived, and Camp Cassadaga.

Walking up the path to where Denise used to live, Office Brown guides Jan to wait on the veranda while he knocks on the door.

The current residents allow her to walk around the centenary wooden house. Walking into a side room, some sort of library or home office, Jan wraps her arms around her torso to fend off a chill crawling on her skin. The owner of the house tells her this is where Denise did her consultations as a medium.

This is the house where Cassandra grew up, as well. Today there are no traces of a child or a teenager ever living here, though. Admiring the more modern furniture in the living room and updated kitchen, Jan walks through different rooms. The owner says she renovated the home before she moved in.

Reaching out to witnesses of Denise's murder and neighbors who were questioned, Officer Brown takes Jan next door to meet Aunt Missy

Richards. At the time of Denise's death, Missy's teenage niece, Jenny, insisted she knew who murdered her. However, Jan wasn't able to speak with Jenny because she no longer lives in the Lake Helen area.

Denise's home stands on the side of a road between Lake Helen and Cassadaga. Mediums in the area still live and operate here, both in the Cassadaga Camp as well as outside the camp limits.

Ever since Cassandra thrust Jan into the vortex of the lifestyle of mediums, unbeknownst even to herself, Jan had refused to inquire about it. The pain of George's deceit blocked her from having any interest in his lover's life or background. Satisfying her curiosity about the life of mediums, she assures herself she's on the correct path. She now knows what she has to do.

Now that everything is said and done, understanding Denise and Cassandra were victims she's inclined to pursue it in her next project. Perhaps Denise's life is more intriguing than she let on to her neighbors and the residents who hated her at the Camp. There seems to be much more to her, and therefore to Cassandra.

Can a nemesis become a friend? Is Cassandra trying to reach out to Jan from where there is no matter, space, or time?

More questions arise as soon as Jan gets answers, a never-ending quest. What about the number twelve? Does it have any meaning for mediums or in the paranormal world? Cassandra and George died twelve days before summer began. Jan also came to realize she met Tim exactly twelve days before summer. For some reason that is tugging at her consciousness and she can't let it go.

Returning to the Police Department after the tour, Officer Brown takes Jan to Charlie's office. When Charlie asks Jan to take a seat she refuses and takes out a box and an envelope from her purse.

Opening the black box, Charlie's eyes widen, 'What is this?'

'Sergeant Wallace, I want you to keep these heirlooms and money safe. They do not belong to me.' Jan hangs her purse on her shoulder and holds both hands in front of her, 'This ring was Cassandra's, as well as the money. 'It should go to her heirs or Denises' heirs. Cassandra gave it to my deceased husband for safekeeping. I know. You will know what to do with it.'

Sitting in the driver's seat of her mini-cooper in the Police Department Parking lot, Jan holds her cell phone tightly in her left hand, her heart pounding in her chest, 'It's done! I did it. I closed that chapter in my life.' Rain pours down her windshield mirroring her emotions. 'I'm so relieved. I feel like a weight has lifted off my shoulders.'

On the other line, Tim steps out of a taxi on 5th Avenue & 5th Street in New York, 'Jan, it was important that you do this. I am sure it was the right thing to do. I'm proud of you.'

Wiping off a tear from her cheek, Jan watches the water spill down the windshield, 'I know. Now I can get on with everything else. Well, I'll let you go. I hear a lot of noise where you are, you must be busy. I have to go now, a long drive ahead of me.'

Before hanging up, 'Yes. I will see you when you get here this weekend. I love you.'

'I love you too.' Shutting off her cell phone, Jan turns on the engine and is startled by pounding on her window right when she's about to put the car in reverse.

Soaking wet a young woman dressed in a long green dress pounds outside her car window again, 'Ma'am. Ma'am, I have a message for you.'

Rolling down her window, water splashing inside, 'What is it? Who are you.'

'Here, this is for you.' The woman with drenched jet-black hair and a tiny black beauty spot on her right cheek hands Jan a brown leather diary, with the number 12 embossed in the center. Wiping water off her face, her black eyes bright, she smiles and says, 'Cassandra says thank you.' The woman turns around and walks away.

Opening the diary, heart pounding, Jan looks at the front page. The first lines read, "If you are reading this it means I'm dead and this should be Cassandra's legacy. I will start from the beginning. My name is Denise Davis. I was born in Peninsula, Ohio…"

Her mouth falling open, Jan sifts through yellowed pages with beautiful cursive handwriting. Some pages in black ink, others in blue, there seem to be a treasure trove of secrets, impassioned references to found love, and tenderness. Toward the middle of the journal, drawn in pencil, there is a sketch of the emerald and diamond ring Jan just surrendered to Sergeant Charlie Wallace. Written in block letters below the sketch is the phrase: "Proof of Denise & Roger's Love"

Staring at the showcase with layers of bands shining under the cabinet's lights, Tim points at one. Holding the teal base, the sales agent with expensively manicured hands and red enameled nails, brings out a platinum ring with a half-circle of diamonds. She places it in Tim's open hand. He smiles.

Gesturing a knowing smile, she points at his hand, 'This is our forever band.' Moving her hand over the cabinet she signals the other delicate platinum rings under the glass, 'It goes well with some of these others, which is a great combination for engagement and marriage bands.'

'I'll take it.'

About the Author

Ann Hoff started her career as a radio announcer and decided to pursue a university degree in the field. She graduated with a Bachelor of Science degree in Journalism /Broadcasting from Utah State University. After graduating she worked as a TV and radio producer and anchor in the Dominican Republic. She also spent many years in corporate communications and translations. After moving back to the United States she has done administrative work, television production, and real estate. Currently, Ann is co-owner of a real estate brokerage and also dedicates her time to writing and service to the community. She lives in Central Florida with her husband, Daryoush.

Still Learning to Love is Ann's first novel to be published. However, her first work, "*Accounting for the Mob,*" is still 'under construction' and projected for publication by the end of 2023. She is also working on a prequel to *Still Learning to Love*, as well as other titles. Ann likes the genres of historical romance and contemporary fiction. She frequently updates her upcoming titles in the Romance genre at www.RomancingSummer.com. Her non-fiction writing can be found on www.Bookstique.com and Medium. Check out a short excerpt of the prequel to this novel, *On the Edge*, at the end of this book.

Acknowledgment

Thanks, Daryoush, for supporting me to finish this. Debbie Geer Hirsh, you turned it completely around, it needed it.

Writing a book entails many long hours, days, months, and in my case years, to reach this point. As I swipe away at the stories lurking in my head, like cobwebs hanging in a dark room, I want to thank so many people who encourage and motivate me to continue shaping these into coherent sentences and paragraphs. I may miss some of you, but you all know I appreciate it, and it means so much.

Thanks to my gang of encouragers, Diana, Hengameh, Melida, Wende, Rosemary, Daniela, Lua, Lida, and Sheri. It means a lot. Navid, Alexander, Jamal, Paul, Juan Manuel, Amin, and Miguel Angel, you mean the world to me. To Yennis, Gg and Amanda.

I also want to thank all those writers who are Twitterers. I have learned and been encouraged by so many comments as I lurk through #Amwriting and #Writingcommunity.

Questions for Book Clubs

1. Can love be deceit? How does Jan and Tim's love affair become deceitful? Should they be together in the end?

2. Did Jan do enough to steer away from trouble?

3. Is Mandy in the right to condemn Jan, to the point of wanting her to go to jail?

4. Do you think Mandy is unreasonable?

5. Why do you think Buford threw his life away? Do you blame him? Should Linda have done more for her brother?

6. What was your "Aha" moment in the story?

7. Agatha Christie wrote in her biography about disliking mysteries to have a romantic sub-plot. How do you feel about romance novels having a thriller or a suspense sub-plot?

8. How do you feel about one-night stands? Is there such a thing?

Turn the page for

an Excerpt from

On the Edge

By Ann Hoff

Prequel to “Still Learning to Love"

Available in e-book and paperback
in 2024

Excerpt of "On the Edge"

Lake Helen, FL

Riding shotgun in Charlie Wallace's police car on Monday morning, Drew Dexter can't hear a word she's saying. He's too busy watching her as she swerves around the curves of the road between the village of Cassadaga and the town of Lake Helen. They're on their way to the park right behind the Police Department. There is lots of grass, trees, and some picnic tables right behind the building where Charlie works. As soon as they get there, she plans to lay out their lunch on one of the picnic tables.

Happy to be out of his Sheriff Deputy uniform on his day off, Drew couldn't wait to see Charlie again. He works and lives in the City of Daytona Beach, which is about half an hour away, but the two towns couldn't be more different. Drew lives with his father, John-John, and brother, Derek, an accomplished race car driver. The family has been involved in the sport of racing since his father was a young man.

Having met a few months ago at a Florida Department of Law Enforcement seminar, Drew was immediately attracted to Charlie. Between his busy life as a deputy and racing season in Daytona Beach, Drew gave his pursuit of Charlie a little leeway. Now, he's riding along in her patrol car, watching her work but he gets to see her again.

Not very familiar with each other, Charlie and Drew aim for comfortable small talk. As she stops at a stop sign she says, 'So, tell me more about the FBI case you had on Saturday.'

'Well, not much more to say. They are pretty tight-lipped. They caught the dead guy's accomplices. They are so stupid. They ran as soon as they saw the FEDs driving up their driveway. All they could get on them was drugs. No jewels. So I guess the FEDs or the Sheriff will continue to pump them for information.'

'Was there any indication in the body they dug up that the jewels had been there and removed?"

'Not that we could find. We will have to wait and see if the lab tells us differently.'

Staring at Charlie's smile, Drew wishes he could reach over and touch her. Charlie doesn't notice as she's looking ahead, 'Exciting stuff, real twisted criminals there in Daytona.'

Still looking at her, Drew chuckles, 'You know, I think I could adjust to the laid-back atmosphere here. Daytona has become too complicated, with beaches, racing, tourism, and all that. I could take a year off the hustle and bustle and come here to the smaller police department.'

Narrowing her eyes with a bit of disdain, she smirks at the comment. He continues, 'I'm serious, I can surely use a quieter pace, believe me. So, is Cassadaga what they say it is? Spirits, ghosts? How is it around here at night?'

Now Taking a basket out of the trunk of her police car unit, Charlie points Drew in the direction of a picnic table under a large Florida Oak tree. As he takes the basket from her hands, she pokes him in the ribs, 'It depends on how you look at it. Of the 50 or so homes, there are about 25 mediums that live in the camp, I am sure there could be some interesting phenomena to be accounted for.'

'What is this camp…a village, a town?'

'Back in the late 1800's a man by the name of George Colby came from the north led to this land by a Seneca guide, or so the story goes. Years later, Colby decided to donate thirty-five acres of his land to his spiritualist church association.'

Whistling, Drew pulls his head back, 'You don't say.'

Laying a tablecloth on the picnic table, Charlie sneers, 'It has its ordinances, but those cover only the homes inside the camp limits. Those other houses around Cassadaga you saw are not under the camp's jurisdiction. Did you notice the big flashy signs?'

'Yep.' Drew's cell phone rings. He holds his hand up and answers, 'Hello Dad, what's up?'

'Do you know where Derek is? I haven't seen him all day and we were supposed to meet here at the shop this morning.'

Winking at Charlie, Drew settles down on the bench, 'No, I haven't spoken to him since yesterday afternoon before I left. We were chatting at the house, he was still a bit bummed out about the outcome of the race.'

'Well, I can't find him. I called Hector and Lisa, and nobody seems to know where he is. I'm not worried. He's a big boy but you know, since the race and the fallout, he's been pretty quiet, not himself.'

'Dad, you know how Derek is. It takes him a while to get over stuff like that. Give him some time. Did you call his cell?'

'Yep, I've left him a couple of voicemails. Do you know Laurin's address in Orlando? Do you think he could be there?'

'I doubt it. She's probably not the person he'd want to see, especially feeling like this. He's a loner. I suggest you give him some time to be alone. Perhaps he's out there walking down the beach or something.'

John-John chuckles, 'Perhaps you're right. Well, have fun. Bye now.'

Shutting off his cell phone, Drew puts it back in its pocket. Charlie has piled up his plate with potato salad, a sandwich, and some grapes. Charlie looks at him inquiringly and Drew holds her stare for a few seconds, a soft forming a soft smile on his lips. She smiles back and takes a bite of her salad. Wishing he could rush things with Charlie, he thinks better and holds off on getting too personal right now. Putting a grape in his mouth, he looks up at Charlie, 'Where were we? Ah, yes, my brother.... My dad can't find him. Nothing much. I wouldn't worry.' He waves the thought off, 'So, you were saying?'

'The camp people are a bit upset with them outsiders. They are very strict about their signs and their image. The people who advertise as mediums outside the camp also charge a lot less than the ones inside the camp. The competition is fierce. The Cassadaga Camp mediums aren't very happy with them.'

Expanding on the history of Cassadaga and Lake Helen, Drew listens to Charlie as they pick at their sandwiches and nibble on some salad and fruit. The radio holstered to her hip crackles. "*To all in and out of code, 23-H 5, 140 Marion Street. Everyone convened by the Chief at 140 Marion Street.*'

Suddenly raising from the picnic table, Charlie starts picking up the food from the table, 'A murder. Hurry up Drew, let's roll.' Drew helps put the food into the basket. Placing the basket in the trunk, she winks at him, 'You'll have to wait outside, though. You don't have jurisdiction.'

Smiling at the comment, Drew gets in the passenger side of the car, 'Well, that's a damper on a perfectly good lunch.' They hurry off.

~

Walking out of the one-story white wooden house with spacious veranda, Charlie crosses the road heading over to her patrol car. Drew is leaning against it with his arms crossed. There are a few other police cars and a large white van parked on the lawn in front of the house as well as across the street next to Charlie's patrol car.

Putting a notepad in her pocket, Charlie wants her head toward the white house, 'Mrs. Davis lives here. I mean she lived here, alone with her cats. She was found dead in her kitchen. It seems there was a struggle with a lot of things strewn about in the kitchen, in the front room she used for her '"consultations," and in her bedroom.'

Raising his eyebrows, Drew wonders, 'Was she a medium? This is not the Camp area? Where's the sign? I don't see one.'

'Well, she was well known.' Charlie turns around to look at the front area of the house and then down the road, 'The owners of the bookstore down around the corner would refer people who wanted a medium to her. Right now we don't know much, not much of a premise. One theory the Sheriff is working with is what I told you about, the rivalry between camp members and mediums on the outside.'

Pointing northward, she invites him to tag along, 'I have to go around and canvas the neighborhood. Want to tag along?'

'Sure…'

As they leave on foot, Chief of Police Walker walks out of the house behind the coroner who is rolling the body out on a gurney inside a body bag.

Arriving next door at Missy Richards home, Drew and Charlie find her standing on the porch. At the front door the elderly cheeky elderly woman shakes her head sadly, 'Denise was very reserved, with the people of these parts. She didn't talk a lot about herself. You know from before she moved here.'

Charlie takes out her notepad and a pen, 'Ma'am, can we come in?'

Moving away from the door, Ms. Richards guides them to her living room. This is also a centenary wooden house with wide and tall windows. A breeze blows through the open window wafting up sheer yellow curtains. Drew and Charlie sit at the edge of a couple of chairs across from the sofa where Ms. Richards sat. She points to Charlie's notepad, 'Missy Richards, my name is Missy Richards but you can call me Aunt Missy. That's what everyone calls me around here.' Smiling, her tiny eyes seem to disappear behind her round wire glasses.

Charlie asks, 'She isn't originally from around here? I've always known her…well, not that I'm that old. How long ago did she move here?'

'We were kind of close, you know, living next door for 25 years, but she had a past before coming to these parts. I know that because she never wanted to talk about it. She and her husband Roger were from Ohio. They were so in love. And there is Cassandra. Their beautiful daughter.'

Walking over from a rear room, a young teenage girl stays in the background. She's a bit pale, distraught as if wanting to say something. She approaches but stands behind her Missy, who says, 'Ah, Jenny dear, these are the police who came to ask questions about poor Denise. This is my niece.'

Trying to get more information, Charlie tries to make the shy girl comfortable. Jenny's lips are trembling and her face is still very pale. Charlie addresses Missy but also looks over Jenny, 'So, can you tell me if you saw anybody come or go from Ms Davis' home since last night?'

'It was Rossana! She killed Ms. Davis!' She starts whimpering.

Turning around with raised eyebrows, Aunt Missy's eyes open wide, 'Jenny, what are you talking about? Who's Rosanna?' She puts her arm around her, 'Jenny!'

Charlie leans closer to the edge of her chair, 'Why do you believe that? Who is Rossana? Do you know her? Where does she live?'

'She doesn't live. But I've seen her, Rossana and Denise were arguing.' Jenny sobs some more.

Frowning, Charlie leans forward and places her elbows on her knees, her notepad and pen in her hands. Aunt Missy looks uncomfortable with her niece's abrupt drivel. Drew stares at Charlie as Aunt Missy still embraces Jenny protectively.

Rubbing her hands on her lap, Charlie tries to make some sense of it all, 'Jenny, are you saying that the last time you were over at Ms. Davis' you saw Rossana's ghost appear? You heard her arguing with Rosanna?'

Sheepishly, Jenny answers, 'Not really like that. Mrs. Davis was arguing. She's the only one I heard speak. But she was kind of screaming at someone named Rosanna. I went over to her bedroom, without her noticing, and through the crack of the door I could see Mrs. Davis sitting on her bed screaming at the wall. She said that she should go away and leave her be, that Roger was gone, that they had loved each other very much, but he was no longer alive. That she should give it up and leave her alone.'

Exchanging looks, Drew and Charlie are certain this line of inquiry will not arrive at concrete answers. Shaking her head, Aunt Missy puts her hand on her forehead and shakes her head; then trying to comfort her, she pats Jenny's lap 'Why didn't you tell me about this?'

Jenny hides her face in her aunt's shoulder, 'I was too scared. I didn't want you to tell Denise I was snooping… it felt like, kind of personal, you know.'

Getting up at the same time, Drew and Charlie begin to leave. Charlie thanks both of them and tells Missy she'll come again if any questions come up.

Walking outside, Drew frowns, 'Well Charlie, looks like you've got yourself your first suspect. I've gotta tell you, your work is surely more exciting than mine, a ghost. Can you explain to me how you're going to put this ghost in jail?' He chuckles. She punches his arm.

You will be able to catch more of Drew's case with the FBI, his brother Dexter's career and where Charlie and Drew's relationship is headed with "On the Edge." You will also get to meet Cassandra and her mother Denise Davis.

"On the Edge" is a prequel to "Still Learning to Love" and I hope you will be interested in picking up a copy next year. It is Charlie and Drew's story surrounded by their families and their work. Coming in 2024.

www.ingramcontent.com/pod-product-compliance
Lightning Source LLC
LaVergne TN
LVHW050613100826
845148LV00011B/1577

* 9 7 9 8 2 1 8 9 5 4 8 8 8 *